Hallmark
PUBLISHING

WRAPPED
UP IN
CHRISTMAS JOY

USA TODAY BESTSELLING AUTHOR
JANICE LYNN

In loving memory of Josh, Erin, & Sawyer Kimberlin
#SawyersSong

CHAPTER ONE

"**I**'LL PAY SOMEBODY FIFTY BUCKS to take my place," Cole Aaron offered his fellow firefighters at the Pine Hill Fire Department.

What were the odds that he would be the one to pull the "winning" green candy cane from the fuzzy red stocking he and the guys had passed around? Not that he felt like he'd won anything. If anything, getting stuck in the role of Santa felt like a huge mistake. Did they really think it was a good fit for a former tough-guy Marine turned firefighter to dress up as Santa in the Pine Hill Christmas parade?

He didn't have any Christmas cheer whatsoever. Christmas generosity, perhaps, such as when he'd offered to pay for poinsettias for the nursing home residents—but trying to make up for all the bad things you'd done in life didn't suddenly make you qualified to be *Santa*.

"This one is all you...Saint Nick," Andrew snickered.

Of course, his best buddy Andrew would find humor in the idea of Cole donning a red suit, fake belly, white beard, and wig. Had the roles been reversed Cole would be cracking up, too. Only, Andrew hadn't gotten the short end of the stick, er...candy cane, in the "Who Gets to be Santa on the Rescue Truck for the Christmas Parade?" lottery. Cole knew they should have gone with rock, paper, scissors. He was good at that.

He turned to Ben, another of his close friends.

"Don't look at me," Ben advised, continuing to help Jules and another firefighter decorate a ten-foot tree to "give the fire station a festive spirit," as the chief had put it. The Christmas music blasting over the intercom system all week had also been Chief's idea. As if to taunt Cole, "Santa Claus is Coming to Town" came on.

The guys all snorted with laughter.

Cole groaned. "I look nothing like Santa."

"Which is what that's for." Andrew gestured to the red suit Chief had sat on the table where Cole had been doing a crossword puzzle just minutes before, trying to ignore how Christmas was taking over his beloved fire-hall. "Come on. You know red's your color."

Glaring at his best friend, Cole peeled the plastic wrapper off the offending green candy cane and stuck the end in his mouth. *Yuck.* He couldn't even determine if it was green apple, watermelon, spearmint, or some horrible combination of all three. It certainly didn't taste like peppermint or anything to do with Christmas.

"That bad, eh?" one of the other firemen asked, looking just as amused as Andrew and Ben. The entire crew found it funny that the new guy had to be Santa. Or maybe they were all just ecstatic they weren't the one stuck with having to put on the red suit and go around saying, "Ho, ho, ho. Merry Christmas."

Not Cole's idea of a good time, either.

Any of the other crew members would be more qualified than Cole to spark the magic of Christmas for the kids at the parade. He suspected most of the guys would even like playing Santa, but were enjoying ragging him too much to step in.

Cole hadn't even celebrated the holiday in years. How was he supposed to pull off being Santa to this full-of-Christmas-spirit small Kentucky town?

"Not nearly as bad as having to wear that." To prove it, he stuck the tip of the candy back into his mouth— and immediately regretted doing so. It should be against the law for candy canes to come in any flavor other than peppermint.

Or for guys with tainted souls to play the ultimate Christmas good guy.

"Come on, Cole. Model the suit for us," Jules said from where she stood on a stepladder placing an ornament of a Dalmatian in a fire helmet on the tree.

Ben handed another ornament up to Jules as he added, "You do need to make sure the costume fits."

Glaring at his coworkers, Cole bit off a piece of the candy and crunched the disgusting stuff between his teeth.

"Ben's right," Chief confirmed, his salt and pepper mustache curling upward as he rocked his six-five frame back on his heels. "Last year, the pants had to be hemmed for Bob. I suspect you'll have to have the extra length let back out."

"Or maybe Bob should just be Santa again this year," Cole mumbled, wondering how long the candy's bad taste would linger in his mouth.

"His daughter is expecting her first baby that week," Chief reminded, his brown eyes twinkling with humor, as well, beneath his bushy brows. "Bob will be in Connecticut to meet his grandchild."

There was that.

"I'll be in my office—I have a meeting in a few minutes." His gaze connected with Cole's. "But for the record, I couldn't have chosen anyone better to be the department's Santa. You'll do great."

Cole wasn't the type to argue with his boss, nor did he usually feel the desire to do so. But, for once, he longed to list all the reasons Chief was wrong.

Instead, he sighed.

Whether he wanted to or not, he was going to be Santa in the Pine Hill Christmas parade. Santa should be some happy, jovial fellow, not a former Marine who'd done things that still haunted Cole's dreams.

No one else at the firehall battled the demons Cole fought.

Thank God.

Cole was proud to have been a Marine, proud of the brotherhood he'd belonged to. He would die filled with love for the good ole US of A and pride that he'd served his country with all his heart. But when it came to the things he'd done…

There was no pride in himself, nor should there be.

"Put on the suit," Andrew repeated, barely able to contain his laughter as all the crew began chanting along with him.

"I've heard about taking advantage of the new guy, but this," he held up his putrid green candy cane, "is ridiculous."

"Hey, I think it's cool you get to be Santa," Ben said, and Cole had no doubt he meant it. Cole's friend would have jumped at the chance to take the role if he'd drawn the green candy cane. Ben always smiled, was friendly to everyone, and would make a great Santa.

"Just think, all the kids are going to love you," his friend continued.

Not one of Cole's life goals. Not that he wanted kids to dislike him—far from it. He just didn't think much about kids one way or the other. He certainly had no plans to ever have any of his own.

No way would he ruin a kid's life by giving him or her a dad as messed up in the head as he was.

Cole still marveled at the life he'd made in Kentucky, at how much he had changed from the civilian drifter he'd been when he'd signed up for firefighter school. Working as a firefighter had given him purpose, and coming to Pine Hill to move into the farmhouse his late uncle had left him had given him a home. The Marines had been his family for more than a decade, and now he belonged to a second family, too. But at times like these, he questioned the motives of his brother firefighters. They sure liked to push him out of his comfort zone, and if he didn't know better, he'd think they'd rigged the stocking draw.

Regardless, being Santa in the parade was what was expected of him. Cole would do his job, and he'd do it well. Never again would he be the weak link of his team.

"Fine. I'll put on the suit. But if I catch any of you with your cellphones out taking pictures, I refuse to be held responsible for my actions."

Andrew grinned. "Just be sure to say cheese when you come back out."

"Instead of 'ho, ho, ho'?" Cole shook his head. "Not happening. If I'm going to do this"—and it looked as if he had to—"then I'm going to do it right, so every one of you clowns better straighten up if you want to stay off the naughty list."

At six foot one, Cole was a good four inches taller than Bob, and the pant legs currently only came down mid-calf. The cuffs definitely needed to be let out, Cole thought miserably as he stared at himself in the mirror. His tall black boots mostly hid the poor fit except when Cole moved and they rode up, exposing his calves.

He noted the tilt of the red hat with its big fuzzy white ball on top, the fake belly that added girth to his middle but did nothing to fill out the sleeves and pants, as his muscular legs and arms were far more toned than Santa was meant to be. Additionally, his furry coat sleeves were also a bit too short, though he supposed they could be made to work with a pair of gloves that covered more of his wrists. The white wig and beard fit right, at least, and covered most of his face except for his eyes, nose, and the top of his cheekbones.

He eyed the furry white stick-on brows and shrugged. *Why not?* He removed the backing and pressed them over his own eyebrows.

With some adjustments and help with make-up from Jules—and a position up on top of the fire truck, where no one could see him all that closely—maybe none of the kids would notice what a terrible Santa he made.

"Here goes nothing," he muttered to his Santa reflection, and then, sucking in a deep breath, he embraced his role.

Like true brothers, the other firefighters would just keep ribbing him about the being Santa if they thought it bugged him, so the best way to get through this would be to show how unbothered he was. As he reentered the break area, he slapped his round midsection and bellowed, "Ho, ho, ho. Merry Christmas. Who's first to sit on Santa's lap?"

"Hey, Cole, there's someone here to see you." Andrew's voice cut through where Ben sang along to the Christmas music still playing on the overhead speaker.

Looking over, Cole saw the pretty young woman standing next to his best bud, looking toward him with wide, surprised hazel eyes and her shiny hair—light brown streaked with gold—falling around her shoulders. She wore jeans, mid-calf boots, and a red sweater with a big cartoonish reindeer face on it, and her jaw was hanging open as her gaze met his.

A hard punch landed deep in Cole's gut, making his breath whoosh out from between the white hair that surrounded his lips.

Sophie Grace Davis.

He almost took a step back from the impact of her expressive eyes. Which was saying a lot because Cole usually ran *into* the face of danger, not away from it. Always had, and he suspected he always would. And for some reason, meeting Sophie's eyes felt exactly the same as all those times he'd seen danger straight ahead.

Not that Cole knew Sophie. Not really. They'd briefly met over the summer at Andrew's Grandma Ruby's Fourth of July picnic and had bumped into each other a few times around town in the months since then. All of which Cole could recount in vivid detail, even if he'd barely said two words to her.

Seeing Sophie always left him a bit discombobulated, uncomfortably aware that he was too stiff and awkward. But seeing her while wearing a furry red suit that didn't properly fit, with the wig and beard that mostly covered his face, and with his great entrance comment...yeah, could this day possibly get any worse?

Not in a million years had Sophie Davis expected to see Cole Aaron dressed up as Santa Claus. Why hadn't Chief warned her?

Of course, Sophie had instantly recognized Cole. As much as she'd tried, she'd not forgotten his pale, almost icy, blue eyes, or how ruggedly well-built he was—which even the costume couldn't fully disguise.

Nor had she forgotten how standoffish he'd been on the few occasions their paths had crossed. She'd taken the hint and avoided him the last few times she'd spotted him around town, and she was well aware he'd done the same.

"Here to give Santa your Christmas list?" Andrew teased, standing next to her with his arms crossed. Their families were friends, but Andrew was several years older than her, so they'd never been close. They just occasionally saw each other at family and town events.

Family friend or not, she felt like elbowing him at his teasing.

Taking a deep breath and forcing a smile, she kept her gaze locked with Cole's. "No, but I am here to return something of Cole's."

Had he even realized what he'd done? That he'd accidentally donated his journal for the church's Christmas fundraising rummage sale?

"Wouldn't happen to be eight reindeer and a sleigh,

would it?" Barely smothering his laughter, Andrew rocked back on his heels.

"She kinda looks like one of Santa's reindeer herself," another teased. "Hey, Cole? You missing a cute reindeer to lead your sleigh?"

Heat rushing into her cheeks, Sophie glanced down at her bright red Christmas sweater with its big, flashing red nosed reindeer. It was one of her favorites, and this was her first time wearing it this Christmas season. Was it too soon to have turned on the battery-operated nose?

On the other hand, Cole was wearing a Santa suit, so what was a snazzy Christmas sweater in the grand scheme of feeling self-conscious? It wasn't as if she hadn't felt self-conscious every other time their paths had crossed, too.

She gave him a pleading look. "Is there somewhere private we could talk a few minutes?"

"Hey, Sophie. Santa Cole been threatening you with the naughty list, too? Doesn't he know your name is written in permanent ink at the top of Santa's nice list?"

At hearing the familiar, friendly voice, Sophie smiled at Ben Preston. How had she not noticed he was helping decorate the cutest fire department–themed Christmas tree ever?

Then again, Cole had always had a knack for capturing all her attention, and that was *before* she'd realized he was her wounded warrior.

"Hey, Ben." Sophie had always liked the good-natured man she'd known since high school. He'd been a couple of years ahead, in her dear friend Sarah's class rather than Sophie's, but they'd all hung out together in their church's youth group. Ben's frequent smiles,

sparkly dark eyes, and his love of God, had impressed
Sophie. She'd crushed on him a bit in high school, but
she'd missed the boat; the only time he'd shown interest, she'd had other obligations. Now, she could only
see him as a friend.

"No, Cole...er, Santa Cole, hasn't threatened me with
the naughty list."

Ben smiled and went to stand near Cole, who'd not
taken a step or said a word since spotting her.

"Good to know he hasn't been bothering you."

Not unless one counted how his written words tore
at her peace of mind and invaded her dreams. If those
were factored in, then Cole had bothered her a great
deal.

Cole studied her with an intensity that didn't at all
match his white wig locks, bushy white brows, and
thick fake mustache and beard. "There must be some
mistake," he said. "How could you have something of
mine?"

Not wanting to explain where everyone could over-
hear, she replied, "I promise I'll only take a few minutes
of your time if you'll humor me a bit in private, please."

"See, that Santa suit is already bringing you good
luck." Ben elbowed Cole's arm and earned a quick glare.
"Go talk to the lady."

Ignoring Ben and looking puzzled, Cole's gaze held
hers. "Okay if I go change first?"

Sophie nodded, because, really, what else could she
do?

One of Sophie's favorite Christmas carols came on
and she attempted to let the song ease her mounting
nerves at just standing in the large, open area of the
firehall where the men were gathered. Surely, thoughts

of Santa being up on the housetop would calm her jitteriness.

But it wasn't working. Because Cole was now Santa in her head. A Santa in desperate need of a good seamstress, which she just so happened to be.

Sucking in a deep breath, which triggered a grin from Andrew who still stood next to her, Sophie ditched him to walk over to where Ben had returned to decorating the tree. "How's LaTonya doing?"

Ben smiled at the mention of his twin. "Living the lawyer high life in Louisville as she fights for justice for all." Visibly proud, Ben told of his latest phone conversation with his sister.

Sophie tried to keep her attention on him, but her mind kept straying to Cole. Maybe Ben wouldn't notice how many times she said *Mm-hmm* and *Oh, really?*

When Cole came back into the festively decorated firehall, he glanced around at the others who were watching them intently, then frowned. "We can go outside. It's not private, but it's better than being the main event in here for these jokers."

"Yes. Going outside sounds like a great idea."

Maybe she would be able to breathe better outdoors.

Sophie waved goodbye to Ben and Andrew, then smiled at Cole, grateful that she'd be able to give him the journal privately so he could tuck it away if he didn't want the others to see.

His coworkers might already know about his time in the military, but if not, he should be the one to decide who knew about the things he'd gone through. No one else.

Which made her feel a smidge guilty at having read his journal in the first place, but there had been no name. She'd only meant to read enough to try to figure out whose diary it was, but once she'd started, the pages had beckoned to her with a call she hadn't been able to resist.

Even after reading it completely, she'd still not found a name. All she'd known was that the author was a male Marine who'd seen and endured too much, just as her father had. Not having a name or a face to assign to the journal meant that the connection between the two men had blurred.

For a week, the intense journal had haunted her. Nightly, she'd picked it up to reread passages that had left her chilled and aching for the man who'd written the heart-wrenching words. Who was he? Where was he? Had he pieced his life back together or...or had the darkness overtaken him as it had her father?

Only when she'd found the Christmas card tucked into a crossword puzzle book that had also been in the donated box had she realized the writer's identity. Discovering that the quiet, stoic man she'd briefly met at Ruby Jenkin's Fourth of July party was the wounded warrior monopolizing her every waking thought had been a surprise.

Apparently, Cole was full of surprises. She certainly wouldn't have expected to find the man whose journal she'd read wearing a Santa suit and teasing his coworkers.

Maybe she should have insisted that he keep wearing the suit. Talking to Santa Cole had to be easier than talking to Gorgeous Fireman with a Tormented Past Cole.

Her stomach was a fluttery tangle of nerves.

She shouldn't be nervous at all. Her palms shouldn't

be clammy. Her heart shouldn't be racing. She snuck a glance toward Cole and gulped.

He made her feel giddy and feminine and a whole lot nervous. He'd had that effect on her even before she'd read his journal, and now that she'd read it, she wanted to help him.

Needed to help him.

Not that he looked as if he needed help. Now that he was out of his Santa suit, he looked tough, handsome—a bit dangerous, even, as if he could take on the world and win.

He wore the standard black uniform pants and a polo shirt with the firehall emblem over his heart and short sleeves that accentuated his muscles. His dark brown hair was cut in a no-nonsense short style. His eyes—a Siberian Husky pale blue with a darker, deep blue rim—flashed with intelligence, curiosity, and annoyance.

On the outside, Cole was a good-looking, well-put-together firefighter who had probably started more than a few fires in the hearts of Pine Hill's female population. Hadn't she noticed him at the picnic and every time their paths had crossed since?

But now, Sophie knew the heartache his handsome exterior hid.

Catching her not-so-sneaky peek in his direction, Cole's brow rose. "Did I misunderstand you a minute ago? Are you here to pick something up from me rather than give something back? I told the lady on the phone I'd drop the money for the poinsettias by the nursing home. Did they need the check right away?"

Poinsettias? He was the one who had donated the

money to buy the poinsettias for the nursing home residents? She'd heard someone had, but—

Sophie half-tripped over her own feet and almost face-planted on the concrete firehall floor. She steadied herself in time that she didn't think he noticed her lapse as they stepped outside into the sunshine. Or if he did notice, he didn't let on.

A soft mid-November breeze blew, tickling her face with her hair.

"I'm not here about the poinsettias or money," she began, tucking the stray strands behind her ears in hopes of keeping them at bay. "And you didn't misunderstand me. I found something that belongs to you, and I'm here to return it."

She reached into her bag and pulled out his journal that had the Christmas card tucked inside it.

"This is yours, isn't it?"

Cole's gaze dropped to what Sophie held. A sucker punch rammed into his stomach, knocking his breath out of him and leaving him going-to-retch-his-insides-out nauseated.

He could stare down an enemy holding an AK-47 and not flinch, but the book that Sophie held made his knees weak.

"Where did you get that?" he growled, barely managing not to snatch the book from her hands to hurl it aside, like a grenade that needed to be thrown as far away as possible for everyone's safety.

For *his* safety.

Sophie winced. He felt a pang of regret over the

harsh tone he'd used, but he couldn't formulate words to apologize. The beauty from the BBQ had his journal.

"I found it at Pine Hill Church in a box of books."

The sinking sickness pitched back and forth in his stomach, making him wish he'd forgone his protein shake that morning. His journal had been in the stuff he'd dropped off at the church?

"I, well, when I realized whose it was…" Her nervousness was palpable as she sank her teeth into her lower lip and looked up at him with hesitation. "I knew you'd want it back." She gave a little shrug of both shoulders. "So here I am."

"You were wrong." Bile rising in his throat, he gestured to the abomination she held. "I don't want that."

Further confusion darkened her eyes. "But…"

"Look." He ran his fingers through his hair, still not completely used to having anything more than stubble after years of keeping his dark hair buzzed. "I'm sorry you wasted your time. You should've just thrown it out. That book's nothing but garbage."

Lots and lots of scribbled garbage a chaplain had suggested he get out of his head by pouring it into the journal the man had gifted to Cole. Not for the first time, Cole regretted giving in to that advice. Seeing everything written out just made him more disgusted with himself, causing the memories to hang even heavier on his shoulders.

Why hadn't he burned the book rather than packing it with the things he'd brought with him to Pine Hill? The mere act of destroying the journal might have gone further in annihilating his memories than putting them onto paper ever had.

"But," Sophie began again, her eyes wide and her voice a little trembly. "But it's...I mean, well, it's—"

"Garbage," he repeated, cramming his hands into his pants pockets and clenching his short nails into his palms as deeply as they'd go. He just wanted away from their conversation, away from the book that felt like his personal Achilles' heel—the weak spot in his defenses that could ruin everything good he'd patched his broken life with. "Throw it away."

"I..."

At her indecision, understanding dawned.

"You read it, didn't you?" Cole felt like a fool for not immediately realizing. A new wave of nausea spread through him, popping sweat beads out over his skin despite the crisp November air.

Wide-eyed, her lips parted but no sound came out. No matter. She didn't need to say the words. The truth was written all over her face.

One of the things Cole most enjoyed about being in Pine Hill was that no one knew of his past. Chief had some idea, and the guys had picked up on a little thanks to Cole's occasional nightmares, but none of them were in on the nitty-gritty details.

In Pine Hill, he was seen as a man who volunteered his time and energy to everything the firehall was asked to participate in; a man who put his life on the line to save others.

If, while out battling those fires, he fought inner de-mons, trying to quench them the way he and his crew squelched nearly uncontrollable blazes from time to time, well, no one needed to know that but him.

Only, Sophie had read about his bleakest mo-ments—and his biggest mistake. She knew the truth.

"I'm sorry," she said, looking truly remorseful that she'd pried between the pages of his private hell. "I opened it thinking I might find a name so I could return it, but there wasn't one." Grimacing, she continued. "And, well, the truth is that once I started reading, I couldn't stop."

She'd read it all. Of course, she'd read it all. She probably thought him a monster.

As much as he wanted to look away, he didn't. Jaw locked tight, he kept his gaze unyielding as it met hers. He could handle whatever judgement she placed on him.

Lord knew she couldn't judge him any more harshly than he judged himself.

"How did you figure out it was mine?"

"There was a Christmas card addressed to you inside a crossword puzzle book that came from the same box. I stuck the card there, inside your journal."

Without looking at the book, he knew the one she meant. Why had he kept the photo card his mother had sent?

"Toss it as well."

"But..." she paused, "You're sure?"

"Positive." He didn't want the sentimental reminder of the family he'd never felt a part of any more than he wanted the journal. His mother had her new life, as did his father, complete with new families. There wasn't a place for him in that picture—but at least they were happy. That was enough for Cole.

"I'm so sorry for what you went through," Sophie said softly, hugging the journal to her as if she was clinging to the book in effort to keep her hands to herself. As if she wanted to reach out to him.

He didn't need or want her pity. He'd rather she screamed and yelled at him for his failures. Feeling sorry for him? That, he couldn't take. He wasn't some emotional charity case needing her Christmastime goodwill.

He was fine.

Frustration and anger that she'd read his journal burned, taking hold and quickly consuming him. The rational part of him knew it was his fault for not realizing the journal was in the donated box, but in this moment, rational thinking didn't matter. That book had never been meant for anyone to read, and especially not the bubbly, full-of-goodness woman he'd met over the summer. She never should have been exposed to the pure ugliness marring the pages. Marring him.

When he spoke again, he kept his voice low and steady. "I get that you didn't know who the journal belonged to, so you read it. Fine. Go back to your life-is-a-bed-of-roses existence and forget everything you read."

Wincing a little, she shook her head. "I can't do that."

Surprised at how her gaze hadn't wavered from his when he'd expected her to walk away and never waste another breath on him again, Cole frowned. "What's that supposed to mean?"

Her chock-full-of-emotion gaze studied his. "I won't forget what you wrote as long as I live."

"Then I'm the one who's sorry." No one should be subjected to his failings. Not in real life. Not in writing. "But that doesn't mean I want the book back. Thanks, but no thanks." He couldn't bring himself to look at the journal clutched to her chest, much less to touch the worn leather book.

"Do the world a favor and throw the thing in the trash. Or better yet, burn it." Even Superman has his

Kryptonite, he reminded himself, determined he would not let this drag him down into a place he never wanted to return to. "I don't care so long as you get rid of it because I never want to see that book, or you, again."

CHAPTER TWO

"**C**AN YOU BELIEVE HE DIDN'T want the journal back?" Sophie mused later that day as she unpacked a shipment of holiday fabric at The Threaded Needle. She and her sister worked hard to keep fresh supplies available to their clients at their boutique-style quilt shop located on Pine Hill's town square.

From the far end of the checkout counter, Isabelle said, "What I can't believe is that you're still talking about him and that journal you found."

Sophie paused from pulling out a bolt of candy cane–print material to stare at her sister. "What's that supposed to mean?"

"You've been talking about him all morning," Isabelle pointed out. She tucked a strand of her shoulder-length pale blond hair behind her ear, then shrugged. "So what if the guy didn't want his journal back? It's his choice, right? Do as he asked and get rid of it."

Horrified, Sophie gasped. "Absolutely not!"

Isabelle didn't know what the journal contained, as

Sophie had glossed over the details when her sister had asked. Even before she'd met Cole, Sophie had felt protective of the book and its contents.

Isabelle arched a brow, frowning in that older sister way she had. "You've got no right to keep his journal, not when he told you to get rid of it."

Purposely not looking at Isabelle, Sophie went back to pulling Christmas-printed fabric bolts from the box and ignored the smidge of guilt she felt at disregarding Cole's wishes.

"I *do* have the right," she said after a few minutes of mental gymnastics. "He donated it to the church holiday rummage sale, and I bought it."

Even though she'd assumed Cole had donated it by mistake, she'd still insisted on paying for it before taking it away from the church. The event helped raise money to give families with limited means grocery gift cards for them to purchase food for Christmas.

"I tried to return it," she continued. "He didn't want it back." Maybe he truly wanted to just forget. She supposed she could understand that. Still, she couldn't imagine tossing out something that contained so much of him on the pages.

She couldn't do it.

"It's mine now."

"Fine." Sighing, her sister shook her head. "It's bought and paid for." Isabelle's eyes crinkled with curiosity. "Tell me, though, what did this guy look like? Was he cute?"

Cute? That was like calling Mount Everest a mound of dirt.

Cole was...feeling her face flush, Sophie averted her

gaze and shrugged. "Um, you've met him. At Ruby's this summer. He's...okay."

"Okay" was a worse description than "cute," but she wasn't telling her nosy sister how disturbingly attractive she found Cole.

"Oh my goodness." Isabelle's voice took on a higher pitch as she came around the corner under the guise of helping with the fabric. "I don't remember him, but he really must be cute. I can tell by your face."

Sophie focused on unpacking the brightly patterned material as if she were unveiling delicate prized possessions that required her utmost attention and care. She kind of did feel that way about fabric, especially this shipment as they prepped for the Christmas season.

"Okay," Isabelle picked up a snowman-printed bolt, "now, I want to know more. Tell me all."

Sophie shoved a cardinal-red bolt of fabric at her sister. "Not much to say. Here, go put this on the shelf. With the upcoming holidays, we're going through this shade like crazy. I bet we use even more after I teach my class on do-it-yourself stockings in December."

Isabelle laughed. "I haven't seen you this flustered over a guy since Jimmy Allbad in the seventh grade."

"His name was Jimmy Algood," she corrected, unable to stop herself even though she knew Isabelle was just teasing her with the mistake. "And thank goodness that didn't work out."

For real, Sophie was thankful for that miss.

Sure, someday she'd like to meet the right guy, marry, and have a few kids, but Prince Charming needed to hold off a few years until Sophie had the time to think about anything other than making sure they could pay the bank note on the quilt shop.

Cole was no Prince Charming. More like a surly brute who'd snapped at her, then walked away, leaving her slack-jawed as she watched him disappear inside the fire station.

Only...no, no, no. Sophie needed to quit thinking about him.

"Yeah, you two didn't make it past eighth grade," Isabelle teased about Jimmy. "So, what was it about this Marine that has you in such a teenage-girl tizzy?"

Was that why Sophie couldn't stop thinking about him? Because she was schoolgirl crushing? She didn't think so since she hadn't been able to stop thinking about the journal's owner even before she'd known it was Cole. His words had reached in and put her heart through the ringer. That he had the most intriguing eyes of anyone she'd ever met had just added to the fascination.

Sophie fought fanning her face.

Okay, so maybe she was schoolgirl crushing.

Not that it would do her any good, if the anger in his eyes had been any indication. She'd read his journal and that apparently made her enemy number one.

He never wants to see me again.

Sophie's face heated as she realized she was still distracted. No wonder Isabelle thought she was in a schoolgirl tizzy.

Rolling her shoulders back to stretch the tension in her neck, Sophie sighed. "I'm just disappointed he didn't want his journal."

"Not everyone cherishes journaling the way you do," Isabella pointed out.

"You keep the birthday dairies Aunt Claudia gives us every year, too," she reminded.

Their aunt had always given the best gifts, and the diaries had been Sophie's favorites. Each year, she'd wondered what butterfly design would be on the cover, what handwritten note her aunt would have penned about emerging from her cocoon and spreading her wings to fly. Her aunt's whimsies had always appealed to the dreamer in Sophie.

She'd kept a diary since receiving her first one on her tenth birthday. She had little bits of herself, her dreams and hopes, scattered over the pages, carefully tucked away in her nightstand, that she'd written for more than a decade. She'd agonize if she lost any one of them. She'd thought Cole would feel the same.

She'd been wrong.

"Yeah. I used Aunt Claudia's diaries," Isabelle agreed drily. "But my entries were more along the lines of 'I can't believe she got me another one of these books when I really wanted new clothes.'"

As Sophie recalled, her practical sister had mainly used the diaries to make lists. Lists of the things she'd done that day and lists of her goals for the following day, goals for the future.

She and Isabelle were as opposite as night and day. Maybe that was why they were so close.

"Say what you will, but I love that Aunt Claudia always gave us diaries. Someday, that's what I'm going to give your kids as gifts, too," she teased, loving how her sister's face contorted in mock horror. "Only, I'll search out ones with dragonflies on them and come up with cool little sayings to write on the inside covers for my nieces and nephews." At Isabelle's "don't you dare" look, Sophie fought giggling and added, "Yep, dragonflies, year after year, with notes about how cool their Aunt Sophie is."

"Dragonflies? Ha," Isabelle snorted and tossing a piece of plastic packaging toward Sophie. "Well, at least my hypothetical kids will be spared that for as long as they stay hypothetical—which will probably be forever. I'll die an old maid living in this town."

"That's not likely to happen," Sophie corrected, frowning at her sister's comment. Did Isabelle regret having moved back to Pine Hill? Did she miss her accounting job in Nashville? She never said so, but sometimes Sophie did wonder. "You're beautiful and smart. Any guy would be lucky to have you. You just have to learn to say yes to a few of your constant stream of date offers."

Isabelle wrinkled her nose. "Have you met the guys who've asked me out? Thanks, but no thanks. I'm fine staying single and never having children, especially in light of your Aunt Sophie gift threats."

The doorbell chimed, indicating they had a customer. Giving her sister one last look, because she would really have liked to question her further, Sophie stopped unpacking fabric to go help the newcomer.

Somehow, she even managed to put Cole Aaron out of her head...until a bolt of Christmas fabric with Santa Claus on it caught her eye.

Living right off Pine Hill's town square had its advantages. For one, Sophie could walk to church and work.

Most days, weather permitting, that was what she did. She spent long hours sitting at a sewing machine and when she was done, she liked to make the most of the fresh air and the chance to stretch her legs.

Sophie had stayed late at The Threaded Needle to use the shop's longarm quilting machine to stitch a queen-sized Double Wedding Ring pattern Odessa Adams had topped as a Christmas gift for her newly-wed granddaughter. The sun had long set by the time Sophie locked up the shop and headed home, but the well-lit streets warded off the darkness.

She made her way up festively lit Main Street with its snow-frosted garlands, each with a bright red ribbon, wrapped around every lamppost. Breathing in a deep breath of crisp night air, Sophie swung her bag over her shoulder.

Despite her pleasure in being outside, enjoying the peaceful setting and the refreshingly brisk breeze, Cole's journal weighed heavily in her bag, just as her heart weighed heavy with his rejection.

If only—

A yellow, furry streak ran in front of Sophie, stopping her in her tracks as she stared down the now-empty street, wondering where the half-grown cat had disappeared.

Speaking of rejections…

"Here, kitty, kitty." She knelt and called in the direction the cat had gone, but to no avail as the cat stayed in the shadows.

"You know," she told the elusive cat, "I've been leaving food for you for over a week. Although I've seen you peeping in my shop window from time to time, I'd like a closer look. A thank-you meow or two would be nice, too."

The cat had been hanging around the square and

surrounding neighborhood for the past several days, but, as tonight, had been too skittish to do more than watch Sophie from a safe distance. Knowing the poor thing had to be hungry, Sophie put a small bowl of food on her front porch each evening and left an old throw out for the kitty to snuggle up in during the cold winter nights.

"Someday, you're going to realize that I'm not so bad, and then you'll want to be my friend," she told the unseen cat as she stood back up and started walking towards her house again.

Would Cole Aaron ever realize the same thing?

The Twenty-Second Annual Pine Hill Christmas Toy Drive was just starting to get underway.

This was Cole's first holiday season in Pine Hill, but from the time he'd moved here, he'd learned this town meant business when it came to holidays. And it seemed that the Christmas season was the be-all end-all. For Cole, it was just another day, but even he wasn't so jaded that he didn't recall the excitement of Christmas morning as a kid.

Kids needed toys.

When Chief said the fire department was taking on an active role in collecting toys for kids, Cole had signed on to help however he could. He had no wife, kids, or significant other to require his time during the holidays like some of the crew, so he volunteered for whatever came up. No one would miss him if he spent more hours away from home. It made sense that he'd volunteer so others wouldn't need to.

Assuaging his ever-present guilt was how he found himself sitting in the church community room with about twenty other people, mostly ignoring what was being said.

He spotted Sophie sitting near the front of the room. Her table's occupants were an odd-looking mix, from Sophie's sunny presence, to Chief towering over the others, to an almost regal woman in her seventies who looked vaguely familiar, to a cyan blue-haired punk granny with glaringly bold lipstick. Apparently not content with letting her bright colors do the talking for her, she also waved her hands frequently while whispering something to a brunette who appeared to be about the same age as Sophie. Whatever she was saying must have been entertaining—and possibly inappropriate, because the young woman kept suppressing her laughter and shaking her head. Andrew's grandparents were there, too.

But the one he couldn't take his eyes off of was Sophie. Sophie Grace Davis. Yep, he knew her full name... because the guys at the firehouse had teased him mercilessly about her appearance yesterday morning. Between that and his bit as Santa, they'd not let up with their Santa Cole jokes. Seriously, couldn't his parents have named him something that didn't sound the same as coal?

Hopefully, Ben and Andrew wouldn't start in again when they spotted him watching Sophie. Because no, he didn't want to take her for a ride in his sleigh, and no, she wasn't getting him for Christmas.

Cole had no intentions of ever settling into a relationship. His friends knew that, although they weren't clued in on his reasons why. As Andrew had also sworn allegiance to permanent bachelorhood, they'd become two peas in a pod, avoiding dates together and openly giving their buddy Ben a hard time as he sought out falling in love and starting a family rather than continuing in their bachelor life.

But lately the teasing had turned to him as his friends seemed to consider it their duty to rag him as much as possible about why Sophie had stopped by the firehall looking for him. He hadn't told them about the journal, or about his telling Sophie he never wanted to see her again.

How many times had those words played through his head?

Too many to count, for sure. Just as visions of Sophie had played through his head too many times.

"Look who's here." Andrew gestured toward her table. "You need to say hi."

If looks could kill, his buddy would need a graveyard plot.

"Hey, if you don't want to talk to her, maybe I should," Ben teased, waggling his brows.

Ben could join Andrew six feet under.

Cole didn't need one of his buddies dating a woman who'd read that journal. He'd hoped his path wouldn't cross Sophie's again anytime soon. He should have known better.

He *had* known better. Pine Hill wasn't that big.

"I asked her out once," Ben admitted, frowning as he stared toward the table where Sophie sat. "In high school. I was a couple of grades ahead of her, but I liked her smile. She told me she was busy attending a sew-in, whatever that is."

Andrew snorted.

Cole frowned. "A sew-in? As in sewing?" he couldn't help but ask, ignoring how strangely pleased he felt that Sophie hadn't gone out with Ben back then.

What did it matter whether or not Ben had dated her in high school?

Ben gave a self-derisive laugh. "Yep. A sew-in. I never asked again. I figured her saying she was sewing was akin to her saying she was washing her hair or some other thanks-but-no-thanks excuse."

"Can you blame her? Who'd want to go out with your ugly mug?" Andrew ribbed Ben, to Cole's relief. If they were needling each other, then neither one of them were giving him a hard time.

"If you think you'll have better luck this time, go for it," he told Ben, secretly hoping that wasn't what his friend would choose to do.

His friend might be single, but it wasn't because women didn't want to be in Ben's life. It was more that Ben dated women just long enough to decide whether or not they were "the one," then moved on to the next woman to catch his interest.

"You're not calling dibs?" Ben eyed him suspiciously.

"I keep telling you—there's nothing there. I barely know her. She just found something of mine in one of the boxes we brought over to the church, and thought I'd donated it by accident. She tried to return it. It wasn't something I wanted back. End of story."

"Yet she wanted to talk to you in private?" Ben raised a brow.

"As private as it gets when standing just outside the firehall in plain sight of anyone who came by or looked out a window," Cole pointed out, clearing his throat for emphasis on the window part.

"I think she just wanted an excuse to get away from you, Benny boy," Andrew added with a grin.

Ben tossed a paper wad toward his friend, which Andrew deflected, sending it flying off in a different direction.

Cole glanced around the church community room floor, meaning to pick up the paper but he didn't see where it landed. Just as he was about to get up to search for it, a woman tapped on a microphone.

The well-put-together seventyish woman from Sophie's table had gone to the front podium, cleared her throat, and almost instantly silenced everyone. Even cyan-blue granny had quieted down.

Cole was impressed. He'd seen less effective drill sergeants.

"Ladies and gentlemen, we're here today to officially kick off the planning for this year's Christmas toy drive. For any of those who may not know me"—she sounded as if she thought that an impossibility, the words a formality she needed to say all the same—"I'm Maybelle Kirby. I've headed up the toy drive since I co-founded it over twenty years ago."

Again, impressive. Obviously, she was a pillar of the community.

Cole liked that about Pine Hill. There were people who'd lived there their entire lives, who'd devoted themselves to making it a better place. It still astonished him that this apple-pie-and-baseball-loving life existed in the world. No wonder his uncle had never moved away from his small farm just outside the town.

"Donations were down last year, probably due in part to the loss of our dear co-chair, Jean Hamilton. We miss her so much." The woman's gaze slid over to the brunette at the table before she gave a slight nod of acknowledgement. Cole took that to mean that the young woman had been a relative of the departed. "We barely had enough toys to meet our requests."

Maybelle's lips thinned, and she lifted her chin with a determination Cole admired, one that said she refused for any child in need to not receive a toy on her watch. No doubt they never would while she was in charge.

"The committee and I have been working to ensure this year's drive is a smashing success," she continued, glancing toward her table that must be the committee. Made sense, given that Chief was seated there.

No surprise Sophie was there, either. Ben had taken great pleasure in telling him about goody-two-shoes Sophie Davis and her volunteering at the church. No doubt she had more than a few gold stars in her crown.

"We appreciate each of you for being a part of this wonderful work." Maybelle smiled at Chief. "We're excited to announce that we've paired up with the fire department this year and will be using the firehall as an additional drop-off point for toys. Sophie, you and Sarah pass out the information sheets."

Sophie and the brunette stood and began handing papers to each volunteer. Cole had hoped the brunette would make her way to their table, but it was Sophie who stopped there, pausing mid-sentence when her gaze met his.

"So glad—um, Cole, uh, yeah, hi." She sounded as breathless as someone he'd just pulled from a burning building.

Seeing him flustered her. Because she'd read his journal, or because he'd been a jerk to her?

He hadn't wanted to see her again. Still didn't want to.

Only...

Knowing any show of friendliness would be exaggerated a hundredfold by his two friends, Cole barely acknowledged her as he took a flyer. As an added bonus, it meant he didn't have to see the pity or disgust that he knew had to be reflected in her eyes.

How humiliating that she knew so many things about him—things he'd never wanted to share with anyone. Best thing he could do was let her go on thinking him a jerk. It would make her less likely to want to cross paths with him again.

He'd seen her, what, a handful of times since moving to Pine Hill? If each of them tried to avoid the other, maybe their paths would cross only rarely.

"Anyone not have a paper?" Maybelle asked when Sophie and the brunette returned to the front. When no one responded, she continued. "As I mentioned, we're doing things differently this year. We're breaking into three committees responsible for covering different needs."

Breaking into groups? Cole had thought he and the guys would just pick up toys around town, put out a few collection boxes, wrap a few presents, and maybe deliver them to some kids.

"If you look at the top of the page, you'll notice a number written on the stocking in the upper right-hand corner. That's your committee number. Those with a number one are in my group, naturally. We'll be handling media for the drive and getting word out via the local paper and online sources, as well as being a contact point for the kids involved." She smiled at the crowd, then at the chief. "Chief Callahan, you're in my group."

Cole's boss nodded at Maybelle. Cole couldn't be sure, given the distance between them, but he'd swear Chief's cheeks had gone pink.

Maybelle smiled at him, then moved on. "Groups Two and Three will be working together within the community. The group leaders have lists of businesses who made donations or collected toys last year. Each group is responsible for contacting all the businesses on their list. Charlie and Ruby Jenkin will lead one group."

"Maybe we'll be with your Grandma Ruby and she'll feed us," Cole leaned over and whispered to Andrew when the couple in their early seventies stood, holding hands as per usual, and smiled first at each other, then at the other volunteers. Andrew's grandmother had welcomed Cole to her fold and invited him to all their family's get-togethers since he'd come to town. He'd actually gone to a few, as well as the Fourth of July picnic. He still remembered the fancy dilled potatoes that were, according to Andrew, Grandma Ruby's specialty.

"Theirs is group two."

Cole glanced at the number three on the stocking in the upper corner of his paper and sighed. No edible perks for him.

"Group Three will be led by Sophie and Sarah."

Naturally.

"Trade with me." He reached for Andrew's paper to snatch it out of his hands, but his friend evaded him.

"How come?" Andrew's eyes twinkled. "You in somebody's group who you want to avoid?"

Deciding to ignore Andrew, Cole focused on Ben.

"I've got a three," Ben said, showing his paper, and

chuckling. "You've got it all wrong, Andrew. Ole Cole's trying to trade *into* someone's group."

Glaring at his friend, Cole held up his paper, displaying the three so Ben would know he was trying to avoid Sophie, not be forced to be in her company.

Seeing the pity in her eyes when she looked at him left him raw and uneasy. And even before he knew she'd read his journal, he'd been committed to giving Sophie a wide berth. He knew her by reputation and he had no doubt that, given the chance, Little Miss Do-Gooder would try to make him one of her many pet projects and attempt to fill his world with snowflakes, gingerbread houses, and Christmas cheer.

A green candy cane forcing him into being Santa was more than enough Christmas for Cole.

He turned back to Andrew. "Come on."

At first Andrew shook his head, then, finally, taking on a more serious expression, he shrugged. "Okay. Fine. Since it's important to you, I'll trade. What are pals for?"

Relief flooded Cole.

That is, until he noted the humor in his friend's gaze and glanced down at the paper Andrew had handed him. A three was in the upper right-hand stocking on his friend's paper, too.

Great.

Cole would be collecting toys with Sophie.

CHAPTER THREE

AFTER SOPHIE FINISHED HANDING OUT the papers, she spotted her sister on the other side of the room. Isabelle must've snuck in late after closing the quilt shop. When Sophie joined her, Isabelle demanded, "That's Cole Aaron?"

"Stop staring," Sophie hissed through gritted teeth, swatting at her sister's arm.

"How did I miss him at Ruby's?"

"He didn't stay long." Sophie had been acutely aware of the firefighter from the moment he and Andrew had arrived that day and had been disappointed at how quickly the two men had left.

When Sophie had seen Chief Callahan here, she'd wondered if she'd bump into Cole.

When she'd stepped up to his table and looked into those icy blue eyes, she'd barely been able to breathe. The man got under her skin, that was for sure.

For his part, he'd barely acknowledged her presence. Guess that told her he hadn't changed his mind about how he felt. He wanted nothing to do with her. Ever.

That left Sophie feeling as if she'd lost something precious. Which made no sense. She didn't know him.

Only...she did. She'd gone through such an intense emotional journey reading his journal that she felt as if he was an intimate friend rather than a simple acquaintance.

Still straining to look toward Cole, Isabelle's brows lifted. "I understand now why you keep talking about him. He *is* cute."

Sophie rolled her eyes. There her sister went with the "cute" talk again. "I haven't mentioned him since the day I went to the firehall."

She hadn't. Not a single word to Isabelle, and barely more than that when her friend Sarah had asked if she'd found the owner of the journal. Sophie had glossed over her meeting with Cole then, and had only told Isabelle that he'd refused the book. Revealing his refusal to anyone else had seemed as if she would be exposing his vulnerability, so she'd kept it to herself.

She might not have mentioned his name out loud, but Sophie had thought about Cole since then. A lot.

As in, way too often throughout every single day.

She'd reread his diary, trying to imagine the quiet man with a pen in his hand, pouring his emotions onto the pages of the book. His fingers gripping the pen tightly as he bore down on the paper, firing words onto emptiness in attempt to rid himself of the nightmares inside of him.

Isabelle said, "I may start schoolgirl-crushing on him, too."

Sophie squinted at her sister.

"Oh, fine. I won't get in a tizzy over him." Isabelle glanced over at where Cole sat with Ben and Andrew.

"Are you going to ask if he's changed his mind about the journal?"

"No." Sophie snorted at Isabella's suggestion. She'd seen the narrowing of those pale eyes when she'd handed him his flyer. It was clear he wished he'd never met her.

In a way, she could understand where that distaste was coming from. What guy wanted anyone to know how vulnerable he was on the inside? Especially a tough ex-Marine firefighter?

Maybe, at some point in the future, she could make him understand that she hadn't judged him harshly because of what she'd read but rather that she viewed him with compassion. Perhaps if she told him about her work with the Quilts of Valor Foundation, he'd understand that she and others like her made quilts for military personnel past and present to comfort and help them heal after traumatic experiences exactly like the ones he'd written about.

Wouldn't it be wonderful to wrap Cole in a quilt?

To drape lovingly sewn material around his wounded warrior shoulders, letting the cotton fabric hug him, as she welcomed him home?

"Sophie? You'd best snap to it before Maybelle calls you out on your daydreaming," Isabelle warned, nudging Sophie with her elbow.

Having no idea what she was supposed to be snapping to, Sophie looked to her sister for guidance.

"Charlie and Ruby's group is over here. Your and Sarah's group is meeting at the back corner table. Perhaps you should join them," Isabelle suggested, filling in the gaps the way she always did when Sophie got distracted. Three years older, her sister had always looked out for Sophie. For their mother, too, really.

"Yes."

She should pay attention. Maybelle wouldn't think a thing of calling her out in front of the entire room. It wouldn't even be the first time for that, either. Maybelle had been her church Sunday school teacher several times over the years and had put a halt to Sophie's daydreaming more than once.

She gave her sister an appreciative smile. "Thanks, Izzy."

Sophie hurried back to where five people waited on her.

Rosie Matthews, Sarah Smith, Ben Preston, Andrew Scott, and Cole Aaron. How had she ended up giving the firemen all threes?

Having Cole in her group made her insides jittery, but it was unlikely she'd get a better chance to let him know his secrets were safe with her, that she knew more about what he'd gone through than he thought.

She'd lived it, too.

Not directly, as he had, but as the child of a father who had been unable to handle the battles taking place inside his head long after he'd returned to civilian life.

Pushing the memories aside before she fell down another rabbit hole of distraction, Sophie took a deep breath and smiled at her group. She knew everyone, of course, but Cole was probably a stranger to Rosie and Sarah. For his benefit, she asked the members to introduce themselves.

Rosie, still a vivacious free spirit even well into her sixties, batted her lashes at the three firemen, fluffed her dyed-blue hair, then held her hand out, palm down, as if she expected one of the men to lift it to his lips. Always the charmer, Ben complied.

"So nice to see you all, I'm sure," she cooed, her Southern accent coming out thick and heavy. "If I'd recalled that Pine Hill's fire department had the likes of you three and was younger, I'd have set my smoke alarm off and had y'all over for some of my grandmother's famous cinnamon bread months ago."

Eyes wide, Sophie and Sarah exchanged looks, both biting back smiles at their audacious older friend—and her well-known technique of using cinnamon bread as the way to a man's heart. Sophie wasn't sure of Rosie's exact age, but the woman was still a teen at heart. A very flirty teen who saw herself so clearly as the belle of the ball that she was still able to convince others to see her that way, as well. She was engaged to a local diner owner who was crazy about her, but she'd yet to agree on a wedding date.

When it came to men, Rosie was more bark than bite—but she was a *whole lot* of bark.

Sophie adored her and had always been a bit in awe of the amount of energy she exuded.

"What Rosie means," Sophie told the firemen, avoiding looking directly at Cole, "is that we're glad to have you guys working with us this year. Welcome."

Sarah and Rosie smiled, as did Ben. Andrew wore more of an amused smirk than a smile, and Cole just gave his friends a look that said he wondered what they'd gotten into and how quickly they could extricate themselves.

Disappointment settled heavily on Sophie.

"So, here's our list of businesses to canvass." Sophie pointed to the paper she held, determined not to let any of her nervousness surface despite the fact she was the source of amusement for two firefighters and the source of irritation for another. Lifting her chin and keeping her smile in place, she continued, "Our first order of business is to go by and talk with each one to see if they'll let us put out collection boxes again this year, and if they'll match last year's cash donation or consider increasing."

She glanced up, noted that everyone was looking at her—except Cole, who appeared as if he'd rather be anywhere than her group.

How awkward would it be if she offered to let him change? Would he even want to, since his friends had ended up in Group Three, too?

"We'll divide the list, pair up, and go by each business over the next two weeks," she told them, pressing forward. Maybe she could still salvage the situation and avoid seeing him for the most part. "Then, we'll get together for coffee to compare notes and reassess what's needed most."

"Rosie," Sarah stepped in before the older woman could offer to go with the men. "You're with me. The extra time together to talk about wedding plans would be wonderful. You know how much I value your insight since Aunt Jean isn't here for me to talk to."

Along with Andrew's grandmother Ruby, Rosie belonged to a group of women who called themselves the Butterflies. Sarah's late aunt, Jean Hamilton, had also belonged to their group, along with Sophie's Aunt Claudia, which was why she'd always given her nieces gifts decorated with butterflies. After Sarah's mother had died, the Butterflies had taken her under their wings, and since Sarah had gotten engaged, all the Butterflies were eagerly contributing to her wedding plans.

"Oh, yes, that would be nice," Rosie admitted.

"I rode over here with Andrew, so I'll partner with him," Ben offered, looking amused as he continued. "Guess that leaves Sophie stuck with our buddy."

Smile instantly fading, Sophie's cheeks heated as her gaze went back to the firemen. "I rode over with Andrew, too," Cole said, frowning at his friend.

"Ben called dibs first, though." Andrew pointed out with a grin.

"Um, well, we could divide up into two groups, the women and the men," she offered, thinking that would give both Cole and her an out. She'd go with Sarah and Rosie, and Cole could go with his coworkers. Problem solved.

"I think the three pairs we have now will be perfect," Sarah said, not quite meeting Sophie's eyes.

Sophie shot her a look to say she was supposed to be on her side. Just because Sarah was happily in love with her fiancé, Bodie Lewis, she apparently thought she qualified as a master matchmaker. She was wasting her time. Cole couldn't stand Sophie.

"Me, too," Andrew added, crossing his arms.

"Makes sense to stay as we are," Ben pointed out, not pulling off the innocent look any better than Sarah or Andrew. "Three groups can cover a lot more ground than two."

"Plus, Sarah and I will be discussing her wedding." Rosie waved her hand dismissively, apparently climbing on the matchmaking train. "We'd bore you senseless, Sophie."

"I doubt anyone has ever been bored around you, Rosie," Sophie corrected.

"Yes, so true." Rosie's face lit with delight. "But Sarah and I have lots to talk about before she says 'I do.' Bodie still hasn't told us where he's taking our girl on their honeymoon. Sarah and I can plot to find out how she should pack."

Could they be any more obvious that they were throwing Cole and her together?

"Bodie is a wise man to keep his honeymoon plans a secret from you Butterflies," Ben said, earning a scowl from Rosie and a smile from Sarah.

Realizing that, no matter how much she argued, she and Cole were paired together, Sophie longed to find the nearest hard surface and bang her forehead against it. Didn't they see how embarrassed she was? Or the sour look on his face at the prospect of being stuck with her?

He'd been through enough. Being near her bothered him. How could she let him be forced into this situation?

It wasn't as if she was eager to be stuck with him, either.

What woman wanted to be around a man who detested the mere sight of her?

Sophie felt obligated to save him. Cole could see it written all over her rosy-cheeked face, could see her racking her brain for a way to get out of spending time with him.

Good. He didn't want to spend time with her. Nor did he need her to save him as if he was some charity case.

He was a proud Marine. He'd been in much tougher situations than being forced to spend time with the likes of sweet, feminine, nosy, Christmas-y Sophie.

They'd visit the businesses on their section of the

list, do their holiday duty, and then be finished. Afterward, they could go their separate ways. No harm done.

Better to just give in gracefully and get it over with, since any protests they put up would just add fuel to the fire their friends were tossing them into. And in the end, they'd still be stuck together with no option other than to grin and bear it.

If things were different, they might've been friends. But things weren't different. Sophie had read his journal.

The less he had to do with her, the better. Which was why he needed to get through this as quickly and painlessly as possible.

Striking a pose similar to Andrew's with his arms crossed, Cole shrugged. "No problem. Sophie and I will tackle our portion of the list."

Her name, said out loud, felt odd on his tongue. Not that it should with as many times as her name had been on his mind. Everything to do with that book seemed permanently etched in his awareness.

Ignoring Sophie's surprised look, he kept his gaze trained on his friends. "Just make sure you keep up with how many more donations we get than you two clowns."

"Game on," Andrew and Ben said almost in unison and fist bumped.

The group made plans to divide the list of businesses, then to meet up as Sophie suggested in two weeks. Cole wasn't on schedule to work at the firehall that day. Too bad, as it would've been a perfect excuse to skip out.

After Maybelle made a few more announcements, the meeting officially ended. Cole had ridden over to the church with the guys and hoped they'd immediately leave. Unfortunately, they'd gotten pulled into a conversation with a guy from another group about Andrew's pride and joy: Big Bad Bertha, aka his motorcycle.

Cole sighed. They were going to be a while.

Sarah and the blue-haired granny were talking wedding stuff with another woman who'd joined them, the blonde Cole had seen Sophie with earlier. She kept glancing his and Sophie's way.

Sophie, who was still right beside him.

What did you say to someone after telling her that you never wanted to see her again?

Taking a deep breath, she found words before he did.

"I'm sorry." She truly looked remorseful and a whole lot embarrassed.

"For?"

As he'd donated the journal, he couldn't really blame her for having read what he'd written. He'd given it away and she'd gotten it. End of story.

Logically, he acknowledged that. Logic didn't make it any easier being around her, though. Her presence made him uneasy, as if he was walking into a burning house that threatened to consume him at any given moment.

Studying him, she shrugged. "That you're stuck in my group."

"It is what it is."

Pink tinged her cheeks. "Okay. I just thought...well, I didn't want you to think I purposely gave you a sheet that put you in Group Three."

"I don't." The true remorse in her eyes convinced him as much as her words.

"Good."

"We'll do our part to make the toy drive a success," he continued. "We're here for the kids. Everything else is secondary to them."

It hit him that maybe she wanted nothing to do with him, either, after their latest encounter. Who could blame her?

"Unless you'd rather not?" he suggested. "If that's the case, I'll find a reason to bail on volunteering and you can join up with the other ladies. No harm done."

Her eyes widened.

"Oh no. That's not it at all. I just didn't...well, you... I mean, I know you said you never wanted to see me again and I..." Looking as flustered as she sounded, she turned her palms up in a helpless motion. "Can we just start over? Pretend I never came to the firehall, that I never found your journal, and that we're meeting for the first time today?"

He regarded her a moment, then shrugged. "Works for me."

After all, they were going to be stuck working together on at least a couple of occasions. This would simply be making the best of a bad situation.

Looking relieved and smiling once more, she stuck out her hand.

"Hi, I'm Sophie Davis, one of your group leaders and your Christmas toy drive partner. We're going to make a great team." She flashed a smile. "Just so you know, we're going to blow away the other two pairs with all the donations we get."

Cole's gaze dropped to her outstretched hand. If she was willing to call a reset, why not go along? What was he afraid of?

He took her hand.

That. That was what he'd been afraid of. Afraid her hand was soft, warm, feminine.

Touching Sophie's hand made him feel. Cole didn't want to feel.

He'd been right to say he never wanted to see her again, should never have agreed to be her partner, but it was too late for second thoughts now.

He pulled his hand away, resisted the urge to wipe the scalded skin across his jeans, but the way his palm tingled made him question if he should.

Something flickered in her eyes, but quickly disappeared as she smiled again. Too brightly for him to think she'd been unaware of how uncomfortable their touching had been.

Did her hand burn, too?

"And you are?" she prompted, continuing with her starting-over pretense.

He was feeling ridiculous, frustrated, and was currently wishing he wasn't there, but whatever.

"Cole Aaron." He didn't sound friendly, but he'd managed not to snarl.

"Hi, Cole." Her smile was dazzling as she went into full sunshine mode. He fought the urge to put his hands up to block her radiant glow. "I've lived in Pine Hill my whole life and don't believe we've met."

Fine, he'd play along. Why not?

"Moved here earlier this year," he admitted.

"Well, I'm glad you're here and that we finally met."

In another lifetime—if he hadn't been warped, if there'd been no journal full of grim thoughts for her to have read, no grim life experiences to fill a journal with—he'd have been glad to meet her. Ecstatic.

Too bad they couldn't really erase that they'd met or what she'd read.

Self-disgust filled him and he glanced around to see if Andrew and Ben were ready to leave yet. He needed to get out of the community room and away from Sophie and those sympathetic eyes of hers that he didn't understand or like.

Knowing what he'd done, how could she even stand to be polite to him, much less act as if she wanted to be his friend?

CHAPTER FOUR

"THAT FIREMAN DOESN'T SEEM YOUR type."

At Maybelle's comment, Sophie paused from straightening up the church community room to gawk at the older woman.

They were wiping down tables and running a sweeper over the floor to leave the area clean and ready for its next use.

"You've lost your eyesight in your old age," Rosie accused Maybelle. "That hunky man is every woman's type."

"I never said Cole was my type," Sophie told Maybelle. When Rosie opened her mouth to protest, Sophie held her hand up. "Just because you and Sarah are playing matchmaker doesn't mean I approve."

Carrie, who'd joined them in their cleaning, raised her head. She was Sophie's fellow church member, friend, and more recently, business associate, since her pet store was selling Sophie's handmade pet bandanas. "You're interested in Cole Aaron? The grumpy firefighter in your group?"

"He's not grumpy," Sophie defended, even though she knew she was at the risk of adding fuel to the gossiping fire. At least, he hadn't been grumpy until he'd realized she had read his journal.

"He's just, well…" She pushed a chair back beneath a table and tried not to let too much show. "He's more the strong, silent type. That's all. Besides, he's been through a lot."

Sophie glanced toward Sarah for help. If anyone should understand what Cole had been through, Sarah should. Although her fiancé now worked for the sheriff's department, in addition to acting as Sarah's handyman at her bed and breakfast, Hamilton House, Bodie had endured some rough times during his own military career. Sophie didn't know the details, but Bodie's emotional recovery had taken much longer than his physical one from an explosion where he'd been the sole survivor.

As she had hoped, Sarah joined them where her friends now circled Sophie.

Sarah gave an empathetic nod and patted Sophie's back. "Sophie's right. Our brave military sacrifice a lot."

She'd known she could count on Sarah.

"I'm sure Carrie didn't mean any disrespect to Cole or his service," Sarah continued. "But I have to agree with Maybelle. Watching you with Cole surprised me, too. He's nothing like any of the guys you've gone out with over the years. He's cute, though."

There Sarah went with the "cute." What was up with everyone calling Cole cute? He was so much more.

Besides, in and of itself, that Cole wasn't like any of the other guys she'd dated wasn't a bad thing. Obviously, none of them had been all that amazing, which was why, for one reason or another, she wasn't with any of them now.

"I'm not interested in Cole," Sophie insisted. Then, realizing no one was buying her quick retort, she added, "Not like any of you are implying or trying to set up. I don't want to date him." She didn't. "Nor does he want to date me." That was the understatement of the year. "But I do feel badly for him after all he went through when he was deployed. He's still new to Pine Hill and it can't be easy making a life for himself here." She shrugged. "I wish I could make things better for him."

Which was the absolute truth. Her heart broke for the things he'd suffered during his time in Special Ops and wished she could take away his inner turmoil.

Just like Dad.

Sophie gulped back the thought.

Sarah's brow rose. "Did he tell you something about his past or do you know about it because of what you read in his journal?"

"What journal?" Carrie asked as she bent to pick up a stray piece of wadded-up paper off the floor.

Sarah glanced over the room to make sure they'd restored it to pre-meeting cleanliness, then said, "Sophie found Cole's journal in a box of donated books when we were getting ready for the church rummage sale. She returned it to him."

Sophie started to tell her friends that Cole had refused to take the journal, but then decided to continue to keep that to herself and hope her sister did the same.

If she told them, they'd be more curious about what he'd written, might even ask to read it, and she had no intentions of telling anyone the things she'd read or of sharing the book.

"He's easy on the eyes, but not much of a talker," Carrie mused, putting her hand on the back of a chair. "Jeff volunteered with a group of kids to wash the firetrucks for a community project over the summer." Jeff was her teenaged son. "I was one of the parent volunteers, and I remember noticing how quiet Cole was. Polite, but quiet. Is he more expressive as a writer?"

Not meeting her friend's eyes, Sophie shrugged. Cole's story wasn't hers to tell, and he obviously didn't want anyone to know about it, including Sophie.

"I'd like to make him a quilt for him," she said to distract them, knowing bringing up their shared passion should do the trick. Carrie wasn't a quilter, or even a seamstress, which was why she had Sophie making the bandanas to sell at her pet store. That didn't keep Carrie from volunteering with them during sew-ins to help in other ways, though.

An avid quilter, Sarah's face shone with excitement. "Oh, that would be wonderful. We could..."

Sophie shook her head. "You, my friend, have a wedding to plan. Christmas Day is barely over a month away and will be here before you know it."

Sarah had chosen to become Bodie's wife on her favorite day of the year, which Sophie found perfect for the couple as their romance had started during the Christmas season a year ago.

"So," Sophie continued, "'we' won't be doing anything."

Happily in love, Sarah laughed. "Okay, you're right, but I do think it's a wonderful idea to award a Quilt of Valor to Cole."

"Me, too." After reading his journal, she couldn't imagine anyone more deserving or in need of one. "I'd like to make him a quilt myself."

Everyone in the room's eyes bore into Sophie and she fought to keep her expression casual.

"Because you feel badly for what he went through?" Carrie asked.

Sophie bit the inside of her lower lip, then nodded. "Yes. If ever a Marine needed to be wrapped in a quilt of healing, Cole Aaron does, and I want to be the one to make his quilt."

"Well, you know what happened when I made Bodie's quilt," Sarah reminded with a smile.

Sophie fought bursting out laughing at Sarah's insinuation. Bodie had come to Pine Hill to say thank you to his quiltmaker and he'd ended up falling in love with Sarah.

Forget coming to town to thank her—Cole seemed more likely to leave town to avoid her. Sophie could wrap Cole in a dozen quilts, and she doubted he'd forgive her reading his journal, much less feel gratitude and love toward her.

She'd never made a quilt with the expectation of receiving either of those. She made them because of the gratitude she felt, the love she felt, toward the military who gave and sacrificed so much for their fellow countrymen.

She made each and every quilt for her father.

She would make Cole a red, white, and blue quilt and maybe, since she might never be able to say the words, doing so would let him know he was appreciated.

Dreading the next couple of hours, Cole parked his SUV in the only vacant parking spot in front of Sophie's quilt shop.

The store was located in a row of similar buildings that ran the length of one side of the town square. Its antique brick exterior had been painted a country blue trimmed with white, giving it a unique look. The quilt shop's windows shone with a colorful display of red, green, and gold fabrics and a Christmas quilt was displayed over a rocking chair with a message about being thankful. The tan awning above the entrance was pristine.

Garlands festooned with lights wrapped around the windows and door and a big wreath hung on the door, matching several other businesses around the square. A bench sat out front and someone had tied big red bows on each end. Old fashioned lamp posts lined the street and were heavily decorated with snow flocked garland and ribbons of their own.

The whole place looked like something from a magazine article about small towns or like it belonged on a Christmas postcard where someone jotted a happy note about days gone by. Warm, inviting, nostalgic, festive.

A sign with a large needle with a thread looped through it was painted onto Sophie's shop's window front. The Threaded Needle.

Catchy. Had Sophie chosen the name or had the shop been around longer than she had? Despite its spotless refurbishing, it appeared as if it could have been a cornerstone of the square since the town had been established in the eighteen-hundreds.

A quilt shop.

Perhaps her excuse to Ben of being busy sewing made more sense than Cole first thought.

Thinking of his friends made him grimace. They'd not let up on the Sophie jokes since they'd bumped into

her at the toy drive meeting on Tuesday evening. No, before that. They'd been at it since her firehall visit. Which
was why he'd offered to meet Sophie at her workplace
rather than his when she'd wanted to immediately start
crossing off businesses on their list during her lunch
break.

He worked twenty-four on, forty-eight off most of the
time, so meeting her hadn't been a problem. He didn't
have to be back at the station until the following morning.

Climbing out of his SUV, he glanced around, a cool
breeze whipping at the flannel shirt he'd thrown over
his T-shirt before heading out. He'd driven through the
square many times, had frequented the local pawnshop
located on one side for used farm equipment, had even
helped put out a fire in an upstairs apartment above
one of the businesses, but he paused to take in the
stately courthouse that was the center of Pine Hill as he
always did.

Automatically standing a little taller, full of pride,
he lifted his gaze to the flag that flew high and majestic
at the top of a pole out front, seeming to stand guard
above the small town.

God Bless America was printed on a large wooden
sign on the courthouse yard, surrounded by miniature
wreaths with flags in recognition of local heroes, past
and present, that had been placed as part of a Veterans
Day service the previous week. Cole had intentionally
stayed in the background, but had otherwise proudly
attended that ceremony, paying his respects to his com-
rades, his flag, and his country.

Even if he'd never really thought he could belong

anywhere, he'd come closer than he'd believed possible in this friendly little town.

He'd been right to stay rather than immediately sell his uncle's place, as he'd initially considered. The farm was where he was meant to be. On his off-work days, he was slowly updating his late uncle's house. He figured if he did decide to sell, to move on someday, the repairs and modernization would speed things along.

He hadn't gotten anything done that morning, though, as he'd been too preoccupied with thoughts of Sophie and trying to figure out how best to make the Santa suit fit him.

A chime went off as he walked into a pine-and-cinnamon scented, color-coordinated world of fabric, accessories, and various knickknacks. Several sewing machine displays stood on one side of the shop. Other sections featured stylishly decorated shelves packed with various how-to projects. To his right were a pastel section with various baby quilts and even a patriotic section with a few red, white, and blue quilts that were perhaps leftover from celebrating Veteran's Day. One area boasted Christmas fabrics and hand-crafted Christmas items. Although it was still November, he supposed one had to plan ahead when making homemade items for the holidays.

Cole could sew on a button or hem a pair of dress blues. Otherwise, he knew nothing about sewing or quilting, as proven by the mess he'd made that morning attempting to rip out the hem on the Santa pants. But even his untrained eyes recognized the aesthetic appeal of the well-stocked and well-organized shop. No doubt just stepping through the doors made crafters' pocketbooks empty themselves.

Christmas music played in the background and he could hear Sophie singing along to the upbeat tune about rocking around a tree, though she wasn't in sight.

"Good morning," she called from somewhere behind a display shelf to his left.

Hearing her voice kicked his pulse up several notches. He paused, sternly reminding himself that all they had to do was go drop off toy collection boxes and pick up a few checks. It was just another mission, one where he'd keep his eyes on the objective. He'd get through this and be done with Sophie once and for all.

Or at least until the next time they bumped into each other.

"Feel free to look around. Our remaining Thanksgiving material is on clearance and we've got some pre-Christmas specials going," she called, obviously unaware of who exactly had entered her shop. "I'll be with you in a few, but if you need me before I get there, just holler."

Cole wouldn't be needing her or any of her holiday specials. What he needed was to get this over with so he could get back out to the farmhouse before someone made him hand over his man card. He headed in the direction her voice had come from, rounded a display and paused.

Wearing jeans and another red Christmas sweater, this one with three presents on the front, a slightly-swaying-to-the-music Sophie leaned over a second cutting table and ran a rotary tool along a straight edge, making a perfect slice along the fabric. She moved the straight edge, double checked the width of the material the cut would create, then made another swift swipe of the sharp-bladed tool.

"You sure you're licensed to wield that thing and dance at the same time?" he heard himself ask, instantly regretting the teasing note in his tone. He needed to keep their interactions simple, minimal, and completely professional.

"Oh!" She jumped at his voice, turning toward him as she did so. "Cole! You startled me."

"No kidding."

Uncertainty shone in her hazel eyes as her lips curved in a tentative smile. No doubt she wondered if he was friend or foe.

He was neither, but for the duration of the toy drive, they were stuck together.

Sill looking a little flustered, she glanced at her watch, then up at him. "You're early."

By ten minutes. He arched a brow. "Should I have waited outside?"

"Oh, no, definitely not. I...just, um, let me finish these strips, if that's okay? I'm almost done. I'll run them through the cutting machine later this afternoon."

"Cutting machine?"

She gestured to a table set up to one side of the open work area. "We sell packages of precut shapes like flowers, stars, leaves—that kind of thing. During down time, I put quilt and table-runner kits together."

He supposed a small-town specialty shop would need to find creative ways to stay in the black and be competitive with chain stores.

"Quilters don't want to cut their own material?"

"Some do." Her tone said she couldn't imagine why. "But cutting material can be tedious work, so our pre-cut packages sell well. Plus, our dies cut precise shapes and patterns. A buyer doesn't have to worry about miscut pieces throwing off the pattern and things not lining up properly. Precision cutting is everything in quilting." Pausing her activity, she glanced his way. The earlier uncertainty from her gaze was gone, replaced by an excitement for her subject. Her face practically glowed as she added, "For the quilt kits, I color-coordinate everything, package the precut pieces with step-by-step directions, and include everything to make the quilt top. A customer has the option to include material for the back of the quilt, batting and thread. They can opt out if they already have their own, or want to choose something different, but for those who want a full kit, we make it easy by putting it all together."

She barely took a breath the whole time she talked.

"Seems to me," he began, "that if someone was going to buy all that done by someone else, they'd just buy a premade quilt and save themselves even more time."

Sophie gave him a horrified look. "Why would they do that?"

Cole eyed her at her total bewilderment. "Why wouldn't they?"

"Because quilting is fun, brings people together, and is a useful work of art," she defended, her hands going to her hips.

"Artwork even when everything is precut?"

"A painter may purchase paint in various shades rather than mixing his own, but that doesn't make him any less the artist when he puts all those premixed colors on a canvas."

Not quite sure he followed her explanation, Cole just shrugged. "If you say so. Cut your strips so we can get to our toy drive business."

She glanced back at the bolt of fabric she'd been working with. "In a hurry to get started?"

"In a hurry to get finished," he corrected, looking at his watch.

"Oh. Yeah, I guess so." Her gaze flickered to him and she flashed one of her full-dimpled smiles. "We have that friendly competition to win."

Cole shouldn't have tossed out the challenge to his friends but at least it had diverted them from their matchmaking teasing—for the moment, anyway.

"Finish your strips," he repeated. "I'll wait outside."

Giving him one last curious look, she nodded and went back to cutting her material.

Rather than leave, as he should have, Cole watched her mumble to herself while making quick work of the bolt of fabric she sliced and diced into nine-and-a-quarter-inch wide strips. When she'd unwound the final bit from the cardboard base, she made one last swipe of her rotary cutter, folded the fabric, then placed it on top of her stack. She jotted a note on a small piece of paper and pinned it to the leftover material, giving the size of the remnant.

"I thought you were going to wait outside," she remarked when she turned to face him. Her eyes glittered as if his having stayed amused her, but he could tell she was still trying to decide how to take him, too.

"So did I," he admitted, surprised he hadn't escaped the shop immediately at the first opportunity. Curiosity had gotten the best of him. "What is it you're going to do with those strips you cut?"

Giving him another full-on I'm-so-glad-you-asked smile, she picked up the stack of strips.

"It's easier to show you. Follow me." She walked over

to a machine that wasn't much bigger than a computer printer. Folding one of the strips back and forth over a die, she layered it multiple times, placed a rubber mat on top of the fabric, then pressed a button that pulled the fabric sandwich through the machine. Once it had reappeared on the other side, she lifted the mat, pulled away a tiny scrap of excess material, then showed him perfectly cut four-and-a-half-inch squares.

"Impressive."

"And a lot faster and more accurate than cutting them by hand with a rotary tool. That just made twenty-four squares."

"I'm not so sure it would have taken you any longer to cut it all out yourself. I've seen you with that rotary cutter."

Her eyes danced with delight at his comment, causing Cole to plant his feet to the ground to keep them from stepping back. She tossed the excess bits of scrap material into a cloth bag attached to the end of the table.

He asked her, "How good are you at Santa suit repairs?"

Her gaze lifted to his. "Excellent. You know someone needing longer sleeves and an adjustment to the pants hemline?"

"I might," he admitted.

She eyed him up and down, then spouted off some numbers.

"What's that?"

"Your pants size. I'm right, aren't I?"

"You have a side gig at the fair guessing age and weight, too?"

"No, but I like to keep my options open. Get me your

Santa suit and I'll have it looking as if it was made for you."

"Deal." Because he sure hadn't had any luck with it. After the mess he'd made, he had bagged it up, planning to bring it back to the firehall to see if one of the others knew what they were doing. "I'll pay you. What's your rate?"

"That depends. Why *do* you have a Santa suit?"

"Didn't you hear the good news? I'm the fire department's Santa in the Christmas parade."

Sophie's jaw dropped. "Seriously? You?"

"My sentiments exactly."

She flushed, as if she was worried she'd offended him. "I'm sure you'll do great—it's just that I wouldn't have guessed you for a stand-in Santa."

"It's not by choice."

Her lips twitched. "Ah, I see. You lost a bet?"

"You might say that. One involving a green candy cane."

She eyed him curiously. "I suspect there's a story there. Let me tell Isabelle I'm leaving, then we'll get this party started. You can fill me in on the juicy details while we're on the road."

He hadn't realized there was anyone else in the shop and glanced around, still not seeing anyone.

Sophie grinned. "You may not see her, but I'm sure that she saw you the moment you walked in."

"The security cameras?" He'd noticed them upon first entering the shop but had figured they were there for theft prevention and detection—the kind of thing you checked after the fact if there was a problem rather than actively manning them during store hours.

Sophie nodded. "She insisted we have them since

she works from the office a lot and doesn't like me out front by myself. Frankly, I think she really just wants to keep an eye on me at all times."

"She's the boss?"

"She thinks she is," Sophie laughed, but her gaze was still wary, as if she expected him to roar at her at any moment and was braced for such. "From the time I was born, she's been bossing me." At his blank look, she added, "Isabelle is my sister as well as business partner. She's three years older and thinks that makes her smarter and better at all things in life. I let her keep thinking that."

Sophie put her thumbs to her ears and wiggled her fingers around, making a face toward the ceiling camera, much as a child might do.

Completely caught off guard, Cole arched a brow. "What was that?"

Sophie shrugged. "Our secret code that I'm ready to go to lunch—and also that I know she's been watching my every move, and it's time to stop. I call it the Ready-to-Go Reindeer."

"Are you kidding me?"

She gave him a pointed look. "Please. Have you seen some of the secret signs baseball players use? Think of this as a sewing store secret sign that you were lucky enough to witness."

Cole stared at her. "I'm one hundred percent sure no baseball player in the history of mankind has ever used that particular sign for anything—and they never will."

"No?" She gave him a pert smile. "Well, they should. It would catch the other team off guard and give them a huge advantage."

"No doubt." Suppressing an unexpected almost-laugh, Cole shook his head. "Or have the umps tossing them from the game."

"There is that possibility," Sophie agreed, still smiling.

"I can't believe you just did that in front of a customer," the blonde he'd seen at the toy drive meeting said as she came out onto the sales floor.

While he'd noticed her before, Cole hadn't realized the woman and Sophie were sisters. But that explained why Isabelle had kept glancing over at them at the meeting. Sophie had probably told her what a piece of work he was, and the woman had been keeping a watchful eye on him in case he got out of line.

Whereas Sophie had sun-kissed light brown hair and hazel eyes, this woman was all pale blond locks and blue eyes. He could see some similarities in their facial features, though.

But more than their coloring, their personalities seemed to set them apart. Sophie was happy rainbows and sunshine. Her sister was more no-nonsense.

"No worries, Isabelle," Sophie assured, not looking the slightest repentant. "Cole has no intention of purchasing fabric, precut or otherwise. He prefers buying his quilts premade."

Isabelle shook her head, then glanced toward Cole. "She's been like this her whole life. Good luck. She's all yours."

I wish.

Cole fought flinching at the unexpected thought. No, he did not wish Sophie was all his.

What he wished was that he wasn't here, that he'd never gotten to know the smiley, surprising woman who read his journal. But the thought of not having met Sophie left him as unsettled as the thought that she'd read his journal. Which didn't make sense.

She was a talkative, bubbly person...who might be a little crazy, given the face she'd made at her sister.

Not that he should, nor that he wanted to, but Cole sort of liked her kind of crazy.

Chapter Five

S OMEDAY, SOPHIE WOULD QUIT GIVING in to her impulses, but apparently that day wasn't today. She had no idea why she'd just made reindeer antlers and an immature face at the camera in front of Cole.

Not completely true. She hadn't liked the nervousness of thinking she was going to do something embarrassing—so she'd taken the pressure off by getting that behind her. Plus, she'd wanted Cole to relax.

So, yeah, Sophie had behaved childishly, but catching both Cole and her sister off guard had been worth it. Given the chance, she'd do it again.

She snuck a glance at Cole and would swear he was fighting a grin. If it would make him smile, she'd make a dozen faces at the security cameras.

"You'll be back by two?" Isabelle asked as a not-so-subtle reminder that Sophie and Cole were on a time crunch.

The words sounded almost like a warning, but Sophie knew they weren't—or at least that they weren't meant to warn *her*. Despite Sophie's impulsivity, Isabelle knew Sophie took their business seriously; she worked long hours toward making it a success. Her sister's question was directed more at Cole, much as a protective parent might remind a prospective date of curfew time.

Her sister had nothing to worry about. Cole was too honorable to bail on the toy drive, but that didn't mean he liked being paired with Sophie. He was clearly in a rush to be done so he could walk away from her as soon as possible.

Ignoring Isabelle's furrowed brow, Sophie asked Cole, "You ready?" His look said he was as ready as he'd ever be to spend time with her. "You've got the collection boxes with you?"

Cole nodded. "Everything's in my truck."

Sophie grabbed her cell phone, then snagged her coat before waving bye to Isabelle. Hopefully, she wasn't overly stressing her sister by taking a few hours off. She'd bring back a piece of key lime pie from Lou's as a peace offering.

"Our list has most of the businesses on the square, so let's start here, then we can swing by Lou's Diner, put out a box, get his donation check, and grab lunch at the same time."

Cole's expression flickered briefly, as if he was going to refuse her suggestion—probably objecting to the "grabbing lunch" bit she'd thrown in—but then he nodded, as if he was resigned to whatever the day brought.

"I bet Rosie is in a tizzy that Lou wasn't on her list, although for Lou's sake, that's probably best. If she tried to convince him to sign over the diner, he might actually do it, because he's crazy in love with her," she rambled on as they stepped out into the surprisingly balmy November day. Unable to resist, she lifted her face toward the sky, spread her arms, and soaked up the sunshine.

"Working on your Christmas tan?"

Cutting her gaze toward him, she laughed. "Ha. That's funny. Just upping my vitamin D level. First up is Paw Parties." Sophie giggled at his expression. "It's a pet specialty store run by one of the ladies I go to church with. You may have met the owner at the toy drive meeting. Pretty blonde named Carrie, in her late thirties, maybe early forties. Super great lady. She specializes in parties for pets and organic treats."

He didn't look impressed. "Parties for pets? Are you kidding me? People around here go for that kind of thing?"

Pausing on the sidewalk, Sophie's hands went to her hips. "People around here? What's that supposed to mean? That we're too backwoods to properly pamper our pets? I'll have you know we adore and celebrate our furry family members in Pine Hill."

His lips twitched. "Tell me, just how many parties have you thrown for your pet over the past year?"

"Well, none, but that's because—"

Looking amused, he held up his hand. "Stop right there. I've made my point."

"But that's not fair."

His gaze cut toward her, and he shrugged. "Life isn't fair."

Sophie sighed. "You're missing the point."

"Which is?"

"I don't have a pet." Not that she didn't want a pet, but every time she fostered one with thoughts of keeping it, Isabelle promptly found it a forever home. She suspected it had something to do with how many tears

Sophie had cried years ago at the loss of their beloved Snuggles. Isabelle didn't seem willing to risk that again. Other than Sophie and their mom, her sister tended to shut everyone and everything out that might wiggle its way into her heart.

If Isabelle knew Sophie was feeding the yellow cat on their front porch nightly in hopes of befriending him, Isabelle would no doubt lecture her. Thankfully, her sister didn't make use of the porch during the winter months, so she hadn't noticed the food and water dishes, or the small flannel blanket, lying just beyond the porch chairs.

"Guess you're right. Hard to throw a party for something you don't have," Cole conceded. "Surprises me, though. I'd have taken you for someone who had a dozen animals."

Barely restraining her smile, Sophie narrowed her gaze. "Are you saying I look like a crazy cat lady?"

One side of his mouth lifted. "You said it, not me."

Bees buzzed in Sophie's belly at his half-smile.

"Maybe someday I will be a crazy cat lady. A girl can dream."

She imagined what it would be like when she had her own place. Currently, she and Isabelle put all their profits back into the shop, making small strides on their very big loan toward the goal to be debt-free. Someday, after the note was paid, Sophie would start saving for a house. Somewhere close, though, in case Isabelle moved, too, because Sophie wouldn't leave their mother alone. Darlene would be lost if both her girls left home.

"Hey, Carrie," Sophie called when they walked into the shop. "I don't even know why they have you on our list when you were at the meeting the other night."

"I wasn't officially there, just dropping off some dog treats Sarah had ordered for Harry—and then I stayed to help with clean up." Carrie's gaze went to Cole and she smiled. "Hi, nice to see you again. We met over the summer? My son volunteered with the high school football team to wash the firetrucks."

"Jeff seemed like a good kid."

Carrie beamed with pleasure that he'd recalled her son's name. "He's a great kid. Best thing that ever happened to me."

Cole was polite enough, shaking Carrie's hand, but rather than continuing their conversation, he turned to look at a sealed bag of organic sweet potato doggie bites, letting Sophie take over.

"I figured you'd be by. I have a check already made out," Carrie told her, giving a questioning look toward where Cole was seemingly ignoring them.

Sophie shrugged, giving her an I-have-no-idea look, and then took the check Carrie pulled out of a drawer.

"Thanks so much for this." She put the donation in an envelope she'd labeled "Toy Drive Donations," then stored the envelope back in her purse.

"You're welcome. I was going to give you a call this week if you didn't make it by. Your Petdanas are selling fabulously. Everyone loves them and the cute sayings you embroider on them."

It was Sophie's turn to beam. She and Carrie had come up with the idea while volunteering at the church's Halloween Trunk or Treat. Excited, Sophie had gone home and sewn a dozen that night and brought them to church the following day to show her friend. Carrie had loved them. Sophie was ecstatic that first set had sold and that now, the subsequent larger batch had, too.

"I've thought about putting them on the website," Carrie added. "What do you think?"

"Oh, wow. Selling them online would be fabulous." Another step in diversifying their sewing business and ensuring The Threaded Needle's longevity and success. If it helped Carrie, a single mom and small business owner, too, that was an added bonus. "I'm in." Very much so, as she'd had fun making the cute pet bandanas.

When she and Cole left Carrie's store, they stopped by his vehicle to pick up another collection box, then headed to their next business.

They hit most of the businesses on the square. Afterward, they climbed into Cole's SUV and Sophie set the bag with the Santa suit on the floorboard. She noticed a crossword puzzle book on the passenger seat and couldn't resist picking it up and flipping through the pages.

She'd found Cole's Christmas card tucked inside a crossword puzzle book like this one, but if she hadn't been looking for something to identify him then she'd never have picked that book up. Word games had never been her thing. Apparently, not Cole's either, as the puzzles hadn't had a single letter written in any of the blocks. Just as this one didn't.

"Sorry about that," he apologized, reaching for the book, but Sophie shook her head.

"How come none of the puzzles are done?"

"It's a new book," he answered, then gave her a sideways glance. "Why did we decide to pair up partners, again? You didn't need me for any of this today."

"What makes you say that? I'm glad you're here." She tucked the crossword book safely under the edge of the seat so she wouldn't accidentally step on it or bend the pages.

"All I did was carry boxes."

"And be there. Sometimes just being there is enough," she pointed out while buckling her seatbelt. She'd been dreading their outing, but so far, the day hadn't been that bad. "Besides, it's always best to travel in pairs rather than alone."

"Not always."

Sophie waited for him to say more, *wanted* him to say more, but he didn't, just started his SUV.

"Surely when you were in the military, they taught you to travel in pairs."

"You're thinking of the Boy Scouts."

"Seems like the same principle would apply in the military," she countered, twisting in her seat to watch him. "Isn't it better to have someone to watch your back?"

"Depends on what your job is."

Having read his journal, Sophie knew what some of Cole's jobs had been. It seemed that he had been part of a special ops team. Had Cole been alone on some of his missions?

He asked, "Where to now?"

"Lou's Diner would be great." She glanced at her watch. "After that, I'll need to get back to the shop to take over the register so Isabelle can work on the books and online stuff."

She was sorry that her afternoon with him was reaching its end. Because, although he was quiet and stood in the background when they were around others, she enjoyed being with Cole. Especially during the times when he seemed to relax a little.

Lou's was busy with the usual lunchtime crowd, but there was a booth open in the back of the diner. Since Lou was tied up with customers, Sophie and Cole decided to order lunch prior to talking to the owner about the toy drive.

"Lou's joke of the day was funny, don't ya think?" Sophie asked as they made their way to a vacant booth. Cole shrugged. "Did you even read it?"

"'What do you call it when it's raining turkeys?'" Cole recited, proving that he actually had noticed what had been written on the dry-erase board.

"'Fowl weather,'" Sophie answered, grinning at the joke as she sat down across from Cole.

Their waitress took their order, then Sophie went back to talking because that was what she did, particularly when nervous. They'd had a good day, much better than she'd have expected, really, but Cole did make her nervous so she couldn't stop the chatter, not even after their food arrived. Occasionally, he'd comment.

"You run a shop, sell quilt kits online, sell pet bandanas in local shops, volunteer at church and community projects." His eyes glittered. "Tell me, Sophie, is that why you're still single? Because you're too busy for a relationship? Or is a previous bad relationship why you stay so busy?"

His personal question caught her off guard and she paused before answering, taking a bite of her veggie burger. Finally, she shrugged. "I enjoy all the things I do. And I admit to having an attention disorder." There were so many interesting things constantly distracting her. Like him, for instance. "There's no previous bad relationship." Not a lot of previous good ones, either.

"When I meet the right man, making time for a relationship won't be a problem."

Because she figured it would be years and years before she met him. By that time, The Threaded Needle wouldn't be mostly owned by the bank. She and Isabelle would be able to hire more help at the shop than their three part-time employees, which would lessen the number of hours she worked, herself.

Not that she didn't enjoy the work. She did. But she'd love to devote more time to other projects such as church events and Quilts of Valor. Especially at this time of year. The need for volunteers always picked up around the holidays. Plus, she'd been inspired by the man sitting across the table from her to work on a new patriotic quilt. She'd sketched out a pattern on graph paper, had chosen the material, and was mulling the design over in her head prior to making the first cut.

She really would love to make him a quilt but suspected he'd refuse. Maybe with time, he'd warm to the idea, though.

"What?" he asked, obviously noticing her scrutiny.

"Nothing," she said, taking another bite of her sandwich and smiling at him from across the booth's table.

Nothing except he might not have been looking for a friend, but too bad, because he'd found one.

Sophie's smile was making Cole nervous. Why did she keep looking at him that way? The way that said she knew something he didn't and if he *did* know her secret, he wouldn't approve.

Sophie liked to push people outside their comfort zone.

No doubt going with her today had been a bad idea... but not going would have been worse. The guys never would have let him live it down. They didn't dictate his every move—far from it—but they were his only close friends outside of the service, and he'd rather not have them on his case.

He was thankful for the bond he'd formed with Andrew and Ben. He'd lay his life down for either one of them, and knew they'd do the same for him. It's what they did.

But that didn't mean they wouldn't hassle him about going to lunch with Sophie. Which was why he kept his end of the conversation to a minimum. In Pine Hill everyone seemed to know everyone, and no doubt someone in the restaurant would mention having seen them there.

Not that his disengagement mattered. Sophie talked enough for both of them, telling him about her shop, her mother, her sister, and life in Pine Hill. Cole just listened and enjoyed watching how animated her face and hands were while she talked.

Finally, he had to ask. "Are you always this happy?"

French fry part of the way to her mouth, Sophie paused mid-sentence. "Happy?"

"Happy, talkative, you know."

She laughed, then waved her Parmesan-coated French fry. "These are amazing enough to make the whole world happy. Try one."

Cole could eat anything. Being in the military did that to a person. But for the most part, other than

Andrew's Grandma Ruby's cooking, he ate for health rather than pleasure, so he shook his head.

"Thanks, but no thanks. My arteries would rather I didn't."

Sophie rolled her eyes. "Way to make me feel guilty for enjoying my very, very yummy food." He started to apologize, then paused as she popped the fry into her mouth and grinned. "And for the record, my cholesterol is completely normal and, fortunately, I have no family history of heart disease. Now, do you always eat healthy or do you have food weaknesses like the rest of us mere mortals?"

Cole thought a moment, trying to think of something he'd eaten that had given him pleasure. Memories of his mother baking hit him, and his lips curved.

"Cookies."

Her lips curved. "Cookies?"

"Christmas cookies. The kind that are cut in shapes and decorated with all the bells and whistles," he clarified, his mouth watering a little in a Pavlovian response to the memory of sitting at the kitchen counter, helping his mom make them, decorating them together, laughing, and then demolishing as many as she'd let him have.

"Must be some great cookies, since just thinking of them made you smile."

Smiling at Sophie was dangerous. Being near her was like playing with matches with fingers soaked in gasoline.

His gaze met hers. "They were great."

Although he could tell she was itching to ask for details, she didn't. Just launched into telling him about how vanilla ice cream was her favorite dessert. That surprised him. He'd have guessed any flavor other than vanilla. Sophia seemed more a candy sprinkles and extreme flavors kind of person.

Despite the crowded restaurant, the table seemed eerily quiet when she excused herself to go to the ladies room, leaving him without her chatter.

The quiet didn't last a full minute.

"I'm wearing his ring!" the blue-haired granny Rosie said as she slid into the booth across from him. She flashed a generous-sized diamond on her left hand, wiggling her finger. "He should be happy with that."

Cole stared at her, not saying anything and hoping Rosie didn't expect him to.

"I've been married three times—God rest their souls. He should just trust me on this and quit pushing."

Knowing when to keep quiet, Cole picked up his water glass. Maybe all the Pine Hill women were gifted with the ability to carry on one-sided conversations.

"You can't blame Lou for wanting you to set a date," Maybelle said, pushing Rosie over as she also seated herself at Cole and Sophie's booth.

Would Sophie find him if he paid their bill and headed to the truck?

"Oh, go back to your own table." Rosie scowled at the other woman. "I came over here to get away from Lou and my so-called friends. I'll set a date when I'm ready."

Her seemingly harsh response caught Cole off guard, but Maybelle took it in stride.

Ignoring Maybelle's concerned frown, Rosie reached over to pick up a fry off Sophie's plate. "These things are heavenly, but I'm not allowed to order them. Lou won't let me."

"Because you're acting childishly, and so he has to treat you accordingly." Maybelle plucked the fry from Rosie's fingers before she could bite into it. But rather than put it back on Sophie's plate she bit the end off that hadn't been in Rosie's fingers. "Mmm, you're right. That *is* good."

Rosie shot an evil eye toward Maybelle. Cole leaned back, wondering if he was about to witness a granny catfight, and wishing Sophie would hurry up and get back to the table.

Maybelle just smiled, as if nothing Rosie said fazed her. "Go talk to Lou and I'll give you the other half back."

"As if I want the other half back after you've had your fingers all over it."

Sophie came back to the table, eyed the two women who now occupied her side of the booth, then glanced toward Cole as if to ask how this had happened. He automatically slid over to make space for her on his side of the booth. Not that Cole wanted her that close, but he couldn't just leave her standing there. Besides, these ladies were her friends. Maybe she'd know what to do with them.

With one more questioning look his way, Sophie sat down, then smiled at the women. "What did I miss?"

The bickering grannies launched into a sordid tale of why Blue Hair wouldn't set a wedding date and why Regal General thought she should, before finally saying their goodbyes.

Cole let out a sigh of relief when they'd gone back to their table.

"Don't believe anything they said about each other," Sophie warned. "They're the best of friends, even though you'd never know it from that conversation. Kind of like how you are with Andrew and Ben, I imagine."

With the women gone and the opposite side of the booth empty, Cole felt odd with Sophie still sitting next to him. They weren't touching, but it wouldn't take much to accidently bump against her.

After they finished eating, they drove back to her shop with a key lime pie for her sister. As they drove, Sophie told him all about the ladies and their lifelong friendship and matriarch roles within the town. She told him about her Aunt Claudia, who was also a "Butterfly" and who'd started taking trips with her husband after having dreamed of traveling for many years.

When they got to the town square, he parked in front of her shop to let her out. A fuzzy yellow cat sitting on her windowsill caught his eye.

"I thought you didn't have a pet."

Following the direction of his gaze, Sophie smiled.

"He's not mine and doesn't want to make friends despite the fact I've been feeding him for weeks." She gave an exaggerated sigh. "He comes around, teases me with how close he gets, but has yet to let me touch him. As far as I can tell, he doesn't belong to anyone." She eyed the cat that must have sensed them watching him as he jumped down and took off down the street. "He is beautiful, though."

Cole hadn't had a pet in years—if the random critters he'd carried into his mom's apartment had even counted as actual pets. He never got to keep them for long before she forced him to release them.

Sophie picked up the bag with the Santa suit, but she didn't open the car door, just left her hand resting there as she turned to him.

"I'll get the suit altered in the next couple of days. I know you need it next week."

Still staring at the yellow cat, he nodded. "I appreciate it."

She smiled. "Thanks for helping today. Sorry I have to go back to work before we completely finished."

His gaze refocused on the woman sitting in his passenger seat. As Sophie opened the SUV's passenger door and stepped out, he had a flashback of how he'd feel when his mother took away his latest pet.

"No problem," he mumbled. "I'll take these boxes to the last couple of places on our list."

"It's safer to go in pairs," she reminded with her usual bubbly smile. "If you're free, we could go together after the shop closes."

Safer to go in pairs? Cole snorted. She didn't really he was in danger by himself on the mean streets of Pine Hill. And if they went together and ran into trouble, did she really think *she'd* be the one protecting *him*? What did Sophie think she'd do, talk their assailant into giving up? Unleash her Butterflies on them, maybe? He fought grinning at the notion.

"I think I'll be okay on this one." Delivering toy collection boxes by himself in Pine Hill seemed way safer than spending more time with Sophie.

"I—okay, but I had a good time today and wish we could deliver the rest of the boxes together. I'd like for us to be friends."

Her disappointment was palpable, which had Cole feeling guilty. But today had been a mission, not a precursor to their becoming friends.

She saw him as another charity case, he reminded himself. She could save her charity for someone else who deserved it.

"We're not friends and never will be." Pushing the words out was harder than he'd expected.

Sophie winced, and for a brief second, Cole wished he could take back his blunt words, that he could give in to the desire to be his friend shining so clearly in her lovely eyes.

"I, well, I thought...never mind what I thought. If that's how you feel—" She paused, swallowed, and he couldn't help but wonder if she was fighting back tears.

Yeah, he was a real piece of work and deserved the guilt shredding his insides. Guilt that he'd allowed today to happen without realizing what it meant to her. He'd been trying to get their obligations over with, and instead Sophie had thought they were becoming buddies.

"Then fine, we won't be friends. But for the record," she lifted her chin, "you are missing out, just like that silly cat is, because I'm a great friend."

Cole suspected she was, but he was determined not to find out firsthand. Just like the cat, he didn't need her to come along and try to rescue him. Some things were beyond rescuing.

Sophie couldn't fix the parts of him that were broken.

CHAPTER SIX

THE FRIDAY BEFORE THANKSGIVING, SOPHIE back-stitched her seam, clipped the thread, then pulled the material from the sewing machine and looked at what she'd sewn. Perfect scant quarter-inch seams bound the two pieces of fuzzy red material together. *There.* She was done with the Santa suit.

She shook the material and smiled at how well it had turned out. The pants should fit him perfectly, as should the coat. He'd be a dashing Santa.

Cole was pretty much a dashing everything.

Groaning at the thought, Sophie changed the thread in her machine over to navy, then picked up two pieces of precut navy material. Over and over, she sewed pieces together, adding them to a growing stack. Soon, she'd press the pieces and start combining them together into a quilt of stars and stripes—the best design she'd ever created. Every block needed to be perfect, as she'd likely use it for a prototype block-of-the-month at some point in the future.

The bold colors and design would have been perfect

for Cole if he'd ever let her award a quilt to him. She still held out hope that one day, he'd accept it.

Even if he didn't want to be her friend.

What a mix the man was. Dark and deep, but with a sense of humor that would come out at the oddest moments. During the times he'd dropped his guard, she'd enjoyed delivering the boxes with him and had been thoroughly disappointed he'd rejected her friendship. Again.

She knew why, of course. He was embarrassed that she'd pried into his personal thoughts without his permission. Not that she *could* have gotten his permission beforehand since she'd only read the journal in the first place to find out whose it was.

Sophie had a sewing machine in her bedroom; an old-fashioned Singer model that had belonged to her grandmother. It had seen many hours of use over the decades. Prior to the shop closing, she'd started sewing on the Santa suit, then the quilt, and hadn't wanted to quit to go home even long after Isabelle had locked up and headed out.

She stood, stretched her arms over her head, then behind her back, rolling her shoulders several times. She should've stopped to stretch more. She tried to maintain good body mechanics and habits, but sometimes, she got so caught up in what she was doing she didn't notice how much time had passed and would sew to the point of all her joints going stiff.

Like tonight. It was nearly eleven. She'd have to be quiet when she snuck into the house.

She packed her supplies and stowed them in their bag. No need to bring it home with her as she wouldn't be doing any more sewing tonight.

Her gaze fell on the Santa suit. She'd leave it here, as well, and have Cole pick it up. After all, he'd insisted her repairing it was a business transaction. So she'd be all business.

She set the alarm, stepped outside the front of the shop, then locked the deadbolt. The night air was brisk, and she wished she'd brought a heavier jacket with her that morning. Thankfully, her walk home would take less than ten minutes.

Despite the chill and her rumbly belly from being too busy sewing to remember dinner, she paused to admire the courthouse across the street, majestic as the center of the square and the town. The entire square was well lit, displaying picturesque lampposts and streetlights and Christmas decor, but the courthouse always seemed so grand with the lights shined upward illuminating the flag whipping in the wind.

Pride filled her at the sight of her hometown. She loved Pine Hill so much.

Unable to resist, she pulled her cell phone from her bag and snapped a photo of the building with its haloed-in-light flag, planning to post it on the shop's social media page the following morning, then slid the phone into her back pocket.

She was still thinking about how pretty downtown looked when it was decorated for Christmas as she exited the commercial district and rounded the corner to the residential street where she lived. As with the square, her neighbors took Christmas seriously and almost every house already boasted festive lights. A few had big, blow-up decorations filling their yards, and Christmas trees twinkled from inside windows.

Despite the chill nipping at her, Sophie smiled at

the pretty scenery around her. All that was needed was Santa to make the night complete. Santa Cole, that is.

"Meow."

Oh, no. Guilt hit Sophie, and she stopped walking and looked around for the yellow cat. Her belly wasn't the only thing she hadn't fed that evening. No doubt the poor thing wondered why she hadn't given him dinner yet.

But where was he?

"Meow."

This time, she realized the sound came from overhead. Sophie searched the branches of the old oak trees that lined the street, illuminated by the streetlights.

"Meow."

"There you are."

Way up in the branches, the half-grown cat paced back and forth, looking distressed.

He was stuck in the tree. She'd heard of that happening, but had never expected to experience it in real life. *Eek.* No way could she leave him up there.

Looking at the limbs, Sophie calculated whether she'd be able to climb up to get to the cat. He appeared to be about fifteen feet up, maybe a little higher. There weren't any really low branches on that tree, but the tree next to it had several large, low ones—and then higher branches that reached over into the other tree's space. If she climbed up the one, then crossed over, she thought she could then make it up to where the cat was.

The cat meowed for help. "I'm coming, baby," she promised, dropping her bag to the ground and preparing to climb.

He'd stopped pacing and was now watching her as

she reached for the first branch. It was a struggle, but she got a hold of it and pulled herself up, snagging her sweater in the process. *Ugh.* She really liked this sweater, too. Maybe she'd be able to repair it.

"You know, after this, you have no choice but to like me." Once securely on the branch, she carefully stood, then began climbing. Slowly, but surely, she made her way over to where she could transfer over to the other tree.

"I'm almost there," she assured the cat before glancing down. She immediately regretted doing so as a wave of vertigo hit her. The branches hadn't looked nearly so high when she'd been standing on the street. Fixing her gaze forward, she tentatively made her way through the limbs to the one where the cat perched.

"I'm here," she told him, realizing he'd have to come to her. His branch wasn't big enough for her to climb out on. "Here, kitty, kitty."

The cat blinked, looking a little bored by Sophie's predicament.

"Um, you're going to have to work with me. I mean, this isn't even expecting you to meet me in the middle. I came ninety-nine percent of the way to you. All you have to do is cross, like, three feet to get to me and I'll carry you down."

Although, she wasn't quite sure how she'd manage that, especially if the cat was scared. Maybe she'd put the cat against her stomach and pull her hem up, wrapping him in her sweater to keep him safe until they were out of the tree.

She wouldn't think about just how high up she was or who was going to keep *her* safe.

"Here, kitty, kitty. Come to me so we can get out of this tree, preferably with a nice, slow descent."

He meowed but didn't budge from where he rested on the branch, watching her. Sophie continued to coax the cat to come to her, but to no avail.

"I can't stay in this tree all night," she told the cat, shivering. "For one thing, I'm not wearing a fancy fur coat like you." Just a medium-weight sweater jacket meant to keep her warm during her short walk home. "Plus, we're both hungry."

Obviously, she was no cat whisperer because the cat had the audacity to yawn.

"Don't you realize I'm here to rescue you?" After all, the cat had been meowing like crazy and pacing prior to Sophie climbing the tree. Now, he looked ready to take a nap. Go figure.

Sophie shivered again. Keeping one hand securely wrapped around a nearby branch, she rubbed her free palm up and down her raised arm. Numbness was beginning to set in beneath the sleeve of her jacket, either from the cold or having her arm extended for so long. How long had she been up there? Maybe she should go back down and call someone to come help the cat. Maybe that's what she should have done to begin with, she thought as she glanced down and tried to visually retrace the path she'd taken up the tree.

Dizziness hit, hard and fast and fierce.

She squeezed her eyes shut. How had she gotten so high? Had the cat been climbing higher as she'd made her way up? That was the only possible explanation, because the ground was clearly a lot further away than it should be.

She swallowed and told herself to calm down. She'd

made it up the tree and she would make it back to the ground. Then she'd call someone to come help the cat. No big deal.

Only when she went to let go of the branch, she discovered that she had a death grip on it and couldn't seem to let go. Her brain ordered her fingers to release, but they weren't budging.

Panic began to set in. She couldn't stay in the tree all night. It wasn't so cold that she'd freeze, but she'd likely end up sick from exposure. Already she was sniffling and needed a tissue.

She needed help. From someone with a ladder.

Which ruled out her mother and sister, both of whom were probably asleep anyway. Besides, what could they do? Her mother couldn't climb the tree, and, even if Isabelle could, it wasn't as if she could toss Sophie over her shoulders and carry her down.

Who had a ladder, a very tall ladder, who she could call at close to midnight?

The fire department had tall ladders.

Um, no. She couldn't call the fire department. What if Cole was there? Even if he wasn't, he'd hear about her being stuck in a tree. She'd rather him not know the dilemma she'd gotten herself into.

Sarah's fiancé, Bodie, probably had a ladder for his handyman work…but a regular ladder wouldn't be tall enough to get her down from the tree. No normal person would have a ladder high enough to reach her.

The wind rustled through the dried-out leaves that had refused to fall from the tree, making an eerie sound that that sent shivers down Sophie's spine. Or maybe that was from the cold air cutting through her clothes.

"Look what you've gotten us into," she told the cat.

Glancing toward him, she sighed. "Okay, so maybe it wasn't your fault I thought I could rescue you, but you aren't exactly a bundle of help, either, are you?"

He watched her through half-closed eyes as if he didn't have a care in the world. Didn't he realize that his rescuer needed rescuing? Glancing down one last time in hopes of finding a magical pathway to the ground that didn't involve gravity and broken bones, Sophie fought back tears.

She had to call the fire department. There was no other option. Cole might not want to be her friend or to see her, but desperate times called for desperate measures.

With one hand clasping the lifeline branch, she dug into her back pocket, grateful her phone wasn't in the bag she'd left on the ground. Unwilling to let go of the branch to push buttons, she voice-commanded her phone to dial the fire department and thanked God for modern technology.

Relief filled her as someone picked up the direct line, but her nerves only increased when she recognized the voice.

"Hi, um, Cole?" Lord, help her get through this and live to laugh about it someday. "This is Sophie and uh, well...you wouldn't happen to have your sleigh and flying reindeer handy, would you?"

Cole was shocked to hear Sophie's voice. Was she calling close to midnight to tell him she'd finished altering his Santa suit?

"Nah, the flying reindeer magic only works one night a year."

"Too bad. I sure could use it about now."

Why did she sound frightened? And had she just sniffled?

Was she crying?

His stomach knotted into a tight wad. "Is everything okay?"

"No." That was definitely a sob. "I—I'm stuck in a tree."

"What?" Cole dropped the puzzle book he'd been working on. It had been a slow night, and most of the crew were asleep. Andrew and Ben were in the middle of a video game, locked in an epic battle to save the world from an alien life form, so Cole had picked up the cordless phone when it rang. It was rare that the direct line went off during the night, so he'd been expecting a wrong number or a family member of one of the crew who couldn't get through on their private cell.

"I, um, you know the cat we saw the other day? Well, I saw him on my walk home, stuck up in this tree. I live right off Main Street, and anyway, just after I rounded the corner, I heard him meowing up in one of those big oaks and I thought I'd rescue him." She was talking fast, pausing only to sniffle before continuing. "But now, well, I'm stuck, too. Every time I try to climb back down, I get woozy and just—"

An image of Sophie trying to climb down from high up in a tree and falling flashed through Cole's head. As a firefighter, he'd worked all kinds of accidents, seen some horrible things that shouldn't have happened. This couldn't be one of those things. It…just couldn't.

"Sophie." Her name rolled off his tongue harshly,

brokering no argument. "Listen to me—don't move, okay?"

Cole tapped Andrew's shoulder, motioning for him to come with him. The world would have to be saved from alien invaders on a different night.

"No worries there." She countered. "I can't pry my fingers loose from the branch I'm clinging to. If I survive this, I may have permanent tree bark impressions from this day forward. What if I can never sew again?"

If she survived this? Was she in peril of falling? And who cared if she could never sew again? If she was hanging from a tree limb, she had bigger concerns than whether she'd be sewing once she was safely on the ground again.

Cole had dealt with emergency situations more times than he could count over the years, both during his military career and with the fire department. Not once could he recall having felt the stomach plunge he'd gotten from Sophie's words.

"You're hanging from a tree branch? How high off the ground are you?" How had she called him?

"I'm standing on a branch, hanging onto another branch for support," she clarified, sending a wave of relief through him. The situation still wasn't good, but at least she wasn't dangling precariously from a limb. "Just please come help me, Cole. I know you don't like me, but I'm cold and scared and...Cole, please don't hang up." This was said in a tone of pure despair.

Cole *did* like her. That was the problem. He shouldn't like her, didn't want to like her. But he liked her anyway.

"I'll stay on the phone with you, Sophie." He wouldn't have hung up regardless, unless he thought being on the phone put her in further danger. "But I need to change to my cellphone so I can head your way."

"Hurry, okay?"

"I'm on my way." He disconnected the land line and then punched the number she'd given him into his cell phone. Relief filled him when she immediately answered. "Come on," he told the guys, pointing to the ladder truck. "We've got a cat stuck in a tree."

"You're all worked up over a cat in a tree?" Andrew gave him a surprised look. "That's why Sophie called? For us to rescue a cat?"

His friends must have been listening in on his side of the phone conversation.

"More like we've got to rescue the person trying to rescue the cat. Sophie's stuck in the tree, too."

"Did you have to tell them that?" she said as all three men got into the ladder truck.

"The more the merrier," Cole quipped, hoping to keep her distracted from her fear. He'd never forgive himself if something happened.

"You'll be surprised to hear this, I'm sure, but I'd rather no one know about this."

"Too late for that. Ben's already called the *Pine Hill Herald*. They may beat us there, cameras in hand for a live feed. No doubt you and your furry climbing friend are going to be social media stars by morning."

"The man's got jokes," Andrew snorted as he drove the ladder truck out from the firehall. "Sirens?"

Cole shook his head. Part of him wanted the sirens on so his friend could drive as fast as possible to the corner of Main Street, but they weren't that far away, and for safety reasons, they wouldn't go much faster through the town streets even if the sirens were blaring.

Besides, there wasn't really any traffic to have to worry about at this hour. The sirens would only wake everyone who lived on that side of town and draw a crowd.

How high up was she in the tree? With the way she'd talked about feeding the cat, he was pretty sure she'd have climbed to the top of a redwood had it meant saving the furry critter. Good thing there were no redwoods in Pine Hill; just some decently tall oak trees right off Main Street.

Sophie sniffled again and Cole's ribcage crushed in on his lungs. What had she been thinking to climb a tree after a cat who wasn't even hers? Her impulsiveness was going to get her into trouble one day.

Today. Her impulsiveness had gotten her into trouble today.

"You're going to be okay, Sophie. Just stay put, and I'll get you out of the tree."

God, please let her be okay.

Not that God had heard any of his prayers in years.

Not true, his conscience reminded. *You're here, aren't you? Alive and healthy and making a decent, peaceful life for yourself? You've got a home, friends, a job you love.*

Sophie.

No, he didn't have Sophie.

"I'm here and I'm not going anywhere," Sophie assured, her voice sounding small and jittery. "You're bringing a ladder, right? You're going to need a really big ladder, Cole. The longest ladder the fire department has."

"How high up are you, Sophie?"

"I don't know." Her teeth chattered. "It didn't look like much from the ground, but now that I'm up here,

93

I feel like I'm in the nosebleed section...I see the fire-truck!"

"Slow down," he told Andrew, his gaze skimming the shadowy, lamplit trees. The Christmas lights that already had been put up all over town helped in finding her right away. She stood on one branch while clinging to another nearby smaller one. "There. Pull over."

Andrew pulled the truck to the edge of the street just in front of the tree where Sophie was. Not waiting for his friends, Cole was out in a flash.

"I see you. Oh, Cole, I'm so glad I see you." Her voice sounded choked, and he couldn't quite tell if she was crying or laughing. "You really came."

"Did you not believe me when I said I was on my way?" He stared up the tree at where she appeared precariously perched.

"I believed you. You're too honorable to have left me stranded. It just felt like forever before you got here."

Honorable? She knew better, but he wasn't going to argue with her.

He knew what she meant about feeling as if the drive had taken forever. The past five minutes might have been the longest of his life, and that was saying something.

"Where's your phone?" he asked, realizing both her hands were wrapped around a branch. How had she even gotten up that high? There were no low branches on the tree. Assessing the situation, he noted a large limb snaked over from a neighboring tree. She must have gone up that way.

"On speaker inside my sweater pocket so I could hang on with both hands."

"Smart thinking."

"Desperate thinking," she corrected. "Hurry up and get me out of this tree, please."

"The things chicks will do to get your attention," Ben mused coming to stand next to him as they studied the branch configuration to gauge how close they'd be able to get the bucket to Sophie.

"Tell Ben I heard that, and that when I get down, I'll pray really hard to forgive him for making fun of me when I'm half-terrified."

Ben chuckled, put his hands on his hips and continued to stare up the tree. "Sorry, Sophie. We'll get you down in a jiffy."

"Sophie, I'm hanging up now since you can holler down at me if you need to. Ben's right, we'll have you down in a couple of minutes."

Only, rescuing Sophie took longer than Cole would have liked.

Andrew put the truck in the best position for getting the ladder to her, but a lot of small branches were in the way. While Ben shined a spotlight on the branches, Cole cut a few of the limbs away to move in as near as possible.

Finally, he was close enough that he could reach her.

But when he stretched to help put the security harness around her waist, she didn't budge from where she grasped the tree branch.

"Sophie? I need you to help me help you."

CHAPTER SEVEN

SHIVERING, TIRED, SO READY TO be out of the tree, Sophie bit into her lower lip as her gaze dropped to the harness in Cole's hand.

He was right there, waiting to pull her onto the ladder with him. All she had to do was let go of the branch, put the harness on and let him assist her onto the ladder. Easy peasy.

But she couldn't let go.

She felt as if she'd been clinging to the branch for hours. Maybe she had been. Her entire body ached with cold and stiffness. She wasn't even sure if she felt her hands anymore, or if her brain just told her she still held onto the limb.

"Sophie," Cole's voice was low but urgent. "You have to put the security strap on, then let me help you onto the ladder with me."

"I—I can't," she admitted, wishing it weren't true. She wanted to be on that ladder with Cole. But no amount of wanting seemed to send the signal to her hands to let go.

"I know you're scared, Sophie, but you have to trust me." His voice was calm, steady.

"Rescue the cat first," she suggested, stalling for time. How could she want down so badly and still be so afraid to take the help offered? Shouldn't she be leaping into his waiting arms?

"I've yet to see your cat."

Sophie glanced toward where the animal had been. Nothing.

Horrified and fearing the worst, she glanced to the ground below. Big mistake, as it made her head spin. There was no cat fallen to the sidewalk, thank goodness, just Ben and Andrew shining a spotlight up at her.

"He was here," she insisted, squeezing her eyes closed as she fought off the new wave of dizziness. "When I climbed up here, the cat was stuck, too."

"Likely story. You sure you just didn't want to see me tonight to tell Santa your Christmas wish list?"

Sophie's gaze shot to Cole's pale eyes, barely visible in the light. He was teasing her, probably trying to startle her out of her nervousness. She was okay with that because it was working.

Eyes locked with his, Sophie shrugged and let out the breath she hadn't realized she'd been holding. "Like Ben said, the things chicks will do to get your attention." Her teeth started chattering.

"Sophie," Cole's voice was low, his hand stretched out to her, "You have my attention. My full attention. Put the harness on and trust me to take care of you."

She *did* trust him. Silly, because outside of his journal, she barely knew him, yet she trusted him completely. Probably just her impulsiveness getting her into trouble again. Or maybe that was her heart pitter-pattering at what he'd just said.

She breathed in deeply, the cold air settling heavily in her lungs. She had to let go of the limb.

Keeping her focus on Cole, she pried one hand loose from the branch, brushed the bits of bark and moss off on her jeans, then grasped for the harness. Following his instructions, she put it on, then took Cole's hand.

"I've got you. Thank God," he breathed, as he helped her onto the ladder.

Sophie was the one thanking God as the realization hit that she was alive and in one piece and Cole's arms were around her, warming her chilled body.

For the briefest moment, she thought his lips brushed against the top of her head.

They hadn't, of course. That she'd thought they had was pure craziness. Fear had obviously muddled her mind and she was in shock and hallucinating.

Such a sweet hallucination to have his arms around her and him kissing the top of head, though.

Sophie shivered.

"I've got you," he repeated. "You're safe now."

She leaned back against him, thankful to be off the branch. Thankful he'd come for her.

"I'm going to lower us down," he told her. "Are you ready?"

She nodded but felt wobbly, as if she'd fall if he let go of her. He must have known because rather than the ladder moving, he leaned in and turned her chin so she could look at him over her shoulder.

"I take it you didn't climb many trees as a kid?"

She hadn't expected his teasing tone now that she was out of the tree. But his silly question was exactly what she'd needed as laughter bubbled up inside her. Perhaps it was tinged with a bit of hysteria, but hysteria apparently went well with hallucinations, because she felt better than she had since realizing she couldn't get down from the tree.

"It's not the climbing that was the problem," she managed to bite out, resting her chin against his warm fingers where he held her face. "It was the threat of a rapid descent."

His eyes twinkled in the glow of the streetlight. "Gravity is so overrated."

His face was so close to hers, the warmth of his body around hers comforting. She couldn't have stopped herself from smiling even if she'd wanted to.

Her heart ka-thunked as Cole's mouth curved in a grin back.

Yep, she was suffering from a complete and total mental breakdown, because she'd swear Cole looked at her with...well, something way more than just relief that his current assignment had ended well.

"Everything okay up there?" Ben called from the ground, obviously wondering why they hadn't moved.

"She's just getting her bearings," Cole answered. The warm look in his eyes dissipated so quickly that she almost thought she might have imagined it all as he said, "We better get down there before they call for backup."

Feeling as shaken from her encounter with Cole as she did from being stuck in the tree, Sophie nodded, and they began their trip downward.

"I may or may not have taken pictures," Ben teased as Cole helped Sophie to the ground.

"You would," Cole shot back.

"I *did*. It isn't every day I get to see you rescue a beauty from a tree."

"You just wish it had been you," Andrew accused.

Ben grinned at Andrew. "I'm not the one who was dateless this weekend."

Andrew rolled his eyes. "Here we go again about you and your date. Take out a billboard or something."

Sophie appreciated the guys' banter as it gave her a minute to collect her wits. She was on the ground. She was glad she was on the ground.

"Wasn't there something about a cat being in the tree, too?" Andrew asked, obviously tiring of his conversation with Ben.

"Sophie's cat abandoned her," Cole told them.

"I hope he's okay," she fretted, looking around but not seeing any sign of him. "I don't understand how he just disappeared."

"You're sure a cat was there, and you didn't imagine that there was an animal stuck in the tree? Maybe the wind or something sounded like meowing?"

She glared at Ben. "Don't ask me what I'm imagining right now."

Andrew laughed.

Wrapping her arms around herself for added warmth, Sophie sucked in another steadying breath. "I'm sorry y'all had to come out to rescue me, but thank you for doing so. I'm so glad to be out of that tree."

"Broke up an otherwise boring shift," Andrew admitted.

"Not that we don't appreciate boring," Ben added.

Sophie's gaze went to Cole. He'd grown quiet, distant. Nothing of that earlier light in his eyes was visible now that they'd returned to earth.

"Thanks. I don't even know where to begin to repay you for saving me."

Cole looked uncomfortable at her praise. "We were just doing our job."

"Well, thanks for doing your job." Her gaze went back and forth between the three men. "I guess I'll head home now."

Because the longer she stood there, the more awkward the moment was becoming, and her shivering was getting worse.

"Which house is yours?"

Sophie pointed down the street. "I, uh, thanks, again. Y'all are my heroes."

"What are you doing?"

"Baking cookies." Sophie didn't turn to look at her sister, just kept doing what she'd been doing prior to Isabelle coming into the kitchen.

"Okay, let me rephrase my question. Why are you baking cookies first thing in the morning?"

"I'm bringing them to the firehall as a thank you for rescuing me the other night," she admitted, cutting another cookie, tweaking the shape with a fork tine, then placing it onto the buttered cookie sheet.

"For Cole?"

"For Andrew, Ben, Cole, and whomever else is there today."

Sighing, Isabelle shook her head. "I know what you're doing."

"Showing my appreciation?"

"Looking for an excuse to see Cole Aaron is more like it."

"That's not why I'm baking cookies. Besides, if that was what I was after, I wouldn't need an excuse. I'll see Cole this weekend when our group meets to go over what still needs to be done for the toy drive."

True. She would see him that weekend. It was also true that she hadn't seen him since he'd rescued her. For whatever reason, it felt as if weeks had gone by instead of merely a couple of days.

"So, thank him. Send a card. Write a letter to the newspaper editor about how great our fire department is. Email Chief Callahan singing praises about his crew. There's no need to go there."

"I can do all those things, too," Sophie agreed. "But why not do this? They came to rescue me late at night because I was too petrified to climb down by myself. The least I can do is make them cookies."

Isabelle leaned back against the kitchen counter. "I'm worried about your fascination with Cole."

"It's just a thank you, Isabelle."

"What about the quilt you're making?" her sister pushed. "You've not said anything about it to me, but it's for him, isn't it?"

"I make quilts all the time. You know how involved I am with Quilts of Valor." She played dumb because she didn't want to argue with her sister. Isabelle meant well. "Besides, I don't understand what the big deal is about my being nice—especially to someone who deserves my kindness. And yours, too, for that matter."

Guilt momentarily flashed onto Isabelle's face, but then she shook it off. "I don't want to see you get hurt."

Sophie didn't want Isabelle to worry, especially when there was no reason to. Cole barely tolerated her company.

Only, when she'd been up in the tree, when they'd been on the ladder, there had been something in his voice, in his eyes, in his touch...something that had probably only existed in her imagination, but oh, how sweet the seemingly impossible moment had been.

"By Cole?" she scoffed, knowing she needed to reassure Isabelle. "The man came up a tree and rescued me. Why would he hurt me?"

"From what I've gathered from what little you've told me about reading his journal, he has a lot of issues. We both know what the fallout from those type of issues can lead to. Dating him wouldn't be smart of you."

"I'm making the man cookies, not dating him," she reminded, placing another cookie on the sheet pan.

"Do you *want* to date him?"

Sophie chose that moment to turn to put the pan into the oven before carefully turning back to her sister's intense blue gaze.

"I feel badly for him. He's a good person. He went through a lot, lives in a town where he only knows a few people and is obviously working hard in an honorable profession in his civilian life. Not to mention, he's making a choice to give back by helping with things like the toy drive. It's what we both wish Dad had been able to do."

All true, and probably why she was so invested in Cole.

Especially after reading his journal and knowing he fought the same mental battles her father had.

"Besides, I need to drop off his Santa suit, too," she reminded. "There's no way I can charge the fire department for the alterations after they rescued me."

"Someone here to see you, Aaron."

Again? Cole straightened from where he'd been bent next to the tower, cleaning the truck, and knew who he was most likely to see when he turned around.

Which explained why his heart had zoomed into overdrive.

"Again?" Ben echoed Cole's thought as his friend glanced up from where he was rubbing the truck down with a cleaning cloth.

"Maybe there's another cat stuck in a tree," Andrew suggested when he spotted Sophie. "Nope, looks like she brought you something again, though. If you don't want these, I do."

"Hi, guys," Sophie greeted, brandishing a smile at each of them, but pausing as her gaze connected to Cole's. "I've finished the Santa suit alterations and thought I'd deliver it. I brought these for you, too."

Her tone was upbeat, friendly, but her eyes held questions. Questions Cole had asked himself over the past couple of days. He always came to the same conclusion.

He needed to stay away from Sophie. For both their sakes.

His gaze dropped to the plastic container she held. "What are they?"

"Cookies."

"Cookies?" His gaze lifted to hers. She had that about-to-bubble-over-with-excitement look shining on her face, and he guessed what she'd done.

Her smile had enough wattage to power the whole town's supply of Christmas lights as she nodded. "I baked them this morning."

Cole popped the lid and was met by a heavenly scent. First wiping his hand over his pants leg, he lifted a perfectly decorated sugar cookie Christmas tree from the container and took a bite. It tasted even better than it smelled.

"Pass 'em around," Ben demanded.

Cole grabbed a second cookie, a reindeer face, just in case the container came back empty, then handed it off to Ben, who walked away with it to share the wealth. Andrew followed close behind, snagging a couple of cookies.

Which left Cole standing alone with Sophie.

"I hope they're okay." Her smile was still in place, but he'd swear she just bit into her lower lip.

"I like them," he assured. *Oh, Sophie, what are you doing here?*

"Oh, good." She smiled again. "They're a thank you for rescuing me."

"No thank you was necessary for just doing our job. Besides, you've already thanked us."

She shrugged. "Words didn't seem enough."

"These," he held up what was left of the reindeer, then finished it off, "are enough. They're amazing. I haven't had any fresh-baked cookies in years."

"Does your mom not make them anymore?"

She probably did. Cole just hadn't been home to eat

them. How could he when his family treated him as a hero and he knew that was the last thing he deserved?

"Not sure. I haven't seen her at Christmastime for a few years."

Sophie raised her eyebrows. "What? You don't go home for Christmas?"

"Uncle Sam doesn't make assignments based upon where mothers live."

She studied him, wanting to ask more, he was sure, but rather than point out that he no longer worked for the government, she sighed. "I shouldn't have pried. Sorry."

Popping the rest of the cookie into his mouth and hoping the sugary sweetness abated the remorse Sophie's expression filled him with, Cole shrugged. "You brought cookies. You're forgiven."

Her smile returned. "Is that all it takes to get your forgiveness? Cookies?"

"Can't say, really. First time it's happened," he admitted.

"Then I'll be thankful it happened with me."

Sophie's pleased expression making him uneasy, Cole turned to see where the cookie container was. Every firefighter on duty had made their way to the table where Ben set the dish. "I'd best go grab another or they'll all be gone. Thanks for fixing my Santa suit."

"Oh, yes, well, you're welcome. I should be going, too. I still have a lot to do before opening the shop."

"Doggie bandanas to make?"

Her eyes twinkled. "Amongst other things."

"Do you ever do something just for you, Sophie? Something that's not volunteering for a project or sewing something for other people?"

She looked indignant. "Sewing is for me just as

much as it's for the person who'll end up with the finished product. Creating works of art that are useful makes me happy; knowing that what I've made will bring joy to someone else makes me happy, too."

Because Sophie was a giving person.

She'd made him and the guys Cole's favorite kind of cookies. Not since his mother had someone done something kind just for him. It was a bit humbling. Everything about Sophie humbled him.

"I truly appreciate you rescuing me, Cole. As silly as it sounds, I can't recall being so terrified as when I glanced down and realized how far away the ground was."

Sophie stuck in the tree had scared him, too. Fortunately, everything had turned out okay, but it easily could have been otherwise. "Just in case the need arises, I want you to promise that you won't go attempting another cat rescue on your own."

"Cole," she began.

"Sophie," he countered, before she could refuse his offer, "I've trained for tree rescues, roof rescues, you name it. If your cat needs rescued, I'm your man."

Her brows lifted and mirth filled her eyes.

"Professionally speaking, of course," he felt the need to add. He couldn't have Sophie taking what he'd said the wrong way.

"Of course," she said with an adorable grin. "And you have my word. Should the situation ever arise again, I promise to call."

Good. He didn't want her risking her life for the cat. His concern was for her safety. Just a firefighter trying to keep a community member safe. Nothing more.

Yeah, right.

CHAPTER EIGHT

"So, THAT'S TWENTY-FIVE BOXES TOTAL at various businesses," Sophie informed the group that weekend, taking a sip of her cocoa as she glanced over the paper she held in her other hand. She was grateful for the way the hot cocoa warmed her insides. She couldn't believe how far the temperature had dropped that week.

It had even started spitting snow that morning and hadn't let up yet. There wasn't any significant ground cover yet, but there was starting to be a white dusting—with more scheduled to come throughout the day.

Sophie loved snow. They usually only had a few good snows each winter, and per the forecast, this one could be a big one.

She forced her attention on the paper she held so she wouldn't focus on the man sitting across from her. Cole had been the last to join their group. When Ben and Andrew had arrived without him, she'd had a moment of wondering if he'd be a no-show. Relief she shouldn't feel had washed over her when the café's door had opened, and it had been Cole shaking snow from his boots on the Merry Christmas rug just inside the doorway.

He'd been nice enough when she'd brought the cookies to the fire station, but his friendliness had been on the surface only. She figured that was because he'd not wanted to encourage her.

"Next weekend is the Christmas festival," Sophie reminded, tapping her pen against the tabletop as she studied the list she and Sarah had put together earlier that day. "Donations always peak that weekend. We'll need to go by and collect them so we'll have an idea of what we still need to fulfill requests."

"Good idea," Rosie praised, waggling her penciled-on brows at the men. "Sarah and I may need one of the men to go with us to carry all the donations that are sure to come in at the businesses on our list."

"I've got that covered, Rosie," Sarah informed her toy drive partner. "Bodie will be helping us go to the businesses, and he will carry anything we need carried."

Rosie gave an oh-well-I-tried shrug. "If the two of you are too busy planning your wedding, I could always take care of things, so you don't have to worry your pretty head about it."

"Our wedding is all planned," Sarah assured, a dreamy look settling onto her face. "Just a few more weeks, and Christmas Day will be here."

"You're getting married on Christmas Day?"

Sarah nodded at Cole. "I can't imagine anything more perfect than marrying the man of my dreams on the most magical day of the year. Can you?"

Her glowy words and expression had Cole averting his gaze. He didn't answer her question, but then,

Sophie didn't imagine Sarah noticed as she was all Bodiefied—the term Sophie and Isabelle had invented for when Sarah got all wrapped up in thoughts of her soon-to-be husband.

They ran through the rest of the meeting agenda, making plans to drop off everything to the firehall where Sophie and Sarah would make an inventory of the items collected.

"Did the Santa suit fit okay?" Sophie asked, glancing toward where Cole leaned back in his chair, quietly taking in the meeting.

"Like it was made for him," Andrew answered for him.

Cole nodded. "He's right. It fits perfectly. Thank you."

"Pretty sure Bob's got competition for next year. No green candy cane needed," Ben added.

Cole frowned at his friends and shook his head. "The snow has apparently given you all brain freeze."

Rosie's phone buzzed and a smile spread across the older woman's face as she read the text. "Sorry to bail on y'all, but I've got to run."

They said their goodbyes as Rosie bundled up, then left.

Sophie grinned at Sarah. "Wonder who that was?"

Sarah sighed. "Hopefully, it was Lou, and she's on her way to finally set a date to marry the poor man."

"He sure does love her."

"That he does, and he might have more patience with her than she deserves," Sarah agreed. "Speaking of love, Bodie and I are having a little get-together later this evening at Hamilton House." She ran the bed and breakfast out of the home she'd inherited from her Aunt Jean. The house held special significance for Sarah and Bodie, since he was the one who had helped her renovate the place and get her business started. "Our booked guests checked out early last night because they wanted to head home prior to the snow, so we've decided to have some friends over. We're going sledding, so come dressed for playing outdoors, and bring something to change into afterwards for games at our place, because you're all invited."

Sophie's gaze immediately went to Cole.

"Thanks, but I've got plans."

Plans? Sophie's pulse quickened. Not that it was any of her business, but what kind of plans did Cole have? With whom?

Why did the thought of him having plans make her so uneasy? She should be happy for him that he had plans. Unlike her. Unless you counted sewing a Christmas quilt for the shop. She'd finished the top, had the batting and back sandwiched together, and planned to load it on the quilting frame soon to quilt it.

An exciting Saturday night ahead of her, for sure.

"Not finished with those hardwood floors yet?" Andrew asked.

Cole shook his head. "Purposely saved them for after I had all the painting done except the baseboard trim work. I'm trying to decide the best way to redo them. I've watched several how-to videos on refinishing wood floors but I'm still not sure."

"You should talk to my Bodie," Sarah told him, her chest puffing with pride. "He's excellent around the house. That's how we met. He answered my handyman help-wanted ad." Her gaze cut to Sophie and she giggled. "Well, I *thought* he was answering my ad. It's a long story, and a great one, but now's not the time for that." She smiled. "Anyway, you should definitely come to the house tonight. Bodie grew up working for his stepfather, who's a professional handyman. He's bound to have great tips on how to do your floors."

"He did an excellent job on Hamilton House," Sophie added. "The place looked amazing when I was last there."

"You should see it now that we have it decorated for Christmas. It's so gorgeous with the garland and lights and wreaths with bright red bows on every window," Sarah sighed with pure delight. "With Bodie's help, I was able to go all out this year."

"I can't imagine anything better than how it looked at your open house last Christmas. Everything was so beautiful," Sophie recalled.

"Thanks." Sarah beamed. "I love Christmas so much and can't wait for you to see the house tonight."

Which put Sophie in the "going" category, even though she hadn't been sure. She could work on the Christmas quilt later. An evening with friends would be fun, even if Cole didn't plan to go.

Since when did she decide her social calendar around what Cole was doing, anyway?

Sophie lifted her chin, almost in defiance of her thoughts. "I look forward to seeing Hamilton House, and spending time with you and Bodie. I imagine the closer it gets to Christmas, the busier y'all are going to be."

"We're fairly booked, but we did block off the week prior to Christmas just in case anything unexpected comes up prior to the wedding."

"I hope you blocked off the week *after* the wedding, too," Ben teased.

Sarah's cheeks grew as red as a holly berry. "No worries there. We're going to be closed until after the new year. Bodie is taking me on a surprise honeymoon."

Sophie was happy for her friend. Sarah was as sweet as Christmas candy. She deserved every good thing that came her way. But Sophie could be happy for her friend while still feeling a little sad for herself that she didn't have anything like that. Cole silently stared into his coffee.

Let him be a lone wolf fuddy-duddy. Sophie liked having fun and didn't intend to let his lack of participation stand in her way.

She said, "I haven't been sledding in a few years, but I remember some fun times on Thrill Hill during that big snowstorm we had back seven or eight years ago."

"Oh, I remember that year," Sarah said. "It was the whitest Christmas we'd ever had in Pine Hill."

A conversation comparing different snowstorms ensued. As Cole had only moved to Pine Hill earlier that year, he didn't join in the conversation. Sophie didn't have much to say, either, so she found herself studying Cole instead.

When he looked up and caught her staring at him, her breath stuck in her chest, and she fought to look away from those haunting blue eyes.

The conversation continued around them, but Sophie couldn't follow anything being said. What she'd told her sister flashed through her head. She didn't want to date Cole. She felt badly for all the things he'd been through and wanted to do something nice for him, to make him smile, and to show him that there were those who cared for what he and others in the military had gone through.

She wanted him to have a good life in Pine Hill, to

enjoy the holidays, and to feel like he was a part of their community.

Only…

She also wanted to be his friend.

That he was a beautiful man and enthralled her in ways no man ever had was an inconvenient detail.

Cole was ready to leave. And not just because Sophie had been watching him for the past five minutes rather than talking with her friends about their hometown's past snows.

"Are there any big snowstorms where you're originally from, Cole?"

He should have known Sophie would attempt to pull him into the conversation. It was all part of that emotional charity she constantly dished out.

"It rarely snows where I'm from."

"Which is where?"

"Northern Georgia."

"He's a Southern Peach," Ben teased.

"The phrase is Georgia Peach, and I'm not," Cole corrected, scowling at his friend even though that accomplished nothing other than triggering a smirk from Andrew.

"Cole's one of them Southern Belles," Ben continued.

"Beaus," Andrew corrected.

"Belles are girls," Sarah agreed.

"Cole's definitely not a girl," Sophie added, then proceeded to blush.

Which Cole found interesting. Why had Sophie blushed?

Her expression had been one of a woman who was interested in a man. Her blush hinted at the same. As did the way she'd looked at him after her tree rescue, which he'd written off as gratitude after a highly stressful event.

She couldn't really be interested in him as anything more than a charity project, could she? No, of course not.

Men had died because he'd made a bad call. Sophie knew that.

Memories tightened his throat, making him antsy.

"I'll take that as my cue to leave," he said, pushing his chair back from the table and standing.

"What's your rush?" Andrew asked, eyeing Cole with too-penetrating eyes. Cole needed friends who were less perceptive.

"Say you'll come to Hamilton House tonight, please," Sarah implored.

Cole glanced toward Ben to see what he'd add. His friend flashed perfect teeth in a big grin, then turned to Sarah.

"We'd love to. What time do you want us to arrive?"

"I told you I was busy," Cole reminded him. Going anywhere Sophie was going to be was a bad idea. He just needed to get through the toy drive, then he'd be more careful with future volunteer work.

His buddy harrumphed. "Even you have to take a break every now and then."

"I've been on break all day."

"You really should get Bodie's advice," Sarah said. "He did such a great job on our floors. Plus, he's former Army, so you have a lot in common."

"I was a Marine," he reminded.

"Army, Marines," Sarah waved her hand in the air. "You're both former military. With you sharing that background, I'd imagine you and Bodie would have a lot to talk about."

"Cole doesn't talk about his military days," Sophie said softly, as if she wished the conversation would end as much as Cole did.

She was right.

"Some things are better not talked about." He avoided looking toward Sophie as he silently added, *Or written about.*

"Bodie is that way, too," Sarah informed, her expression a mixture of pride and sadness. "He doesn't like to talk about his time in the military, but I know there isn't a day that goes by that he doesn't think on his time there and the friends he made and lost while in the service."

Cole fought wincing. This conversation had taken a horrible turn. Why hadn't he left already?

Why had he bothered to come?

Oh, yeah. Toys. Kids. Christmas morning.

Still, they were finished with toy drive business.

He pulled his coat off the back of his chair. "Thanks for the invite. Maybe next time."

"What he means is that he'd be glad to come to Hamilton House tonight," Andrew corrected, standing and grabbing his coat, too. "Ben and I are headed to his place to check out these floors and see what needs to be done. With the three of us there, he'll have plenty of time to go sledding later today if this snow holds out.

What time should we have Cole at your place to get some expert advice from your fiancé?"

What Sophie had thought was going to be a small get-together had turned into a group of over twenty-five people. Leave it to Sarah to turn an impromptu gathering into a full-blown "It's Snowing" party. She couldn't help but be impressed with how beautifully her friend had managed to pull everything together. Then again, Sarah had worked as the church's program director for years and was experienced in putting together events. She had a way of making things fall into place.

Sarah had created a party to celebrate the snow, so snow it had. Pine Hill had become a winter wonderland. There was a good four inches of soft powdery snow covering the ground and light fluffy flakes were still falling.

The group had met at Sarah's, loaded into as few vehicles as possible and traveled the short distance to Thrill Hill, which was the most perfect location for sledding. Not only was there a wonderful long slope, but there was also a gravel road that led back to the top of the hill. Once at the bottom, it was easy to hook the sled to an all-terrain four-wheeler and pull the sled back to the top. There were couple's sleds, single-person sleds, and a few tubes. A few more friends had shown up since their arrival.

Bodie, Andrew, Carrie's son Jeff, and one of Jeff's friends had each brought four-wheelers and were pulling the sleds back up the hillside, traveling way clear of where the sledders were zooming down the hill. Bodie's dog, Harry, stayed close to wherever Sarah was, even riding on the sled with her after Sarah's maiden voyage down.

"Sophie," Sarah called after she'd made several more trips. "You haven't been down yet, have you?"

Sophie glanced toward her. Sarah was barely even recognizable, bundled up as she was in hat, scarf, gloves, boots, and waterproof puffy jacket. Sophie shook her head. "I'm in no rush, though. Let everyone who wants to keep going go. I'm good."

Thanks to her own cozy fleece-lined pants, jacket, boots, gloves, scarf and knitted toboggan, she really was. She loved playing in the snow and knew how to dress the part as she didn't like to be cold.

"What about you, Cole? You've not gone down the hill yet, either, have you?"

Sophie did not glance toward the man Sarah was addressing. He'd been quiet since arriving at Hamilton House just as they'd been getting ready to depart.

As promised, Andrew had brought him, so he was trapped into staying until his friend decided to have mercy. Since Andrew appeared to be enjoying hauling the sleds back up the hill, Sophie didn't think that was going to happen anytime soon. Which left Cole standing off by himself, watching the others.

Sophie had seen Bodie talking to him earlier, and the two men had seemed to hit it off. But once the sledding had started, Bodie had been tied up with sledders, and when he wasn't busy with that, his attention had been on Sarah playing in the snow with his dog and two kids from church.

As Ben had ended up bringing a date with him, that left Cole on his own since he didn't seem interested in making new acquaintances.

He didn't appear to mind, but Sophie's heart had squeezed every time she'd glanced his way, which was why she'd tried to keep from doing so.

If he was lonely then it was his own fault, going around and telling people he didn't want to be their friend.

Remorse hit her.

She knew better than to have such negative thoughts. She knew why he didn't jump in and join the fun. She'd watched her dad struggle with the same types of things, always uncomfortable when it came to interacting with others, not knowing how to be social. Even as a small child, she'd recognized that her father was usually an outsider on the rare family outing.

A two-person sled became free, and Sophie ended up on it with her sister.

"How is it I got stuck with you?" Isabelle complained, although Sophie knew she was teasing. Her sister had probably arranged it that way.

"You love it, and you know it," Sophie retorted. "This way you can make sure I don't do anything too daring."

Looking guilty as charged, Isabelle laughed. "Just like old times."

"I only tried to stand up on the sled once," Sophie defended.

"Once was enough for us to end up in the emergency room," Isabelle reminded her.

"To be fair, I was only ten. And it wasn't that big of a deal. I'm no worse for wear because of it." Sophie ran her tongue over the scar on the inside of her upper lip. "Not much worse for wear, at any rate."

"Wish I could say the same."

As they settled onto the sled, Sophie turned to

look at Isabelle. "I don't recall you being hurt when we crashed."

"You think I came through that unscathed? Seeing you all bloody-faced gave me a heart attack."

"Sorry," she told her sister and meant it. "I imagine looking after the likes of me all these years can't have been easy."

"You're not too bad. Most of the time."

"Ready?" one of the guys asked.

Sophie nodded and he pushed them off the side of the hill.

Laughing, Sophie embraced the cool air rushing around them as they zoomed down the snow-covered slope.

"Oh, that was fun!" she declared when they got to the bottom. She climbed off the sled and pulled it over to where the guys were waiting for the trip back to the top.

"You'll have to go again," Andrew said, hooking the sled to the back of his four-wheeler.

"This is kind of fun, too," Sophie mused as they rode the sled back to the top.

"I think I've gotten old," Isabelle mused as she climbed off the sled once they'd reached the summit and rubbed her bottom. "Either that, or I should have worn padded pants."

"Try going down on one of the singles and lie on your belly," Sophie suggested. "Or use one of the tubes. Oh, there's one empty now."

Isabelle looked as if she was going to refuse.

"Go," Sophie encouraged her. "Let loose and have some fun. Who knows when we'll have another snow this awesome?"

Isabelle's brows creased in consideration, and then she nodded and took off toward the empty tube.

Andrew unhooked the two-person sled. With a mischievous look in his eyes, he called, "Hey, Cole, Sophie needs a sledding partner and I nominate you."

Sophie's face grew so hot she was surprised all the snow didn't melt.

"I just went down—someone else may want to use the sled," she suggested, fiddling with her gloves.

"You go, and I'll drive the four-wheeler to the bottom to pull you up afterwards," Cole offered, coming to stand closer to them.

Andrew shook his head. "Sophie wants you to sled with her."

Jaw dropping, Sophie stared at Andrew. She hadn't said that.

"She was a little shaken up by her sister's wild steering on that last ride down. Now she says she's not going to go again unless you go with her." Where was Andrew getting this stuff? "Something about feeling safe with you because you rescued her from the tree."

Cole glared at his friend, but when he glanced toward Sophie there was question in his pale eyes, and she didn't have the heart to respond to by denying any of the things Andrew had said.

Unless she pushed Cole to sled right now, he wouldn't sled, but would continue to stand on the perimeter of the outing. She wanted him to have fun, to sled and interact with the others. She wanted him to feel the exhilaration she'd felt when the wind had been whipping at her as she raced to the bottom.

"Please," she added, earning a nod of approval from Andrew.

Cole looked undecided for a brief moment, then sighed. "You should know I've never sledded before."

"Never?"

He shook his head. "So, if you're looking for a smooth ride, you'd be better off convincing Andrew to go with you."

She shook her head. "I want to sled with you. I've got enough experience for both of us—I'll steer."

Cole visually examined the sled. "I don't see a steering wheel."

"Even better, there's a steering strap," she teased, bending to show him. "You can also use your feet to guide the sled in the direction you want it to go. Left heel down to go left. Right heel down to go right."

"Have fun, Santa. I'll see you at the bottom of the hill," Andrew said, taking off on the four-wheeler.

"You're sure about this?" Cole asked the minute Andrew was gone.

"Positive," Sophie nodded. And she *was* positive that Cole needed this. Needed fun and interaction and for her to help him. "I'll climb on, then you climb on behind me."

Sophie got onto the sled, then looked up at Cole expectantly.

Was he going to back out?

Eyeing the sled hesitantly, he said, "Give me a quick low down on the do's and dont's."

Do spend time with me and be my friend. Don't push me away.

The thoughts were so strong in her mind that for a moment Sophie worried she'd said the words out loud.

"Um, so most important thing is that if you put your

feet down to try to stop us, use your heels, not your toes. Otherwise, you'll flip us."

"Heels, not toes. Got it."

"If you want to slow down, lean back and it'll decelerate us a little. There aren't any trees, but if for any reason, we're about to get too close to anyone and you think we'll hit them, bail off the sled," she continued. "We're much less likely to be hurt bailing than crashing into someone."

His brow rose and he frowned down at her. "You're making this out to sound dangerous. I thought we were supposed to have fun."

"Scared?" she teased.

His gaze narrowed and Sophie laughed.

"Just wait and see. You'll love it." Sophie glanced to see who was close, then called, "Ben, will you give Cole and me a push?"

Grinning, Ben looked back and forth between them. "Sure thing."

Though obviously reluctant, Cole got onto the sled behind Sophie, his body instantly blocking some of the cold as he settled around her.

Oh my, she thought. She hadn't been close to him, hadn't touched him, since he'd rescued her from the tree. Settling back against him, his legs around hers on the sled, Sophie fought sighing.

Ben and another guy got behind their sled.

"The things I let you talk me into," Cole mumbled.

"I'd say for you to blame Andrew, not me, but I don't mind taking credit for this because you're going to love sledding. Hang on," Sophie warned as they were given a hardy push over the edge of the hill. "Wheeeee!"

Sophie held onto the strap. Cole had one arm around her waist and gripped the side of the sled with his other.

Sophie would give Andrew credit for being right, though. She really had wanted to sled with Cole. Now that she was soaring down the hillside with him, she acknowledged just how good it felt to be near to him, to be held by him.

"You're enjoying this?"

Sophie laughed. "Aren't you?" She let go of the steering strap and threw her arms up into the air, leaning first one way and then the other.

"Sophie, hold on," Cole bit out.

His barked, serious-sounding command surprised her.

"I used to stand up when I got close to the bottom," she teased. It had actually only happened once, but that counted, right?

"Don't do that this time."

He was right. Hadn't Isabelle just reminded her of why she shouldn't?

Sophie put her arms down, realized he'd tightened his hold around her. Even if she'd attempted to stand, he'd have stopped her.

He'd been concerned for her. Him. A big, tough former Marine. She'd scared him by letting go.

She smiled. He really was a protector. And she really wanted her protector to relax and have a good time.

CHAPTER NINE

RIDING A SLED DOWN A snow-covered hill was nothing scary or shocking in the grand scheme of things Cole had done during his lifetime. It was just new.

New didn't bother him. Sophie possibly getting hurt, however, did.

Not that she'd seemed in the slightest concerned, unlike when she'd been stuck in the tree. No, his sweet, talkative, impulsive Sophie had a bit of a daredevil spirit. She enjoyed the adrenaline rush of flying down the hill.

Cole liked that unexpected side of her personality more than he should. At the same time, that side terrified him as he didn't want her taking unnecessary risks.

When their sled came to a stop, he got off quickly and extended his hand.

Rosy-cheeked, eyes twinkling, she smiled up at him as she placed her gloved hand into his. "What'd ya think? Wasn't it wonderful?"

She was what was wonderful. What was beautiful inside and out.

God help him. He shouldn't get emotionally entangled with any woman, but especially not Sophie.

Step away, Cole. Just step away and keep your distance, he ordered himself.

"I might have to go again to be sure," was what he said out loud, though, stunning himself as much as her.

She squeezed his gloved hand with excitement. "Really? You want to sled again?"

Her excitement was palpable, making her look like a little kid begging for a favored treat. Only, Sophie was no child. She was a grown woman.

An enchanting woman who knew about his past and looked on with friendliness all the same.

Pity, he corrected himself. That's what Sophie looked at him with.

The cold apparently had frozen his good sense, though, because he pulled his hand free and shrugged. "If you want to sled again. Now that I know what to expect, I'll enjoy it more."

He'd enjoyed it the first time around, except for when Sophie had let go.

"Then what are we waiting for?" She practically bounced. "Let's get back to the top of the hill."

Cole turned to grab hold of the sled's strap so he could pull it over to where the four-wheelers were waiting to haul them up the hill. When he turned back toward Sophie, a snowball hit him square in the chest.

"Gotcha." She broke into laughter but was smart enough to step back as she did so, widening the distance between them as her eyes danced with pure delight.

Cole prided himself on his quick reflexes, but he'd been distracted. Her snowball had caught him off guard.

Sophie had him off his game in just about every way possible.

"I can't believe you did that," he pretended to complain. That Sophie nailed him with a snowball didn't actually surprise him, really. "You know that automatically puts you on Santa's naughty list, right?"

He bent to scoop up a handful of snow. A big handful.

Laughing, she took another couple of steps back but didn't look afraid. Instead, eyes twinkling with mischief, she was very clearly packing together a second snowball behind her back. He'd bet she was planning to nail him again the second he let his guard down. Did she think he didn't realize?

"Oh, come on, Santa," she teased. "Leave me on the nice list. You know there's nothing like a good old-fashioned snowball fight."

"No?" Cole arched his brow. "That means I have your permission to throw back?"

"If you're asking my permission, then no, absolutely, not." Her laughter threatened to spill from her smiling lips. "Don't you dare throw snowballs back at me, Cole Aaron."

Then she nailed him again.

While she danced a happy little snow jig in celebration of her successful aim, Cole stood his ground, not moving toward her, just waiting.

"Tell me I can fight back, Sophie."

She quit dancing around, gathered up another

handful of snow and then stared at him in wonder. "Are you seriously not going to throw any snowballs back unless I say you can?"

"That's right."

"Well, where's the fun in that for you?" she huffed. "Because if you think I'm going to give you permission to throw snowballs at me, you're crazy."

"I see." Cole tightened his grip on the snowball in his hand. "So you intend to fight dirty?"

Sophie glanced down at the powdery white snow, then gave him a faux innocent look. "Doesn't look like a dirty fight to me."

"No?" He took a step toward her.

About six feet separated them. She didn't move, just waited, tempting him.

"You should run, Sophie."

Her eyes widened. "Because you're going to make me face plant in the snow?"

He shook his head and took another step closer. "Tempting, but no."

"Then why would I run?"

"Because you're going to give me permission."

Howling with exaggerated laughter, Sophie slapped her leg. "You must be suffering from brain freeze, because why would I do that?"

"Because you feel guilty."

"You think I should feel guilty?"

He was a foot away from her now. "Definitely."

"Too bad, because I don't."

Cole kept his gaze locked with hers, kept his voice low, steady as he said, "Give me permission to defend myself, Sophie."

"I think I'll pass." Lips twitching, face full of sunshine

despite the cold night air, she met his gaze. "Thanks anyway, though."

Cole was mesmerized by the sparkle of her eyes, the kissable fullness of her lips. He paused on her mouth and swallowed at the nerves attacking his stomach.

He shouldn't think about that. Ever.

Sucking in a lungful of cold air, hoping it would shock his brain back into good sense, he directed his focus back to her eyes.

The laughter was gone, replaced by curiosity. Her gaze locked with his, searching for answers to questions he didn't even want to contemplate. She swallowed, then parted her lips.

"Cole, I—"

"Hey, you two ready to head back up the hill?" Andrew called, breaking the bubble they'd been inside.

Cole's eyes didn't shift from hers as he called, "Be right there."

Sophie's tongue darted out, moistening her lips, reminding Cole of where his brain had gone, of what he'd almost done.

What he was glad he hadn't done.

Her rapid breaths could be readily seen between the light of the almost-full moon and artificial lights from cars and four-wheelers.

"I didn't believe you, but you're right," she said.

His brow lifted as he waited for her to tell him what he was right about.

"I also can't believe I'm doing this, but..." She gave him a nervous look, her eyes big, her lower lip disappearing between her teeth.

"But?" he prompted, barely managing to stop himself from reaching out to tuck a stray strand of hair back into her toboggan hat. Her cheeks were rosy from the cold and her nose matched. But her eyes were warm and threatened to thaw everything deep inside him.

"But..." She sucked in a deep breath, looked torn, then lifted her chin as if gathering her courage. "Because you're Santa Cole and I want back on the nice list...I'm giving you permission."

As soon as her words registered, so did the snowball she lobbed toward him that smacked into his right shoulder.

"Gotcha!" Laughing, she broke into a run toward where Andrew waited with the four-wheeler.

"Start your engine," she yelled to his friend. "Hurry. Hurry. Get me out of here. Quick."

"Don't involve me in this," Andrew answered, sounding amused.

Shaking his head and not even trying to contain his laughter, Cole hit her mid-back with the first of his snowballs. He hadn't thrown very hard as he didn't want to hurt her, but the snowball had been big enough to have a sizeable impact.

Still on the move, she scooped up snow and tossed it behind her. It fell in more of a shower spray than a ball.

"He's gaining on you," Andrew warned just as Cole grabbed her waist and spun her toward him.

Laughing, Sophie stared up at him. "Uh-oh. I'm in for it now."

He pulled her to him. "I didn't know you could predict the future."

Her eyes twinkled. "Would it help if I said I was sorry?"

"*Are* you sorry?"

She gave a faux-innocent look, then shook her head and attempted to kick snow at him. "Not in the least."

Cole couldn't suppress the laughter that broke free from his chest. "Then you understand and forgive what I'm about to do?"

She twisted her mouth, considering. "I didn't say that."

"But you will."

"Now who's predicting the future?" She didn't look the slightest bit daunted despite the fact that he held her and threatened her with snow.

"I shouldn't have turned you to where I could see your face," he admitted out loud. It would have been much easier to retaliate if he wasn't looking into her lovely eyes.

"Why's that? You going soft?" she teased.

He shook his head. "Nope. It's just a shame such a pretty face is about to make a snow angel."

"I like snow angels," she said softly, her breath making a cloud puff in the air.

"You look like a snow angel," he admitted, then held up the snow cupped in his other gloved hand. "At least, you will in just a few seconds."

Her mouth opened in protest and she wiggled against him in her first attempt to free herself. "Cole!"

"Hmm?" he said, as he slowly moved his hand toward her.

"Please don't." She made a pretense of shivering, her movements way too exaggerated to be real. "I'll be cold."

Even though he knew what she was doing, Cole paused, letting her think she had the upper hand.

Knowing he was enjoying himself more than he had in a long time.

"I wouldn't want that," he answered honestly, taking note of her breathing, everything about her, so he'd know the precise moment she planned to make her move.

Just as he'd expected, Sophie wiggled enough that she thought she'd freed herself, batted her lashes, then, quick as a flash, dove for the snow.

Cole let her.

But as she came up with her hands full, he tossed his snow first.

As the spray of snow covered her, she sputtered, then, losing her balance, fell back onto her bottom. Despite bursting into laughter, she flung snow at him as quickly as she could from her seated position.

Cole dodged her onslaught and got in a few more snowballs of his own.

"You were messing with me," she accused, laughing as she flattened her palms against the ground to push herself up. When her foot slipped and she plopped right back down, smiling, she shook her head. "Now look what you've gone and done. Knocked a girl down so hard that she can't get up. You were just waiting for me to do that, weren't you?"

Cole reached for her hand. "Did you really think I didn't know what you were planning? Subtlety isn't one of your virtues."

Her gaze flashed to his as she let him pull her to her feet. "What are my virtues, Cole?"

Without having to think about it, he said, "Joy."

"Joy?"

He should have kept his mouth shut, but he'd already dug this hole for himself so he might as well lay down in it.

"You overflow with joy," he admitted.

Obviously pleased at his answer, she rewarded him with the biggest smile he'd ever seen.

"That," her eyes shone with happiness, "just may be the greatest compliment anyone's ever given me."

"Hand me those binoculars," Rosie ordered, attempting to grab the pair Maybelle held with her fuzzy white gloves that matched her white playing-in-the-snow ensemble.

"You shouldn't have forgotten yours," Maybelle reminded from where she sat in the driver's seat of the four-by-four diesel mule, slapping Rosie's hand away with her own white-glove-covered hand. "I'm trying to watch Cole's facial expression."

"I can see his face," Ruby said, looking through her own pair of binoculars from the back seat. "His smiling face. I just knew there was something happening between those two."

"You're sure about him?" Claudia asked, sounding worried. "Sophie and Isabelle are my favorite nieces. I'd never forgive myself if I let something happen to either one of them."

"Ha," Rosie scoffed. "You couldn't stop that freight train even if you wanted to. Our girl is hooked."

"It's not Sophie being hooked that I'm worried about," Claudia clarified. "What I need to know is, what's in his eyes when he looks at her?"

"Snow," Maybelle said drily. "Because she just pelted him with another snowball."

"I just love winter romances," Rosie sighed, rubbing her gloved hands over her white faux-fur jacket.

Maybelle snorted. "You love romances in any season. It's the follow-through you have problems with."

"Oh, don't you go harping on me about setting a wedding date again tonight," Rosie scowled. "It's not as if I didn't hear it enough while we were borrowing this fun little gas-powered buggy from Sheriff Roscoe. I can't believe he insisted you drive, though. Doesn't he realize that you can barely see a thing even with your glasses on?"

"Just because I squint when I look at you doesn't mean I can't see. More that I'm looking at something I don't want to see."

Ruby and Claudia giggled from the backseat.

"Yes, it must be difficult to see all this and then have to look in the mirror," Rosie retorted, puckering up her bright pink lips and air-kissing Maybelle.

"Speaking of difficult to see, I don't think our all-white camouflage worked," Maybelle warned. "We've been spotted."

"I told you we should have wrapped the Mule in white butcher paper," Rosie reminded. "What was the point in us wearing all white if we're in a black vehicle?"

"As if butcher paper wouldn't have blown off by the time we drove here."

"Or gotten wet and made a mess," Ruby added.

"Well, with the way you three work, your pieces probably would have blown off or made a mess," Rosie agreed. "Still, it would have been just like decorating a float for the Christmas parade. We could have even cut out paper snowflakes to hang from these bars."

"It would have been festive," Claudia agreed.

All four women watched Andrew's four-wheeler get closer to where they were parked.

"Grandma? What are you doing up here?"

"Hello, Andrew," Ruby waved at her grandson. "We brought warm blankets and hot chocolate! Aren't you glad to see us?"

Snuggled beneath one of the quilts the Butterflies had delivered to the sledders, Sophie took a sip of cocoa and stole a look at Cole over the rim of her mug. They'd stripped out of their wet outer snow gear prior to coming into a fully-decorated Hamilton House. A dozen or so people had come in with them, and Bodie had gotten a fire roaring in the living room fireplace.

Now, the fire was blazing, and the majority of guests were in Sarah's kitchen, with its large built-in dining nook, waiting while she threw a batch of cookies into the oven. But a handful had brought their drinks to the living room to warm by the fire, Sophie among them.

She huddled on the hearth, quilt draped around her shoulders, drinking her cocoa and letting all of it warm her insides.

Truth was, her insides were feeling pretty toasty already. All thanks to the man sitting in a chair near her, drinking his cocoa. Unlike her, he was blanketless as he'd denied needing one.

Of course he'd say that when the Butterflies had claimed they were fresh out and suggested he could share with Sophie.

Could they have been any more obvious?

She'd seen the extra blankets—had known there

were plenty for Cole to have one to himself—but he hadn't been shivering at all, so she hadn't insisted. The cold probably had been no big deal to someone who'd been in the military and seen and done the things he had.

It was so difficult to imagine this handsome, relaxed-looking man sitting in jeans, a long-sleeved T-shirt, and socked feet being the same one who'd written the anguished journal. Her brain struggled to connect the person who'd played in the snow with her with the journal writer who'd been tormented by the images in his head, and likely still was.

Yet, they were the same.

"Warm?"

He must have caught her watching him. Well, of course he had. He was a highly skilled former special ops Marine whose senses had been honed to pick up on things far stealthier than her. And as he'd said, subtlety wasn't her strong suit.

Which made her feel pretty proud she'd gotten those few snowballs in...although, she suspected he'd let her. She couldn't recall ever having so much fun playing in the snow.

"All warm except my toes—they still feel frozen."

Instinctively she wiggled them in the thick, fuzzy socks Sarah had loaned her to replace the slightly damp ones Sophie had pulled off with her boots on the front porch.

Concern flickered in Cole's eyes. "Do I need to rub them to get circulation going again?"

Stunned, Sophie blinked. "Would you?"

In response, Cole put his mug on a coaster and knelt

beside where she sat on the fireplace hearth, clearly intending to take her feet into his hands.

"I didn't mean that you should," she clarified, tucking her feet as far back against the hearth as she could. "I was just surprised that you would be willing to do that for me."

"If your toes are cold, then the best way to restore circulation would be for me to rub them. It's not a problem."

He sounded logical but she'd...well, she hadn't been logical at all at the thought of Cole rubbing her feet. The mere idea of him massaging them, even through her socks for therapeutic purposes, melted her insides.

"I thought you just wanted to play piggy with me," she teased. This time it was him who blinked, looking thrown by her comment. "You know, this little pig went to the market? This little pig stayed home?" she prompted at his continued silence.

"I knew what you meant."

Enjoying teasing him, she arched her brow. "But that wasn't what *you* meant?"

He shook his head. "My intentions were medicinal only."

Smiling, she took another sip of her cocoa, then gave a little shrug. "Good job. They say laughter is the best medicine."

"Seems I recall hearing that somewhere."

"If it's true, then I'm doing my part to improve your health," she mused, proud she had made him laugh.

Cole's lips twitched. "Is that what you're doing? Improving my health?"

"I'm trying, but you don't always cooperate."

Then he smiled.

Warmth spread throughout her chest in ways that had nothing to do with her cocoa or the fire and everything to do with the man kneeling beside her, smiling at her with what could only be described as tenderness shining in his amazing eyes.

Emotions erupting inside her like a Fourth of July firework finale, Sophie smiled back, thinking that tonight, in her butterfly-embossed diary, she'd write that today had been the best day of her life.

Oh, Sophie, don't go falling for Cole. He runs hot and cold and may never be able to let go of the nightmares barricaded within him. He could be a repeat of your father.

"Okay, guys, it's game time," Sarah announced as she came into the living room. "Let's divide up into teams."

Sophie loved games, but Cole's smile instantly disappeared. He must not care much for them. No surprise there.

"Where's Andrew?" he asked, obviously deciding it was time for him and his friend to leave.

"Miss me?" his coworker asked, coming into the room with a freshly baked cookie on a napkin.

"Ready to head out?" Was that hope or desperation in Cole's voice?

Sophie's brows knit together, almost to the point of causing her forehead to hurt. Whatever magical cocoon they'd been inside moments before had dispelled, and now he wouldn't even look towards her.

No. No. No. Sophie refused to let Cole throw walls back up. She didn't even understand why he had.

Well, that wasn't entirely true. His reasons were exactly why Isabelle would warn her to erect walls of her own.

Andrew's lips pursed, then he shook his head. "Naw, I think we're going to stay. These cookies are too good to leave until I've had a few more. Besides, it's been a while since I've played a game."

Cole's gaze narrowed. "You played video games two nights ago."

"Video games aren't the same as board games," Sophie added, earning herself a nod of approval from Andrew.

She suspected she'd played a role in Cole's friend's decision to stay. She wanted to feel at least a little guilty, especially since it was clear that Cole would rather go, but she'd been enjoying his company so much that she wasn't going to look a gift firefighter in the mouth.

Especially when that firefighter was Cole.

"You don't even know that we're playing a board game," Cole insisted, his tone dry. "Sarah might be hooking up a virtual reality game for us."

Shaking her head, Sarah laughed. "Sorry, Cole. No virtual reality games here. We're board game people."

Sarah opened a cabinet and pulled out a word game Sophie had played many times before. A team drew a card and had to get their teammates to guess what the word at the top of the card was, but they couldn't use any of the most common clue words—which were also listed on the card—to prompt them. An hourglass timer would be going and whoever's turn it was had to get through as many cards as possible in the allotted time.

"Oh, this is fun," she assured. "I like this game."

Cole looked resigned to enduring the next hour or so.

Sophie laughed and, without thought, patted his knee. "Don't worry, you'll have fun, too."

They divided into two teams. Sophie, Cole, Andrew, Carrie, Ben, and his girlfriend, Susan were on a team together along with Sophie's former schoolmate Lilly Stevens.

"I'm pretty sure y'all should just give up now," Sarah informed them as she opened the box and explained the rules, sending a besotted glance toward her fiancé. "With Bodie on our team, we're a shoo-in."

Looking up from where he knelt petting Harry, Bodie grinned at his fiancée. "I'm only good at this game because Sarah knows what I'm thinking even before I do."

A few chuckles rang out around the room.

"Which is why he's marrying me. That way, he can stay a man of few words," Sarah teased.

Sarah was right about how good their team was. Bodie and Sarah truly did seem to have a silent language going between them as no one else understood the obscure clues that would trigger the other to provide the right answer.

"They got six points that round," Sophie said with a little bit of a pout, then took a deep breath. Six was a really good number. "No worries. We can do this."

Sophie's team got four words on their first go around. Three on their next. When it was Sophie's turn to look at the cards and give clues for the others, she made a show of stretching her shoulders and cracking her knuckles, then picked up the box with the cards.

"Ready?" Isabelle asked, preparing to flip the sand-filled timer.

"Ready." Sophie pulled a card from the box, glanced at the first word, and smiled. She couldn't say December, Santa, holiday, or presents, but she had this one. "When Sarah and Bodie are getting married."

"Christmas," Carrie immediately shouted, excited at knowing the answer.

"The best day ever," Sarah added from the other side of the coffee table, causing a round of laughter from the others.

Not Sophie, though. She was all business and pulled the next card.

She couldn't say cup, drink, water, plastic, or transparent.

"What a window is made of. Pour myself some sweet tea in this," she rushed out.

"Glass," Andrew answered correctly.

Sophie pulled more cards, gave more clues, and her team answered. Time had to be getting close, she thought as she pulled another card.

When she saw the word, happiness bubbled inside her. She couldn't say giggle, funny, joke, mirth, or chuckle, but she knew exactly what clue she could give.

She looked directly at Cole. "The best medicine."

"Laughter."

"Time," Isabelle called just as Cole answered.

"Yes! We did great, guys!" Sophie counted cards and jumped up to do a happy dance. "Eight!" she exclaimed. "We got eight words. That ties us up."

Each team had one turn left. On the other team, Isabelle went and had a good showing with four words, an impressive feat especially as her final word had been delinquent.

Sophie loved playing this game, but even she couldn't think up words for that one when you couldn't use any of the main synonyms.

Cole was the last player to go for their team.

He didn't look excited about it. "Can I pass and let Sophie go in my place?"

"Absolutely not," Isabelle and Sarah chimed in unison, then laughed at their synchronized timing.

"They just don't want me to go again because they know how good I am and they don't want to lose," Sophie teased, stretching out the word lose.

Both her sister and her friend rolled their eyes.

"Rules are rules. Each team member takes a turn reading cards," Isabelle reminded.

Her sister was such a sucker for rules. Not that Sophie would have taken Cole's turn anyway. She wanted him to, to see what he came up with on the word cards.

"You got this," Sophie assured him. "Andrew, Ben, Susan, Lilly, Carrie, and I have your back."

She fist-bumped with her teammates as Cole took the card box.

"It's not my back I'm worried about. It's anyone figuring out the words on my cards that's the problem."

"You'll do fine. Just don't say the word or any of the listed descriptive clue words on the card," Sophie reminded. "Even if we don't get the words, it'll be okay. It's all in fun."

"But what she really means is that she wants to win," Isabelle teased from where she sat next to Sarah on the sofa. "Sophie doesn't like to lose."

Sophie made a face at her sister.

"Quit trying to put undue pressure on Cole." She cut her gaze to him and squinted, then gave her meanest look as she shook her fist. "Beat them."

Everyone laughed except Cole.

"Ready?" Isabelle asked, preparing to flip the timer.

"As I'll ever be."

"Do you need to stretch? Crack your knuckles, maybe?" Sophie asked, earning a frown. "Fine, you don't. I was just checking."

Cole pulled the first card, thought a second, then said, "Bodie will put this on Sarah's left digit."

"Ring!" Sophie guessed.

Cole nodded and pulled the next card. "Sophie and I are involved in a toy…"

"Drive," Andrew answered.

Nodding, Cole pulled the next card. "Harry."

"Dog," Carrie exclaimed.

Excitement built in Sophie's belly as Cole pulled the card that would tie the game.

"What Andrew, Ben, and I had for dinner earlier."

"Pizza," Ben and Andrew both answered, laughing.

She glanced at the hourglass. There was only a little sand remaining.

Cole nodded and pulled the card that could win the game. His brows furrowed together.

When he looked up from the card, his gaze met Sophie's and she knew whatever he was about to say would be a clue just for her.

"Your virtue."

"Joy!"

"Time," Isabelle and Sarah said in unison.

"Woot. Woot. We did it." Smiling, Sophie high-fived all her teammates within reach.

"I'll be hearing about this for weeks," Isabelle complained, but with a genuine smile on her face. "You remember that one time when my team beat yours?" she mimicked.

Although her sister joked about Sophie not liking to

lose, it was Isabelle who'd always had to come in first. At everything. She'd been valedictorian of her high school class, even.

Sophie liked to win, but it wasn't the be-all, end-all for her. Not like it was for Isabelle. But she wasn't above teasing her sister.

"Why wait until later to remind you? I'll start bringing it up now. Hey, did you notice that my team just beat yours for possibly the first time ever?" Her gaze cut to Cole. "Thanks to Cole's brilliant clues."

"Yeah, yeah, that and the fact I got delinquent."

"Cole drawing 'joy' was quite lucky."

"But it wasn't luck that you knew what he was referring to when he described it as your virtue?"

Sophie knew what her sister was getting at, and she wasn't going there. Instead, she smiled and shrugged her shoulders.

"What can I say? 'I've got the joy, joy, joy down in my heart' and it shows."

CHAPTER TEN

"**I**'M CALLING OFF THE ENGAGEMENT," Rosie announced as she came into the quilting shop in a blue whirlwind the following Monday morning. Literally, she was decked out in blue from head to toe with the exception of her flushed face peeking out from her hat.

Shocked at Rosie's announcement, Sophie put down her scissors and stared at the stressed woman. "Good grief. What did Lou do?" She couldn't imagine the diner owner having done anything worthy of Rosie calling off their engagement. Not when the man was so crazy about Rosie.

Pulling off her blue gloves, Rosie then undid her parka. "He's driving me crazy with these 'set the date or else' threats. Fine. He wants a date? How about never?"

"You can't mean that, Rosie."

Rosie's face twisted with worry, making her look near her age, which was rare. Rosie usually had such a youthful vivaciousness that it was difficult to believe she was in her late sixties. "Of course I mean it."

Even as she made the claim, she twisted the diamond solitaire on her left hand.

"Wouldn't it bother you more if Lou was okay with indefinitely putting off the wedding?"

Rosie plopped down into a vacant chair next to the cutting table, pretending to be very interested in the pieces of material sitting there.

Sophie had known Rosie for as long as she could remember. In addition to being one of her aunt's dearest friends, the older woman was a mainstay at church and in the community and was too vibrant to have not stood out even in Sophie's earliest memories. Only following the death of her late husband did Sophie ever recall Rosie losing some of her sparkle. Rosie's sparkle wasn't flashing now, though.

"What's wrong? Why don't you want to set a date with Lou?"

Rosie arched a painted-on brow and attempted to wave off Sophie's concern. "Not that I blame the old coot for wanting to rush me down the aisle, but maybe I'm not in a rush to give up my single life."

Sophie leaned against her cutting table and eyed her friend. "Is that it? You'd rather be single than become Lou's wife?"

Rosie hesitated just long enough that Sophie had her answer regardless of what words were spoken.

"I'm wearing his ring. That should be enough."

"Most people believe wearing an engagement ring indicates a commitment to end up with a wedding," Sophie reminded.

"So you think I'm being ridiculous, too?"

Too? Sophie's eyes widened. "Who said you were being ridiculous? Maybelle? You know she doesn't mean the things she says to you."

"It's not Maybelle. I know that old biddy is just jealous of me being more than a decade younger than her and," Rosie fluffed what little of her hair stuck out from beneath her hat, "always finer."

Sophie smothered a smile at the comment that Rosie would just as readily have said in front of Maybelle as not. Too bad Maybelle wasn't there to come right back at her with a return jab. The two women were a hoot when you put them together.

Only, it wasn't her friendly rivalry with Maybelle bothering Rosie. It was Lou.

Sophie's heart gave a squeeze. She adored the big-hearted diner owner. "Is something wrong with Lou?"

"Just that he thinks he's in love with a foolish old bat like me."

It was unusual to hear Rosie say anything that wasn't flattering of herself, so Sophie was stunned by her friend's comment.

"I'd say that it's a good thing that he loves you." Sophie placed her hand over Rosie's. "I've seen you two sitting in church together, so I know how Lou lights up when you look at him, and how he always makes a big deal of opening doors for you and holding your hand."

Sophie had felt a pinch of jealousy a time or two at how the older man doted on Rosie. Rosie kept him on his toes, for sure, but the diner owner was happier than Sophie had ever seen him now that the two of them were together.

"Lou is a lucky man to have you, Rosie."

They were lucky to have each other. Not that Sophie wanted...she stopped the thought because maybe she *did* want what Rosie had with Lou. Maybe she wanted it a lot. With Cole.

When Rosie's eyes lifted to Sophie, they were watery, and that was something Sophie had rarely seen.

"Only, he's not a lucky man," Rosie deflated with a long sigh. "He wants to get married and says if I don't hurry up and set a date, he's going to take my ring back and ask that Alberta Jennings to marry him instead."

What? Lou wasn't in love with Alberta. Why would he even threaten such an absurd thing?

Rosie crinkled her nose. "Can you imagine him replacing me with her? Why, that would be like having vanilla pudding after being privy to the finest restaurant's prized tiramisu." Sophie suppressed another smile. "Or more like bland stale bread after sampling some of my grandmother's cinnamon bread," Rosie said with a burst of fire. Apparently, even mentioning Alberta's name had riled her up.

Sophie nodded in agreement. "Absolutely."

"I just don't see what the big rush is."

"Lou has wanted to marry you for a long time," Sophie reminded, thinking perhaps there was more going on than met the eye. Why else would Lou threaten Rosie with Alberta? "Remember that romantic carriage ride he took you on and then popped the question? And the dozen or so times he proposed after that before you said yes?"

"I haven't forgotten."

Sophie nodded. "That was almost a year ago, Rosie. Lou isn't wrong to want the wedding to take place, or to at least have a date set, after all this time. Many would say he's been quite patient in waiting on you."

"I suppose so, but we have our whole lives." Rosie

wrung her bejeweled hands. "What's the problem with waiting a little longer?"

Sophie imagined that when she met the man of her dreams that she'd want to be with him as much as possible and would barely be able to wait to walk down the aisle to be his forever. Just as Sarah felt about walking down the aisle to Bodie. Shouldn't Rosie feel the same excited anticipation?

Rosie let out a long breath. "I'm going to have to marry him, aren't I?"

That didn't sound encouraging, either.

Sophie scooted her chair over next to Rosie's and placed her hand over the older woman's. "I guess I'm a little confused. Don't you *want* to marry Lou?"

Rosie stared at where Sophie held her hand. "Of course I want to marry him. The big ole teddy bear loves me with all his heart and is just so sweet—usually. It's just..."

"Just what?"

Sighing, Rosie grimaced a little. "You know I've already been married three times."

Sophie nodded.

"Three times," Rosie repeated, shaking her head a little as if she couldn't quite believe the number. "All three of my husbands died, Sophie." Closing her eyes, Rosie took a deep breath. "I just don't think I could go through that again."

"Oh, Rosie." Sophie's heart squeezed.

"That Maybelle would start calling me a Black Widow if it happened, and then I'd have to come up with a name to remind her how much older she is than me and worn out, to boot. Why, it would just ruin a perfectly good friendship."

Sophie recognized Rosie's comment for what it was: misdirection to distract from what she'd admitted. Rosie was scared to marry Lou for fear something would happen to him, the way it had to her other husbands.

"Don't you think you should talk to Lou about this?"

Rosie huffed. "I have. He's the one who told me I was being ridiculous." Sophie didn't say anything. "Don't tell me you think he's right?"

"I didn't say that."

"You didn't *not* say it, either."

Sophie shrugged. "I think this is something you're going to have to figure out for yourself. There are no guarantees in life, but I do know love when I see it. Lou loves you and you love him. It would be a shame for him to have to settle for stale bread after sampling your grandmother's famous cinnamon bread."

Rosie pouted a perfectly lipsticked lower lip. "That darn cinnamon bread is what got me into this predicament to begin with. I never should have made it for him when I know its power."

Rosie's grandmother's cinnamon bread reportedly made men fall in love with the baker. Sophie wasn't superstitious, but she knew that many a woman around Pine Hill would love to get their hands on the recipe so perhaps there was something to it.

"Speaking of that cinnamon bread, do you need me to whip you up a batch in honor of your date to Sarah and Bodie's little winter wonderland party this past weekend?"

Sophie's cheeks heated. "It wasn't a date. And I absolutely do not need you to make me any cinnamon bread."

"No? You and Cole looked quite cozy riding on the

sled together, and you know the way to a man's heart is his stomach."

Sophie thought back to the cookies she'd made Cole. His favorite type of cookies. They'd been good, too, as she knew because she'd had to sample a few, just to make sure they'd turned out right. But she hadn't made them because she'd been trying to find the way to his heart. She'd just wanted to express her gratitude for his coming to her rescue.

"Sledding with Cole was no more a date than when Isabelle and I went down the hill on the same sled." She felt dishonest saying it. Technically, it was true that she and her sister had ridden on the same sled just minutes before she'd taken the trip down the hill with Cole, but the ride with Isabelle hadn't made her insides feel as light and fluffy as the snow that had been drifting down from the night sky.

Sophie was glad her sister could only see her and Rosie if she glanced at the security camera feed, and that even if she looked, she wouldn't be able to hear this conversation.

Her sister had had more than enough to say about Cole already.

"You Butterflies shouldn't have tried to get him to share a blanket with me, either. Poor Cole."

"Poor Cole? Honey, haven't you ever heard that the best way to warm up after some time out in the snow is to snuggle up next to someone? We were just trying to make sure you stayed warm."

"Please don't try matchmaking us. Cole is my toy drive partner, nothing more."

Even if he felt like much more.

Which was only because she'd read his journal.

And because she felt so good inside when she was with him.

And on the occasions that he let loose and smiled... okay, so Cole was more than just her toy drive partner.

She wanted to be his friend. There was nothing wrong with wanting to be his friend. He was newish to town and needed more friends. Sophie was a good friend. Just ask anyone—well, anyone except the cat that continued to evade her attempts at friendship. But no one should ask the cat that was as elusive as Cole had been since leaving Hamilton House on Saturday night.

Shouldn't he have at least texted to see if she'd been sore from when she'd fallen back in the snow during their snowball fight? Okay, so that was stretching it, but he could have texted to ask her that.

Or any other of a thousand things, such as why do birds sing? Why do Butterflies matchmake? Or something just as inane.

Or he could have asked her to dinner under the guise of working on the toy drive. Or not used a guise at all and just asked, telling her he wanted to spend time with her, too.

He could have done that.

"Child, you're blushing."

If Sophie hadn't been, she would be after Rosie's words. Eek. How had she gotten so lost in her thoughts under Rosie's eagle eye?

"I'll tell you what, Rosie. Let's not talk about Lou, weddings, or Cole anymore today. Instead, we'll focus on what we're going to do to make sure this year's toy drive is the most successful ever."

Rosie laughed and clicked her tongue at Sophie.

"Don't think I don't see what you're doing here, but, yes, let's brainstorm on ideas for the toy drive, clever girl."

Thanksgiving Day arrived and Sophie, Isabelle, and their mother had dinner at Aunt Claudia's. It was a huge gathering of family and friends that included Maybelle, Rosie, Sarah, Bodie, Sarah's dad, Claudia's kids, and her grandkids. The house was pure chaos.

Sophie loved it. The noise. The smiles. The laughter. The bickering between Maybelle, Rosie, and her aunt that was better than any comedy act. As was tradition, Ruby had cooked a big meal for her large family and would get together for a Friendsgiving with the Butterflies at a later time.

They'd just finished eating and some had started migrating from the dining room, where various tables had been set up along with the large main dining table, to the living room.

"Who's hanging around for cards?" Aunt Claudia asked. "I picked up the neatest deck when we were in Alaska over the summer and can't wait to break them in on a game of Nertz." Smiling, she added, "I got a deck in Europe, too, but we broke them in over Labor Day weekend when we were at the lake cabin."

Sophie's aunt had spent most of her life dreaming of traveling the world, but Uncle George had been content to never step foot outside Pine Hill. In his eyes, there'd been no need. Why go somewhere else when everything and everyone they needed and loved was right there? Maybelle had lit a fire under his feet last Christmas and he and Aunt Claudia had gone on several trips that year. He must have liked them as they had more planned for the following year. Or maybe he just liked how blissfully happy they made Claudia.

"No cards for us tonight," Sarah answered, smiling at her father. "Dad and I have our standing Thanksgiving date to put up his tree and watch a movie together. Plus, he wants to run Sunday's sermon by me. I think his topic is on honoring your mother and father, so it wouldn't look good if I bailed on him."

Sarah winked and everyone chuckled. If ever a child honored her father, Sarah honored hers.

Sarah had a great dad and Sophie had a great mom.

Too bad the two had never shown the slightest interest in each other. Sarah's dad seemed content to have loved once and Sophie's mom had gone through too much with Sophie's dad, apparently, to risk loving again. The two were friendly, as you'd expect from two people in the same social circle in a small town, but there had never been anything more than friendship.

Sophie glanced at where William Smith sat talking with Uncle George. Yeah, it really was too bad the two had never noticed each other romantically as she'd applaud that union.

"What about you, Bodie? You and Harry headed to William's?" Maybelle asked, her brow quirked high as she regarded him with great affection. It had taken Maybelle awhile to warm to Bodie, but ever since she had, she'd begun treating him as a favored son.

Petting his dog, Bodie shook his head. "Not this year. Sarah and I decided Thanksgiving night was a tradition we were going to keep just between her and her dad, at least for the time being. Down the road, after the wedding, we may relook at it."

Maybelle nodded her approval, apparently pleased that Bodie encouraged Sarah to maintain her special bond with her father.

"Besides, you've seen the Christmas trees at Hamilton House. I've done more than my share of decorating." He sent an indulgent glance toward Sarah. "Guess I'll be doing lots more over the years to come, though."

Sophie needed to get with it on decorating her own tree. Isabelle and her mother enjoyed the holidays, but not like Sophie. Sophie loved Christmas: the bright lights, the music, the parties, the On-the-Square festival and parade. And the tree lighting. She liked that, too.

She was excited to put up and decorate a tree, but she just hadn't gotten around to it yet. She'd been busy working on her latest quilt; making Petdanas as they'd seen a spike in orders, probably due to the holidays; getting things ready for her Quilts of Valor Foundation booth at the Christmas festival; and planning for the Make Your Own Christmas Stockings class she'd be teaching the following Tuesday evening. And every day for the past week, she'd been putting in extra-long hours at the shop to help others stock supplies for all of their own projects.

Tomorrow, they'd open earlier than their usual nine, having their annual The Threaded Needle Black Friday sale from eight until six, and then another big "shop local" sale on Saturday before they closed at noon for the On-the-Square Christmas Festival, tree lighting, and Christmas parade later that night.

Sophie might not have her tree up at home, yet, but the shop looked amazing. She'd stayed late several nights putting up more decorations for the town's biggest Christmas event. For their window display, she'd done a red pillows-and-fabric fireplace display by pushing two thin shelves together and running a board across the top where she'd placed a row of brown and gray fabric bolts turned on their sides to look like layered bricks as a mantle on which she'd hung several of the stockings she'd made for her class. Next to it, as a tree, she'd created a Christmas-fabric-and-pillows display that she'd placed on a tall tiered triangular-shaped shelf that had the shape of a tree. She'd even put a giant bow on top and draped it downward. A Christmas quilt was draped over a wooden rocking chair in front of the "fireplace." She'd been quite pleased with the overall look.

She loved how every business on the square decorated. The overall effect was a Christmas-card-worthy square that she was proud to be a part of.

As for their personal, family tree, she'd recruit her mother and Isabelle to help, and they'd get their tree up at home soon.

"You're lost in thought. Wouldn't be thinking of a certain firefighter, would you?" Sarah interrupted her thoughts.

Sophie felt heat rush to her face, then shook her head. "I was thinking about the shop and the parade and tree lighting this weekend. I hope I've done enough decorating. It's important for every business to show our support for such a great community event."

"Are you kidding me? I was in there yesterday buying fabric and was blown away by the window display that Isabelle told me you'd designed. Girl, it looks amazing and should be on a magazine cover."

Sophie beamed. "Thank you. I love coming up with

different ways to display our fabrics and sewn goods for sale."

"Do you need me to do anything to help with the booth Saturday night?"

Sophie shook her head. "You're already volunteering with the ornament hunt for the kids and the snowflake sale for the church. The last thing you need to do is volunteer to work the Quilts of Valor booth, too."

"Well," Sarah smiled, "that booth is near and dear to both our hearts. I want to help get word out."

The organization had brought Bodie into Sarah's life after she'd donated a quilt that had been awarded to him. He'd come to town to thank her and had stayed to fall in love. Sophie's experience with the organization had been no less impactful. Her efforts had saved Sophie's life in many ways as making those quilts for soldiers had helped her to deal with her father's PTSD. She'd been so helpless while he'd been struggling, but by making the quilts, she could feel as if she was giving back, could even hope she could make a difference to other military personnel in ways she hadn't been able to help her father. If only she'd been old enough to have made him one back when he'd needed it most, the lovingly sewn fabric could have wrapped him in love.

"When Bodie and I finish working our shift selling snowflakes, we'll stop by in case you need a break."

"Deal," Sophie agreed, grateful she had such a good friend to help promote the wonderful foundation. "I bet y'all will sell out again this year. If I don't make it by prior to you getting low, save me three." She always gave one of the handmade snowflakes each to her mother and sister and held one back to someday use on a tree in the house she'd eventually get. "I just love them."

"I'll pick you out some while we're setting up the displays and put them aside," Sarah promised. "By the way, Bodie went out to your fireman's place for a while yesterday to look at his floors."

"Cole's not my fireman, but that's great." Sophie fought to keep all visible signs of her interest at a minimum.

"Yeah. He says Cole has a great farmhouse that's sitting on the prettiest piece of land, even has a pond where he offered to let Bodie fish whenever he wanted to get away. I think my fiancé might have been a little jealous of the wide-open space."

"I seriously doubt that since Bodie has you, Harry, and Hamilton House." The bed and breakfast didn't have acreage but did boast a huge yard that was more than enough room for Harry to stretch his legs.

"Cole invited him to bring Harry back anytime, whether he was home or not. He said that Harry had the best time running and chasing birds." Sarah smiled. "The farm next to Cole's has cows and apparently Harry didn't know quite what to think of them and kept wanting to herd them even though to our knowledge he's never been around cows—or any livestock at all—in his life."

Picturing the dog herding the cows, Sophie laughed. "I guess it's instinctual for Harry to want to herd them."

"Must be," Sarah agreed. "Anyway, Harry liked Cole, and so did Bodie."

"I'd say Bodie understands Cole in ways you and I never could."

Sarah's smile faded. "Because of what you read in Cole's journal? Is it similar to the things Bodie went through?"

Sophie shrugged. "Maybe." She didn't know specific details of Bodie's military stint. On Cole's end, he'd probably say she knew too much. Maybe she did, since it put him so on guard with her.

"Does he ever talk about his time in the service?" Sarah asked.

"Not to me, but then he wouldn't. We're just acquaintances." She wanted to say "friends," but she wasn't sure they were even that. He'd been very clear that he didn't want to be—but she had a little bit of hope that she'd started to change his mind. The longer she went without hearing from him, though, the more that hope was shadowed by doubt. Did friends have walls the height of Cole's? "Did he mention anything to Bodie?"

"Not that Bodie told me, but he wouldn't have said anything if he believed Cole wouldn't have wanted it repeated."

Respecting and understanding that, Sophie nodded. "Those military guys stick together."

"Bodie plans to go back to help him with a few things that are two-men jobs. He was laughing that they were going to have a good, old-fashioned barn raising this spring with some of the guys from the firehall, too." Sarah laughed. "I'm not sure if building a barn means Cole plans to start farming or what."

Sophie was grateful Bodie and Cole had hit it off and tried to imagine Cole farming. She could see him out, working the land, and drawing pleasure from his fields yielding crops. It was easy to imagine that he'd find the process soothing, a renewing of life.

"It might be difficult when he works twenty-four-hour shifts at the firehall," she mused out loud. "At least, it would be difficult if he intends to have animals."

Although, she supposed he could hire someone to help during his firehall work shifts. Really, what did she know about farming? She'd lived in the house off the square her entire life, and they'd never even had a garden.

Sarah nodded. "I'm glad the sheriff's department has more regular work hours. Of course, Harry's right there with Bodie in his patrol car."

Sophie sighed. "Harry makes me want a pet."

"Every animal makes you want a pet," Sarah teased before she asked, "Have you seen your cat recently?"

"Ha. Every night, but only from a distance. You'd think after I risked life and limb—limb, ha ha—that the cat would love me, but no, he's still playing hard to get. The closest I've gotten to him was in that tree—and sitting a few feet away on the front porch while he eats my friendship offerings."

"Bless him." Sarah patted her hand. "And bless you for taking care of him. He'll come around."

"You'd think he would trust me. I've been feeding him for almost a month."

"Sometimes it takes a while to build trust. Be patient. With the cat," Sarah's gaze cut to Sophie, "and with Cole."

"I told you we're just acquaintances," Sophie insisted.

"I know what you said," Sarah gave a knowing smile, "and I know what I said."

Be patient, Sophie thought later that night, sitting on her bed.

She hand-stitched a block together for the Quilt of Valor she was making, pushing the needle through the navy material and pulling it to the other side, then repeating the process over and over. Most of the blocks were machine-sewn, but the very center one, she'd decided she wanted to hand-piece.

The personal touch was important to her. She could be patient for this and put in the extra, time-consuming effort, even if patience wasn't her virtue.

Which made her smile as the memory of Cole saying her virtue was joy flashed through her mind.

She'd had a great day, a day truly filled with being thankful for all her many blessings. Still, she couldn't say she felt particularly filled with joy just now.

Because she was preoccupied wondering about Cole.

She regretted not inviting him to Aunt Claudia's Thanksgiving dinner. Which was silly. Why would she have invited him? Why would he have accepted? He'd barely even met her aunt.

Then again, her uncle and aunt's home had always been open to anyone and everyone during the holidays, whether family or friend. No one would have said anything had Cole attended other than to welcome him with open arms and a big plate of turkey and dressing with all the fixings.

Okay, so Sarah and Isabelle would have questioned her, and Maybelle would have given a raised eyebrow or two, but other than that...guilt nagged at her.

What if Cole had sat home alone? How awful was that? That someone who'd put their life on the line defending her freedom and safeguarding her ability to gather with family and friends might have had to spend the holiday by himself?

No one should be alone on the holidays, especially not someone who had risked his all and given such big chunks of himself for his country.

Guilt ate at her. Why hadn't she invited him?

Isabelle wouldn't have been happy, as she worried Sophie was getting too invested. But her sister wouldn't have wanted Cole home alone on Thanksgiving anymore than Sophie would have. Isabelle had a good heart, even if she was all business most of the time.

Sophie pushed the needle into the fabric—then, not able to stand inaction a moment longer, she set the quilt to the side and reached for her phone.

Should she call Cole and wish him a happy Thanksgiving?

Why did her belly knot at the thought? Maybe she'd just text him instead, let him know she was thinking about him and hoped he'd had a good holiday.

That didn't quite feel right, either. What she really wanted was to give him a smile.

And, as she often did, she gave in to the impulse to do just that.

CHAPTER ELEVEN

"**A**REN'T WE A PATHETIC TRIO, swapping schedules so we could spend the day at work together?"

Cole snorted at Andrew's observation. Thankfully, it had been a slow day at the firehall, and they were just hanging at the station. Earlier, they'd helped with a minor traffic accident, but otherwise, they'd not had a single call.

Cole worked on a crossword puzzle. Ben and Andrew were yet again saving a video game world from an alien takeover. Overall, the firehall was as quiet as the day had been.

Sometimes, Cole got antsy when there were no calls. He liked to be busy, to be working. When he reminded himself that a call coming in meant someone somewhere was having a bad, bad day, it pulled his wayward thoughts back in line. Quiet was good. Only, sometimes it wasn't as it gave Cole too much time to think.

Thus, the puzzle book.

"You thought I swapped so I'd get to spend Thanksgiving Day with you two?" Looking up from his cross-word, Cole shook his head. "You just keep on believing that, buddy."

Andrew laughed. "More like you hoped it would be slow enough that we could go by my grandma's for a plate."

"There is that," Cole agreed. This was Cole's first Thanksgiving in Pine Hill, but he'd heard several of the guys mention how Andrew's Grandma Ruby always made extra so the crew on duty could swing by and get a plate—or two. He'd been with Andrew and had gone by for Easter dinner and the Fourth of July cookout where he'd first set eyes on Sophie. Grandma Ruby's cooking skills were worth working holidays, and tonight's home-cooked meal, complete with her famous potatoes, had exceeded expectations.

"That's why I volunteered," Ben assured, repeatedly zapping a grotesque-appearing being and high-fiving Andrew when the alien exploded. "It had nothing to do with your ugly mugs."

"You volunteered because Susan wanted you to come to Thanksgiving dinner with her parents," Andrew teased, gearing up for their next big battle as more aliens appeared on the television screen.

"You may be on to something," Ben agreed. "I like her, but I'm not ready to meet her family, especially not at a holiday get-together." He grimaced. "As much as I'd like her to be, I don't think she's the one."

"What makes you think that?" Cole asked, curious as to what Ben meant. Susan had seemed nice enough. The few times Cole had been around them together, they'd seemed to enjoy each other's company. And Ben made no secret of the fact that he hoped to marry and have kids, so this couldn't be a question of not wanting a commitment.

"That she's not the one I'm meant to spend the rest of my life with? Susan's just not—and it doesn't feel right to do things like go to her parents' house for Thanksgiving dinner. She's a great person, though, and I don't have the heart to end things right before Christmas."

Cole started to remind Ben that he and the girl had only been going out a few weeks but held his tongue. If Ben didn't want to end things until after the holidays, that was between him and Susan.

"Unfortunately for you, and us," Andrew teased, rapidly pressing a button on his controller, "you're with the ones you're meant to spend your life with. May as well face it."

Cole snorted, but thought to himself that he was okay with Andrew's observation. Much as Cole had felt about his brothers in arms in the Marines, Andrew and Ben were family. For the most part, Cole was at peace with his lot in life. It was what it was and could be much worse.

"What about you, Cole?" Ben put him on the spot.

Cole looked up from his crossword puzzle again—just as well as he was stuck on a seven-letter word for "strips in geography." "What about me?"

"You and Sophie."

"There is no me and Sophie, unless you're talking toy drive partners. Unlike you, I am not interested in meeting anyone, much less 'the one'."

Quite the opposite, he thought, as he mentally answered "isthmus" on his puzzle.

"So you keep saying, but we were there, remember?

We saw you two together snow sledding and playing word games."

They were never going to let him live that down. He'd known that even at the time, but the temptation of playing with Sophie in the snow had been irresistible. Much about her was irresistible.

Like thoughts of her. They kept slipping into his head, had even invaded some of his dreams, which beat the nightmares that occasionally haunted his sleep.

"Not to mention snowball fighting," Andrew added. "All's fair in love and snow."

Glancing back down at the blank puzzle, mentally filling in that the second letter was an "r" on a seven-letter word meaning "caught", Cole snorted. "Shows how much you two know, or don't know. I haven't seen Sophie since that night."

That night that had been fun and almost carefree at times. He'd enjoyed sledding with Sophie, had enjoyed their snowball fight and then drinking hot chocolate with her while her Butterfly friends kept suggesting they wrap up in a shared quilt together for warmth. Yeah, right. Cole had shot that down real fast. But playing the board game hadn't been so bad. She'd been so ecstatic that they'd beat the other team and, well, he'd enjoyed that, too.

None of which was good. Not when a darkness resided deep within him that could take hold at any time and pull him beneath its depths.

He needed to stay away from her for so many reasons. But when Sophie smiled at him, it wasn't easy to remember that nothing more than pity motivated her kindness, especially when that light sparkled in her pretty eyes as it had when she'd tossed snowballs at him.

"Have you talked to her?"

Ben didn't look away from their game, seemingly fully focused on the television screen, but Cole didn't fool himself. If he ignored the question, both of his buddies would be all over it, accusing him of holding out on them. It was much better to address things directly with them.

"No. There's no need for me to talk to Sophie. Like I said, there's nothing between us other than the toy drive."

Sophie had read his journal. That he had to keep reminding himself of that when he thought of her, because it wasn't what automatically came to mind anymore, said a lot, considering the gravity of what she'd read in that blasted book, considering what motivated her friendliness.

What came to mind first now was her quick smile, her bubbly personality, her exuberance for life, and how the world looked brighter when she was around, as if she somehow had the ability to help others to look at the world through the rose-colored glasses she viewed life through.

Probably because she glowed with happiness and anyone near her couldn't help but be affected with joy.

"Yeah, that's been a whole, what, week?" Ben joked, not sounding impressed by the time gap.

"Not even," Andrew added from where he leaned back in his chair and killed bad guy alien after bad guy alien.

"I mean, if you haven't seen her or talked to her in

five days, then clearly you must be telling the truth and there's nothing between the two of you," Ben continued.

"Clearly," Andrew nodded.

Cole rolled his eyes. "With friends like you..."

"Hey, I provided you with Thanksgiving dinner, didn't I?"

"Grandma Ruby provided Thanksgiving dinner," Cole corrected. "A very delicious Thanksgiving dinner. Is there any of that buttermilk pie left?"

Maybe mention of the pie Grandma Ruby had sent with them would change the current course of the conversation.

"You leave my buttermilk pie alone," Andrew warned, glancing away from the game long enough to shoot a narrow-eyed glare Cole's way.

"I was there," Cole reminded. "I heard her say that pie was for all of us."

"She handed it to me, and I'm blood. I get dibs."

"Trapped," Cole mumbled out loud, the solution to his seven-letter word clue finally hitting him. Rather than writing the word onto the crossword puzzle, he read the next clue. He never wrote the answers in but used the games to help keep his mind sharp, to make himself remember each answer and where it fell on the page. He liked the extra challenge.

"What?" Ben asked, confused at Cole's non-sequitur.

"Nothing." Cole shook his head just as his phone dinged, indicating he had a text message.

Pausing their game, Ben and Andrew exchanged looks, then turned toward him wide-eyed.

Cole's phone never went off. There was no reason for it to when he was at the firehall. He was only ever contacted by his fellow firefighters, and there was no reason for them to contact him on his cell phone when he was already there. The firehall was the only reason he even had a phone in the first place as he had no qualms with living off the grid and had done so in the past. But it was against policy not to have one in case there was an emergency that meant additional manpower was needed.

"My money is on that being from a certain toy drive partner," Ben guessed.

"One who's nothing more than that," Andrew added.

While pulling his phone from his pocket, Cole frowned at his friends. "You two are crazy and have overactive imaginations. Sophie has no reason to text me."

"Maybe she climbed another tree."

Cole rolled his eyes. "It's probably just a wrong number."

Only, when he glanced down at his phone, it wasn't.

It was a funny turkey meme.

Sent from Sophie.

"You do realize wrong numbers don't make you smile, right?" Andrew pointed out.

Cole didn't bother to hide his amusement since it was too late anyway. "This one did."

"You gonna share? I could use a laugh."

Cole touched his screen to keep the meme lit up and handed over his phone.

Andrew snorted at the picture.

"That's a local number," Ben pointed out, leaning over to get a closer look.

"You were supposed to check out the joke, not see if you recognized the phone number."

"Just hit the redial button to find out who it is," Ben suggested.

"He doesn't need to," Andrew assured, glancing toward Cole with amusement filling his eyes. "He knows who it's from."

"Maybe," Cole admitted. He didn't have any programmed numbers saved as contacts in his phone. There was no reason to. He knew all the numbers to the firehall, knew the chief's number, and the crews' numbers. He preferred using his mind, occupying his brain space with facts and figures rather than memories. It was one of the reasons he never wrote in the answers on his crossword puzzles. Having to keep up with a mental map of the answers and where they fell on the puzzle forced him to stay focused.

Usually.

Andrew handed over the now dark-screened phone. "You going to text her back?"

Good question. Doing so shouldn't feel like a big deal. He could just send a funny message of acknowledgement and be done with it.

But texting back felt a very big deal. So much so that the thought of doing so made his blood feel as if it quivered through his veins. Cole slid the phone into his pocket.

"How about that buttermilk pie?" he asked, standing up and tossing the book of puzzles aside. "The two platefuls of food I ate earlier have settled enough to enjoy dessert."

"I know what you're doing, bro." Andrew's gaze narrowed as he set the controller down in his chair. "But I'm okay with it since it means cutting into that pie."

Which was exactly what Cole had hoped.

Maybe the sugar rush would offset the urge to return Sophie's text.

Both were sweet.

Why had she sent him the meme?

Pity, kindness, or the something more that he felt sparking between them despite his best efforts to pretend otherwise?

Black Friday came bright and early, and The Threaded Needle was going to have its best day of sales ever. Sophie and Isabelle arrived at the shop a full hour prior to opening to make sure they had everything ready.

"Today is going to be great," Sophie assured her sister, knowing Isabelle was always crunching numbers in her head.

Isabelle nodded. "It will be. The window display looks wonderful, by the way. I've had a lot of people comment on it."

"Thank you." Sophie beamed at her sister's praise. "I'm hoping it gets a few more folks to sign up for my Make Your Own Stocking class."

"There's only a couple of spots left after the Butterflies signed up."

"All of them?"

Isabelle nodded.

Sophie's eyes widened. "I'm not sure what I can teach any of them. They've been sewing longer than I've been alive."

"They probably just want to show their support."

"Or are up to something." Like more matchmaking. Knowing them, they'd probably signed Cole up, too.

Subtlety was rarely their thing. Come to think of it, she could probably blame them for the fact that she'd never had any subtlety herself. After all, they'd had a formative influence on her while she was growing up.

"Definitely a possibility," Isabelle agreed. "No doubt Maybelle had something in mind when she signed them all up. I'm just glad it's you who'll be teaching the class."

"You're welcome to help."

Maybelle was certainly a mover and a shaker, so if she'd been the one to sign the ladies up for the class then Sophie agreed that there was likely more to it than a simple interest in stocking sewing.

"Thanks, but I'll pass. It's all I can do to keep up with our online presence and sales, accounting, and taxes, not to mention all the other paperwork to keep day-to-day operations going."

Sophie glanced at her sister. They were just preparing to unlock the front door, but Isabelle already looked tired. Had she sat up working last night after they'd gotten back from Aunt Claudia's?

"Maybe we need to hire someone else full-time for out front so you can focus on the business side of things." The back-office work was the part of the business that her sister loved, what she'd trained for with her business management degree.

Isabelle opened her mouth and Sophie sensed the protests that were on their way. She held up her hand.

"I know that the more we do ourselves, the more we have to pay toward the note, but other than church, you have no social life. I was so glad you went sledding Saturday evening. You need to do that kind of thing more often."

Isabelle's brow lifted. "Isn't that the pot calling the kettle black?"

"My point exactly," Sophie countered. "But I do get away from here more than you."

"Work isn't restricted to what you do inside this building while the shop's doors are open. You put in more than double the hours of a normal work week most weeks, coming in early and staying late."

"True, but many of those extra hours are spent sewing, which I love, so it's not really like working," Sophie reminded. "Although, if our Petdanas sales continue to increase, I'm going to have to make some decisions on how I spend my sewing time."

"You think you may cut back on your Quilts of Valor work?"

Sophie shot her sister a horrified look. "Not as long as there's breath in my body."

Isabelle paused in what she was doing and met Sophie's gaze. "You do realize, don't you, that no matter how many quilts you make, you can't save Dad?"

Sophie's heart pinched at her sister's question. Every quilt she'd made for veterans had been sewn for her father, to some degree. It was one of the reasons she often donated quilts to be awarded elsewhere, in hopes that somewhere, some daughter had wrapped her father in a quilt, and that he'd felt the love sewn into every stitch and found healing and comfort.

Fortunately, Sophie was saved from responding to her sister's unwelcome question by her cousin knocking on the front door.

"Hey, Annabelle," Sophie greeted their recruited extra help. Though the high school student was too busy with her own activities to work a regular schedule with them, Annabelle occasionally filled in on the weekends and when school was out, and she was a lifesaver when it came to help with Black Friday and Shop Local Saturday.

Several hours later, Sophie rolled her shoulders, then leaned back over to measure the material yardage being purchased by Sue Harvey.

"I can't wait to make new pillows to go in the rockers by the fireplace. And then I'll make a matching Christmas tree skirt," the woman said.

The Harveys owned a local farm where they specialized in Christmas trees, among other things to keep the farm hopping all year long. Sophie loved going out to the farm in the spring to pick strawberries, in the fall to select a pumpkin, and, of course, in the winter to choose a tree. The most beautiful Christmas trees she'd ever seen had all come from Harvey Farms. In every season, Mrs. Harvey ran a deli and gift shop combo in a converted barn where she served yummy homemade treats and sold local goods.

"You should sign up for my stocking class on Tuesday night and make matching stockings, too," Sophie suggested while cutting the requested length.

"Tuesday night?" Mrs. Harvey looked thoughtful. "I could probably sneak away from the deli long enough to make that work. Sue Ellen could cover for me."

"Ha. I was just about to say you should get Sue Ellen to come with you. Maybe we could get her to sewing yet," Sophie laughed, thinking fondly of her former classmate. Sue Ellen had always been complimentary of Sophie's sewing abilities but had seemed almost horrified at the suggestion of doing any herself.

"Doubtful. She'd rather be out getting her hands

dirty with her dad than anything else, but she covers for me in the deli when needed."

Sue Ellen had been that way back in school, too. If asked to name a real-life tomboy, Sue Ellen Harvey would be the first person to come to Sophie's mind.

"If you want to reserve a spot, just tell whoever checks you out, and they'll save you a place."

Annabelle's giggle from the cash register had both women glancing that way, spotting the girl deep in conversation with Jeff.

Mrs. Harvey smiled at the young man at the counter.

"Carrie sure has done a great job with that one. I had to pick up some heavier items from the feed store, so Mr. Harvey sent Jeff along with me to help with anything I needed." Mrs. Harvey winked. "Little did either of them know, I planned to make a detour to hit a few of the local sales, too."

Sophie suspected Jeff and Mr. Harvey had known exactly what Mrs. Harvey was up to when she'd chosen Black Friday to pick up feed store supplies, but she kept that thought to herself.

"It doesn't look like Jeff minds this particular detour in the slightest," Sophie mused, giving Mrs. Harvey a conspiratorial smile as they watched the two teenagers laugh at something Jeff was showing Annabelle on his phone.

"I'd say not. Claudia's granddaughter is a beauty. I don't think anyone was the slightest bit surprised when she won Little Miss Pine Hill last year." Mrs. Harvey sounded as proud as if Annabelle was her own granddaughter and as if she wasn't talking about Sophie's cousin.

"She's even more beautiful on the inside," Sophie

assured, folding the piece of fabric she'd just cut, then writing the amount on a piece of paper she stuck to the top. "We love her dearly."

"Will she be entering Miss Pine Hill this year?"

Sophie nodded. "Her mother signed her up the day entries opened. I think they caught the pageant bug last year when Annabelle won and were glad she moved up an age category so they could compete again this year."

"She's a shoo-in. I recall your Grandmother Belle was a beauty queen, too," Mrs. Harvey mused. "No one in the county stood a chance if she entered a pageant. All you girls favor her to some degree, but Annabelle is her spitting image."

Sophie smiled. Her mother rarely spoke of Sophie's grandmother's pageant days, but Aunt Claudia loved to go on about them to her daughters, nieces, and grand-children, which Sophie had always found strange. She'd have thought it would be exactly opposite as Darlene had grown up to love make-up and hairstyling while Aunt Claudia wore her naturally gray locks up in a tidy, no-nonsense bun. Sophie couldn't recall the last time she'd seen her aunt's hair down or her mother not done up to a tee outside the privacy of home.

"We all thought she'd go on to do great things, to travel the world and live the life of the rich and famous," Mrs. Harvey continued.

"From what Aunt Claudia says, Grandma Belle never regretted her life choices." Although Sophie had wondered more than once if her grandmother's decision to lead a quiet life had led to Claudia craving to see the world. Thank goodness she was finally getting to realize that dream.

Mrs. Harvey smiled. "It's no wonder. She loved your

grandpa very much and always seemed so happy. It didn't surprise anyone when they passed within six months of each other."

No. Even as a young girl, it hadn't surprised Sophie, either. Her grandparents' love for each other had been palpable and so unlike what she'd witnessed between her own parents. Sophie was thankful for them, because they'd given her an example to strive toward someday.

When Cole popped into her mind, Sophie shoved him right back out and handed Mrs. Harvey's material to her. Cole was not going to be part of any relationship that she should be striving toward. Not today. Not someday. Not any day.

Only, he sure sent her pulse through the roof just at the thought of him.

"Is there anything else I can help you with?" she asked Mrs. Harvey.

Taking the fabric, the woman shook her head. "This is all I need, but, Lord willing, I'll be back for that class. You're right that matching stockings hanging from the mantle at the gift shop would look amazing."

The day passed quickly. Thank goodness they'd had both their part-time helpers and Annabelle there to assist customers. She and Isabelle were both exhausted by the time they'd locked the front doors, but it had been a great day.

While Isabelle worked in the office, Sophie straightened out all the disorder in front, restocking items for the following day's "buy local" sale, then sitting at one of the machines to make a couple dozen Petdanas as Carrie had texted to say she'd sold out again.

Late that night, in the privacy of her bedroom, Sophie sat on her bed, leaned back against the headboard, a light-hearted Christmas movie playing on her favorite television station, while she worked on her quilt.

"Meow."

Sophie glanced over at her bedroom window.

"Seriously?" she said to the cat sitting on the ledge and staring in at her. "Did you come to thank me for the yummy cat nibbles from Carrie's shop I left you on the porch?"

The cat blinked and continued to watch her through the glass pane.

"Just think, if you trusted me, you could be in here snuggled up on this blanket with me, getting some love and attention, but no, you have to play Mr. Hard-to-Get."

Sophie continue to talk to the cat while she sewed, taking care to make sure she got each stitch evenly spaced. She took great care with all the quilts she donated, but this one felt special.

The furry feline settled in to watch her through the window.

"How about Stitches?" she asked, wondering how much the cat could hear through the glass panes. He probably could hear everything she was saying. After all, she'd heard his meow just fine. "Or Bobbin. I like both, for obvious reasons. But I think Stitches fits you best."

Stitches the cat. Yep. She liked it.

The cat must have, too, because he laid down on the ledge, closed his eyes, and drifted off, looking at peace.

Surprised at this change in behavior, Sophie just stared at him.

"Well, how about that?" she mused, wondering if

maybe Sarah was right. Maybe she just needed to be patient and the cat would come around and eventually want to stay. She'd never force the animal to, but if he quit coming around, she'd miss him.

She glanced over at her phone.

And Cole? Was Sarah right about that, too? Did she just need to be patient there, too?

And what was it she was being patient in hopes of gaining, anyway? Cole wasn't a cat that she wanted to bring in from the cold. So what was he? What did she want him to be?

Friend. She wanted to be Cole's friend.

Even if he hadn't texted her back.

Would it seriously have hurt him to have sent some funny little meme back? Or to have at least typed in a LOL or SMH or some other acronym, the way anyone else would? Just something in acknowledgement that he'd gotten her text, that he'd smiled or had a happy thought at the funny picture.

Maybe the firehall had been busy. She hadn't heard of anything that had happened around town, but who knew what all the firemen did that she had no clue about?

Pushing the needle through the material, Sophie jabbed her finger.

"Ouch." She stuck her finger in her mouth, then got up to go to the bathroom to get a bandage so she wouldn't risk getting blood on the quilt.

When she came back into her bedroom, the cat was gone from her windowsill.

And her phone still hadn't dinged with a returned text.

Why couldn't patience have been her virtue?

CHAPTER TWELVE

WHEN COLE HAD VOLUNTEERED TO work during the Pine Hill On-the-Square Christmas Festival, he'd pictured himself manning the firehall, maybe even walking around the square, keeping an eye on things to make sure everyone stayed safe.

He sure hadn't seen himself as being part of the parade.

He wasn't a parade kind of guy. He wasn't a Santa-suit-wearing kind of guy, either, but here he was in the perfectly fitted costume Sophie had altered for him, riding in the Tower, waving and tossing Christmas candy to kids as the bucket truck slowly drove along the crowded streets of the parade path.

"Hey, look who's just a few yards up ahead on your side of the street."

Cole wanted to ignore Andrew, knowing from his friend's tone that if he looked over, he'd see Sophie there, but his gaze automatically jumped in the direction his buddy had mentioned.

His phone burned in his pocket, reminding him he

hadn't texted her back, and that for the past two days, he had spent way too much time dwelling on why he hadn't.

He supposed he could have snuck away from Ben and Andrew to come up with something to say in return. But every time he'd considered doing so, he'd reminded himself that Sophie was just being nice to him because she felt sorry for him. Nothing more.

He'd be a fool to think otherwise.

Which he must be because when they'd been sledding, snowball fighting, playing their game, he hadn't felt anything like an emotional charity case.

He'd felt...like someone she really liked.

Then he'd remind himself of all the reasons why he needed to distance himself from Sophie. Reasons that included his past lurking in the shadows. The last thing he needed was Sophie having that kind of interest in him when he never planned to be in that type of relationship with anyone. Especially not someone as wonderful as Sophie. She deserved better than a messed-up man such as himself.

He'd done her a favor by not texting her back. Once they were through with the toy drive, she could forget about him.

The truck rolled closer to where Sophie stood and as his luck would have it, the parade slowed to a standstill right at the moment when he was opposite from where she stood, wearing a Santa hat and a flashing Christmas bulbs necklace.

From where she was looking straight at him. When their gazes met, she smiled and waved. Not just a little wave, but a big, exuberant one as if she hadn't texted him and been ignored. As if he was a long-lost friend she'd just spotted for the first time in years.

"Someone is happy to see you."

Cole mumbled something under his breath, not even sure himself what he'd replied. Whatever it had been, Andrew laughed.

"Throw her some candy."

"No."

Andrew chuckled. "Ah, now, that's not nice, Santa."

"I never said I was nice," Cole reminded, wondering at how his hands had gone clammy inside his gloves despite the chill from the open truck window.

"You're nicer than you think you are," Andrew pointed out, his gaze back on the truck in front of them.

"I must be to put up with the likes of you."

Andrew snorted.

Cole couldn't resist glancing back toward where Sophie stood. She was still looking his way, still smiling and still waving.

Lord, she must be a saint to stay so positive when dealing with someone as jaded as him.

Unable to stop himself, Cole waved back. He hadn't consciously decided to, but his hand had lifted and done exactly that. Okay, so it had been a one-time shifting of his wrist that almost mimicked a mid-air salute, rather than a wave.

Certainly nothing like the enthusiastic back and forth moving she'd been doing.

What kind of Santa would he be if he hadn't waved back?

A bad one. Which was what he was anyway.

Happy surprise lit on Sophie's face, as if she'd expected him to completely ignore her wave as he'd done with her text. Such a small thing to wave back, yet she truly looked pleased, as if he'd done something wonderful.

Guilt hit him. He hadn't texted her back because he hadn't wanted to encourage the light he saw in her eyes. But not encouraging Sophie had only been one part of his reasoning.

He'd convinced himself she would be better off if he kept his distance, that *he* would be better off if he kept his distance, too, because he didn't want to be one of her do-gooder projects. He wasn't someone she could fix.

But common courtesy dictated that he should have acknowledged her text. That he should toss her some candy.

So, he tossed a handful. Next to him, Andrew chuckled, but didn't say anything further, for which Cole was grateful.

Fortunately, the parade started moving again and Andrew's attention returned to maintaining a safe distance from the truck in front of them and watching for any wayward pedestrian that stepped off the crowded sidewalk.

Unable to resist, Cole's gaze met Sophie's and held until the truck moved beyond where she stood. The whole time, she kept smiling at him as if she was truly glad to see him.

As if she'd missed him that week.

Rather than admit he'd missed seeing her, too, Cole nodded in acknowledgement of whatever it was he was acknowledging and attempted to focus on tossing more candy to parade watchers.

Missing Sophie would mean he cared for her as more

than just a casual acquaintance, and he really didn't need to do that when it would only lead to heartache down the road.

Heartache for Sophie? Or for him?

He'd decided to never have a relationship. There'd been reasons for that. Good reasons. Valid reasons that shouldn't be ignored.

He never wanted to hurt her.

Only, what if Sophie was the one woman who could read his journal and not view him with pity, fear, or disgust?

What if she'd read his journal and still saw the man he was beneath all the things he'd done and seen? A man who'd made mistakes and lived everyday with that knowledge and the desire to make up for what he could?

What if she was the light bright enough to illuminate the inner darkness that never truly let go of him?

"Be leery of candy from strangers and good-looking firefighters dressed as Santa," Isabelle warned from beside Sophie as they made their way back to Sophie's booth just opposite from the quilt shop. The courthouse yard was covered with garland and ribbon-draped tents and the space was full of vendors selling various wares.

Isabelle was splitting her time between the church's bake sale and ornament sale. Each year, the Butterflies made plastic canvas snowflakes that were sold to raise funds for Sarah's special community charity projects. Sophie supported the snowflake cause but didn't volunteer for the booth because she felt the Quilts of Valor booth needed her more. Her sister felt otherwise.

Isabelle never complained about the amount of time Sophie put into the cause she whole-heartedly believed in, but her sister rarely volunteered to pitch in herself with Sophie's Quilts of Valor activities.

Isabelle's reasons for not being as involved were the exact same as Sophie's reasons for wanting to be as involved as possible. Their father.

"You're just jealous because I got the Rudolph the red-nosed gumball from Santa," Sophie accused, blowing a bubble with her gum, and, laughing, quickly sucking it back in when Isabelle went to pop it.

Santa Cole had waved. Silly, but that simple wave had flip-flopped her belly with pure giddiness.

Isabelle wrinkled her own nose. "You know I haven't chewed gum since before I had braces—and I was fifteen when they came off."

"Your loss," she assured her sister, then added, "Besides, you have nothing to worry about when it comes to Cole."

"Other than how emotionally involved with a former military man you're becoming, you mean?"

Bingo.

"Not that we're involved, not like you're inferring, but his being a former military man is a plus to me."

"You've forgotten how our father was?"

Sophie blew another bubble because she knew it would annoy Isabelle almost as much as her sister's question annoyed her. Isabelle knew Sophie hadn't forgotten.

A kid didn't forget that her father had just packed up and left.

"You can't blame me for worrying about you," Isabelle reminded as they entered the tent where Sophie had quilts displayed, including ones attached to each side of three sides of the tent to block the wind, along with a table spread with brochures and pamphlets.

Most of the goods on display in the various tents were Christmas themed or decorated, but not Sophie's. She was all red, white, and blue.

A Quilts of Valor Foundation banner draped the front of the table and Isabelle winced as she stared at it.

"I've been doing it my whole life."

"I know," Sophie relented. "And, I appreciate how much you love me and have always looked out for me. But where Cole is concerned, stop worrying. We're barely more than acquaintances."

"You don't expect me to believe that, surely?"

Shrugging, Sophie straightened a stack of brochures. "Believe what you want."

"You'd like there to be more between the two of you," Isabelle accused, obviously not ready to let the conversation go.

"Of course, I'd like there to be more." She met her sister's gaze. "Why wouldn't I? Cole's a great person. I'd like to be his friend." Maybe more. Maybe a lot more. "I'd think you'd feel the same as me, that we should reach out to him, make him feel welcome."

Isabelle sighed. "I can't stand the thought of you being involved with someone who is destined to hurt you."

Isabelle was wrong. Cole wouldn't hurt her. Yes, he was a bit hot and cold, but it wasn't out of malice. He was just dealing with his own defensive issues.

Leaning over, Sophie hugged her sister. "I'm very lucky to have you to love me and watch out for me. Thank you."

"Just...be careful, okay?"

"That is some good chili."

A de-Santa-fied Cole nodded at Andrew's comment after they'd each finished eating a bowl apiece from Lou's food truck. The hot, spiced-up soup he'd chosen had been some of the best Cole had ever eaten. One thing was certain, Pine Hill had great food.

He tossed his empty bowl into a recycle bin and the two men prepared to walk around to look at the other booths. As part of their firefighter duties, they were required to stay at the festival, search for any fire code violations that might put others at risk, and mainly, just be close in case there were any issues.

They made it about halfway around the square before stopping.

"Hey, Cole! Andrew!" Sarah called from a festively decorated large tent. Garland with colorful Christmas lights and ribbon twisted around each support pole and across the front of the tent. One side of the tent boasted the church bake sale, where several men and women were waiting on customers. The other side was set up as an ornament booth where Sarah and Bodie sold snowflakes that they displayed by hanging them both on live Christmas trees and on a large painted pegboard-type tree that served as a partition between the bake sale and the ornament sale.

"Do you guys need a Butterfly-made snowflake?"

"No."

Those Butterflies made him nervous. Probably because he suspected they were always up to something.

Besides, Cole hadn't decorated the farmhouse and

didn't plan to. Why would he? It was only him there. Other than Andrew, Ben, and more recently, Bodie, he never had company. He'd found a few boxes of his uncle's Christmas decorations in the attic when he'd been going through things, but he hadn't pulled them out and had no intentions to anytime soon.

Hearing Cole's voice, Harry came around from behind the booth partition.

Cole knelt to scratch the dog behind his ears. "Hey, buddy. You remember me?"

"Harry never forgets anyone," Bodie said proudly. "He's probably trying to butter you up for another invite to chase birds at your farm."

"Like I told you, he's welcome, anytime. He's a great dog. Aren't you, boy?"

Harry gave a bark, confirming that he was indeed a great boy.

With his work schedule, Cole hadn't seriously considered getting an animal, but the more he was around Harry, the more he thought he might. If he ever did, he'd just have to make sure he could bring it to the firehall with him as he wouldn't want to leave an animal at home alone during his long work shifts.

"How about you, Andrew?" Sarah turned her gaze on his friend. "Do you need a snowflake?"

"Need?" Andrew shook his head. "I've got dozens of the things. My grandma makes me one and puts it on my Christmas gift every year." He wore a rather lost expression as if he wasn't sure why she did that. "I don't put up a tree, so I just keep tossing them in a drawer because I don't know what to do with them."

"I'd think that was obvious," Sarah told him in a no-nonsense tone. "You need to get a tree and to put them on it. It's why Ruby makes them for you. Shame on you for just tossing them in a drawer year after year."

Not looking up from where he petted Harry, Cole smothered a laugh at Sarah's scolding.

Andrew shook his head. "Not happening. Too busy to mess with all that fuss and bother. My man cave is just fine the way it is—womanless and treeless."

Sarah's mouth dropped open, then taking in Andrew's expression, she let out an exaggerated sigh. "Men."

Cole, Andrew, and Bodie looked at each other and grinned.

"At least you're keeping the ones Ruby makes you," Sarah pointed out, giving credit where credit was due. "That's good. Someday, you'll be glad you did. Still, you should buy a few of these to use on presents you give this year. It's for a good cause and it'll add a festive touch and make your gifts more meaningful."

"I expect meaningful gifts," Cole couldn't resist saying.

Andrew's gaze narrowed. "I'll give you a meaningful gift."

Cole laughed.

Bodie gave Sarah an indulgent smile. "It's okay. Not everyone wants or needs a snowflake."

Smiling back, with her mouth and her eyes, Sarah clicked her tongue at her fiancé. "Your sales pitch needs work, Bodie Lewis."

"Guess you'll have to help me practice," he suggested.

"I could do that." She batted her lashes at her soon-to-be husband.

Cole felt a pang of jealousy at the teasing looks and

banter passing between the couple. When he'd been at the farm, Bodie had mentioned a little of his past, revealing that he'd been busted up during an IED explosion that had left him as the sole survivor of his unit. Afterward, he'd had to deal with a lot of survivor's guilt.

Cole understood the survivor's guilt. He hadn't been the only one to survive the ambush, but he'd been the one in charge. He should have gotten his men out of there sooner.

Cole was happy that Bodie had managed to make a good life for himself in Pine Hill but couldn't help the pang hitting him.

What was Cole thinking? He did *not* feel a pang of jealousy.

That pang had been nothing more than heartburn from Lou's chili.

Besides, Cole had made a good life for himself in Pine Hill, too.

Any jealousy he felt toward Bodie would be over Harry. He'd like a dog like Harry.

As if he sensed what Cole was thinking, the dog nuzzled his head against Cole, then licked his gloved hand.

"Everyone *does* need a snowflake," Sarah insisted, standing on her tiptoes to kiss Bodie's cheek.

Nope. That was not jealousy.

"Some folks just don't realize they need one. It's our job to enlighten them." Sarah's expression said that Bodie could voice no argument that would convince her otherwise. "We're doing them a favor by selling them a snowflake and adding Christmas magic to their holiday season. Plus, they're doing a good deed in helping fund church charity projects." She gave Bodie a pointed look.

"Remember that and you'll do a much better job in selling these snowflakes."

One side of his mouth hiking up, Bodie turned back toward Cole and Andrew. "Sorry, guys, but you heard the lady. Prepare to be enlightened. You may not realize it, but you do, after all, need a snowflake. Your entire holiday season will be lacking in Christmas cheer if you miss out on these extraordinary, genuine Bumblebee-made, snowflakes."

"Butterfly-made," Sarah corrected with an amused eyeroll before turning back to Cole. "But other than that, he's right. Besides," she said, directing her gaze to Cole, "surely you want a snowflake as a reminder of the other night, don't you?" Her eyes twinkled. "Weren't the sledding and games just so much fun?"

Cole didn't need a reminder of that night. Far from it.

"Got to help a brother out," Andrew said, handing over a folded bill to Bodie and taking a snowflake even if he didn't look as if he knew quite what to do with it.

Cole pulled out his wallet, too. "How about I make a donation and you give the snowflake to someone who really does need it?"

Sarah awarded him a smile, took his money, then gave a sly look. "That's an excellent idea. I know just who needs one. It would totally make her night. Would you deliver it for me?"

"Say no," Andrew half-coughed, half-whispered as he slipped Bodie his snowflake back to be resold to raise more funds.

Cole narrowed his gaze at the smiling woman he'd liked until that moment. She wasn't fooling anyone, least of all him. Maybe she was one of those Butterflies, too, only younger.

"Let me guess, Sophie needs a snowflake?"

"I always did say you military boys were quick to catch on." Sarah grinned, then turned to choose a snowflake, her gaze pausing only a moment on the snowflake Bodie had rehung, staring at it just long enough to let them know she knew what they'd done.

"Told you to say no," Andrew said, shaking his head.

Once she'd picked a snowflake, Sarah placed it inside a paper bag, then handed it to Cole with a big smile.

"Thank you so much for your support and for passing on holiday cheer. Merry Christmas!"

Sophie beamed at the two women who'd stopped at her tent and asked for more information about the Quilts of Valor Foundation.

"I'm so glad you asked," she said, meaning every word. She loved talking about the organization that did so much good. "Back in 2003, Catherine Roberts started the organization after she had a dream about wrapping a dejected soldier in a quilt. Since that time, the organization has awarded thousands of quilts and strives to wrap thousands more around past and present military."

Sophie handed the woman a brochure and continued to gush a little as she explained the patterns for some of the quilts she had on display. Although Sophie volunteered her longarm services to quilt others' quilts to be awarded, and though she had several of those at the shop, Sophie had made all the ones she'd brought with her tonight.

"My father was in the Navy," the older woman said. "He served during World War II. I would love for him to have been wrapped in a quilt." Memories of her father shone in her eyes. "He'd have loved that. Despite the hardships he faced, he was so proud of his time in the military."

"My father served, too," Sophie told her. "Not in World War II, obviously." She smiled. "He served in Desert Storm."

And was never the same afterward, according to all who knew and loved him. Still, he'd come home long enough to marry and father two girls prior to taking off for parts unknown.

"Because of his service and the service of those like your father, we enjoy so many freedoms every day." Sophie smiled. "Our goal is to honor their sacrifice and offer healing with the wrapping of a Quilt of Valor around those touched by war."

"That's wonderful," the younger woman said, picking up one of the many photos Sophie had printed and spread out on the table.

Photos of men and women wrapped in their quilts. Men and women whose lives Sophie hoped they'd touched so that, when needed, the veterans felt the heartfelt hug of love and appreciation that was sewn into every quilt.

"Being wrapped in a quilt is something I wish every serviceman and woman could experience," she admitted. "I've met so many wonderful people who have sacrificed so much."

Just as her father had sacrificed so much.

Isabelle blamed him for abandoning them. Sophie tried to view his choices differently, knowing her father had left for reasons that went beyond abandonment.

The utter devastation she'd read in Cole's journal echoed what she imagined had tormented her father.

"They each have a story to tell, memories that are precious to them, friendships made that have lasted a lifetime," she continued. "I'm always in awe at each quilt presentation of the person receiving the quilt. Their accomplishments are extraordinary. We owe so much to our wonderful military and I'm so proud to be the daughter of a man who served his country."

"I wish I sewed," one of the women mused. "I'd love to make a quilt to donate."

"If you're interested in learning, you are talking to the right person. I can teach you to sew. It's what I do. Our local QOVF group meets once a month to sew for a few hours together at my shop, The Threaded Needle, which is just over that way." She gestured in the direction of the shop. "If you want to learn, please come. There are some wonderful seamstresses there who'd love to teach you their craft as much as I would, and we always have a great time."

How could they not with the Butterflies there for entertainment?

"Even if you discover sewing isn't for you, you'll still have made some new friends and so will we." She handed each woman a business card and told them the next date and time. "We'd love to have you join us. There's nothing to compare to wrapping a quilt you've made around a soldier. I don't know how to fully put it into words except to say that it's the best feeling in the world."

Sophie's gaze went beyond the women to a uniformed man standing just beyond the tent. A handsome man in a fire department uniform rather than a Santa suit or the marine uniform she imagined he'd worn with distinction.

"Cole."

Talk about the best feeling in the world.

How long had he been standing there and why hadn't he come on inside the tent?

Automatically she smiled. Crazy, since he didn't smile back. Then again, he didn't most of the time, and that hadn't dissuaded her yet. With as wonderful as his smiles were on the rare occasions he brandished them, she doubted she ever would quit trying for them.

Maybe she was more patient that she'd thought.

Either that, or all the praying for patience she'd been doing was paying off.

CHAPTER THIRTEEN

COLE SHOULD HAVE HANDED THE snowflake to Andrew and let his bud deliver the ornament while Cole did anything other than purposely seek out Sophie.

Instead, Andrew had been the one to bail when Sheriff Roscoe had stepped up and asked if he'd ridden his motorcycle lately.

Once his friend got to talking about Big Bad Bertha, he'd always lose track of time. He and the sheriff would likely still be talking motorcycles when the whole festival was over and people started taking down the tents.

Deciding he'd rather deliver the ornament without an audience, Cole had taken off for Sophie's booth. With each step in her direction, the anticipation had built.

Being near her flipped a switch inside him that was like existing versus living. Really living.

With joy. Sophie's joy.

But after hearing her conversation with the two women, he wondered if he should have stayed put.

No. It was better this way. He'd allowed his head to

get clouded with thoughts and ideas that had no place outside of fairytales. This brought him back down to earth.

So for that, he was glad he'd heard her talking to the women. He'd needed the reminder that Sophie's interest in him stemmed from things other than girl meets boy and girl likes boy despite all the bad things boy has done and all the memories that haunted him.

Sophie wanted to fix him. Probably by wrapping him in one of her quilts. As if it was that easy. She had no clue.

"Thanks for the information. We'll stop by your shop soon," the younger of Sophie's two visitors promised, taking a brochure along with the business card Sophie had given her.

When the ladies left, Sophie turned her gaze back to him and flashed one of her most brilliant smiles. One that he'd swear lifted her whole body until she stood a couple inches taller.

"Hi," she said, sounding a bit breathy.

He stepped to just inside her tent. "Hi back."

"I was hoping to get to see you again in your Santa suit."

He shrugged. "Can't have two Santas running around tonight, and the American Legion sponsored a 'photo with Santa' booth. Plus, I'm on duty."

"Maybe next year."

He didn't bother pointing out that he wouldn't be wearing the suit next year, or ever again, for that matter. He'd have it cleaned, then he'd bring it back to the firehall for whoever got stuck with it next year.

"Thanks for my Christmas candy."

"You're welcome." Cole picked up one of her photos,

eyeing the image of a veteran wrapped in a blanket. An older gentleman in full uniform who was decorated to the hilt from what Cole could see that was not covered by the quilt around the man's shoulders. "I expected to find for sale items from your shop in your booth, not all this patriotic quilt stuff."

"The Threaded Needle is an avid supporter of all things patriotic." Grinning, she saluted him.

"As are you?"

"Of course." Sophie stared up at him, her eyes glittering as she asked, "Did you have a good Thanksgiving?"

Glancing back at the photo, Cole inhaled a deep breath. "It was just another day."

"Did you work?"

He nodded. "Yeah. Thanks for the text."

"You're welcome." Her smile was infectious as she added, "For future reference, it's polite to respond in a timely fashion."

Cole regarded her, taking in her hair spilling from beneath her Santa hat, her still-flashing Christmas lights necklace, and the same puffy jacket she'd worn when they'd gone sledding. Her cheeks and the tip of her nose were pink from the cold.

"Just how long is a timely fashion? Am I still within an okay window?"

Sophie's eyes danced with mischief as she said, "Not even close. Anything beyond twenty-four hours is too long and in bad taste. You should make a note of it."

"I never was good with social etiquette."

"Well, now you know so that the next time I text, you can keep in mind that the clock is ticking." She tapped her coat covered wrist. "Tick tock."

Studying her, Cole asked, "Do you intend to text me again?"

Her cheeks flushed. "Maybe, if you're lucky, but you best not ignore my text next time if I do."

"I didn't ignore your text."

He should just let it go and let her think he had. She didn't need to know how much he'd agonized over her message and what his appropriate response, or lack thereof, should have been.

"No? That's so odd. I don't recall getting a text back." She noticed the small white paper bag he held. "What's that?"

"Sarah sent it for you."

A smile spread across her face. "Oh! It must be my snowflakes I asked her to hold for me. I'm so glad she remembered. Yay!"

Cole held out the bag. "I don't know anything about snowflakes that were on hold for you, but she asked me to give this one to you."

"Oh. Okay." Sophie's cheeks pinkened as she took the bag, opened it, and gently lifted the ornament. "I'd asked her to put three back for me. When you said...I wonder why..." She stared at the single snowflake, then glanced up at him, seeming to realize why her friend had asked the favor of Cole. Her face flushed a deeper pink. "Oh, never mind."

Yeah, this was growing more awkward by the minute.

"Thanks for bringing the snowflake to me." She carefully tucked it into the bag she had stowed beneath the table. "I'll ask Sarah about it later."

She wouldn't have to as her friend would, no doubt, tell her that it had been Cole who'd bought the ornament. Cole was convinced Sarah was either a full-fledged Butterfly or maybe one in training. That Bodie had called them bees fit. They buzzed way too much to be labeled butterflies. The older women probably called Sarah a caterpillar or something just as corny.

Why else would Sarah so obviously matchmake? Perhaps she thought because Bodie was such a good man, Cole must be, too. She didn't know his past to know any better.

Unless Sophie had told her. But no, if Sarah had any idea what he'd been through, what he'd done, she'd want her friend to stay as far away from Cole as possible.

A woman came into the tent, took a brochure, then asked Sophie a question about how to sign up her grandmother, who'd apparently been an Army nurse once upon a time.

Answering the woman's question, Sophie's smile wattage flashed with her excitement over her answer and her enthusiasm for the organization she was promoting.

"What is all this stuff?" Cole asked after the woman left, glancing around at the various patriotic quilts displayed around the tent. Three sides of the tent were covered in red, white, and blue quilts, probably to block the wind and cut down on the cold as much as for décor.

If he'd thought her wattage had been cranked up answering the woman's question, he hadn't seen anything yet. Her current smile was so brilliant that Cole felt as if he'd just stepped into a spotlight. So much so that he fought to keep from taking a step back, feeling like a deer caught in headlights. Or given the season, should that be a reindeer?

If he wasn't careful, Sophie would be hooking him up to a sleigh and saying it was for the benefit of his own Christmas spirit.

Eyes sparkling, she clasped her hands together. "I'm so glad you asked."

Then she launched into a passion-filled spiel about the organization she belonged to that made quilts for the members of the military.

"Our local group awards in this area, as well as sending some to the organization's national headquarters to help meet requests they get for quilt awards." Her eyes took on that about-to-bubble-over, hope-filled look she'd had the first time they'd met, the one packed with so much happiness. But this time, it also held a hint of hesitancy that set warning bells off in Cole's head.

"I want to—" she began, causing Cole's throat to tighten.

"No." He cut her off before she could say more.

Maybe he shouldn't have eaten that spicy chili after all, because he was feeling pangs again. Lots of pangs. Not of jealousy, but of absolute refusal to even consider what she'd been on the verge of saying.

Everything in him rejected the idea of Sophie awarding him anything. Of anyone "awarding" something to him that was meant to convey honor.

He'd done his job. And he hadn't done it nearly well enough—if he had been someone truly worthy of any awards then he wouldn't have let his men down.

He deserved nothing more than what the government had paid him.

They'd given him a medal. He hadn't deserved that, either, even if they'd insisted that he had. Men died on his watch. There was nothing honorable or award-worthy about that.

"But you—"

Every muscle in his body contracted to the point where even breathing was difficult. "No buts."

Frowning, Sophie wasn't ready to give up on what she'd obviously given a lot of thought to long before tonight. He could see that truth shining in her eyes—saw it and felt frustrated by it.

Widening his stance, bracing for her rebuttal, Cole crossed his arms. He wouldn't back down on this.

He didn't want her giving him things. Not quilts. Not pity. Not anything.

"Just hear me out," she persisted.

"Cole!" Rosie said, coming up to the booth in a swirl of perfume and colorful winter attire that made the blue spikes of her hair poking out from beneath her hat seem tame. The older woman dropped an equally colorful purse beneath the table, then turned back to him. "Are you here to take Sophie to get something to eat during her break? Lord knows she probably hasn't eaten a bite all day."

Sophie was about to go on break? And hadn't eaten a bite all day?

Maintaining his stiffened posture, Cole shook his head. "I should get back to Andrew. He's probably wondering where I'm at."

Rosie waved her hand. "I just left him and Sheriff Roscoe. I hate to break it to you, but I don't think they're missing you." She gave a little laugh, then patted his cheek with her gloved hand. "Go, be young. Take this hard-working girl to get some of Lou's chili before it's all gone. I swear that man puts magic into that pot when he makes his Christmas batch."

Cole narrowed his gaze at the older woman. Did everyone in the whole place think they were small-town Cupids?

Scratch that, small-town Butterflies?

"I've already eaten."

Rosie gave him a duh look. "Which is why I didn't say for *you* to go get some of Lou's chili but to feed our girl. Sophie, have you had anything to eat, dear?"

Our girl? Sophie might be Rosie's girl, but she wasn't his.

Looking a bit sheepish, Sophie shook her head. "I haven't."

"Just as I suspected. You work too much," Rosie clicked her tongue. "Now, go and see Lou. Make sure he's behaving himself because I swear, that Alberta keeps coming over there as if we don't all know what she's doing." Rosie's gaze shot imaginary daggers in the direction of Lou's booth. "It ain't like she's actually eating all that chili she keeps buying and giggling over."

Cole gave Sophie a blank look.

Laughing, Sophie linked her arm with his as if it was the most natural thing in the world. It wasn't.

"Come on," she said, "and I'll explain on our way to Lou's. Sometimes it's easier to not argue, and I am hungry. All I've had since lunch is a piece of gum a firefighter tossed out to me during the best Christmas parade ever."

Sophie was right. Sometimes it was easier to just not argue.

But his sense of self-preservation was arguing right and left that he should not have his arm linked with

Sophie's, that he should step away, that he shouldn't be looking into her smiling face.

That he shouldn't be going soft inside just because she walked with her arm hooked with his and seemed oblivious to everything and everyone except him as they strolled toward Lou's food truck.

That her arm linked with his, her warm presence next to him, felt right even when he knew it wasn't.

Sophie talked non-stop while they made their way to where Cole had gotten his chili.

"Mmm, everything smells heavenly." She inhaled deeply, then smiled at the older gentleman in the food truck. "I'll take one bowl of your Spicy Hot Chili and a hot chocolate, please."

Surprised she'd chosen the spicy version of Lou's offerings, Cole got out his wallet. He was still full, but the chili did smell good enough to make his own stomach growl.

Sophie's gaze dropped to where he was pulling out some cash. "You don't need to do that. I don't think Rosie meant for you to buy my dinner." Thinking on what she'd said, she grinned and acknowledged what he'd already known. "Well, she might have, but *I* didn't mean for you to."

"Rosie sent y'all over here?"

Sophie's gaze shifted to Lou.

"Of course. Don't you recognize spies when you see them?" She winked at Lou. "We're taking notes on how many bowls of chili Alberta buys while we're here."

Lou grinned. "Be sure to tell her that Alberta bought a few dozen, and that I threw in a pie for free. That should get Rosie's goat good."

"Now, Lou," Sophie mock-scolded. "You wouldn't be purposely trying to make Rosie jealous, would you?"

"Darn tootin' I am. It's past time for her to make an honest man out of me."

Sophie sighed. "Agreed. I'll make it sound good and tell her about the twinkle I saw in your eyes."

"Thatta girl." Lou grinned, then gave her the total for her items.

"Here. I've got this," Cole stepped forward, handing the man a twenty.

"Cole," Sophie began again, but when her gaze met his, she paused and seemed to come to a conclusion, because rather than argue further, she smiled and said, "Thank you. That's very sweet of you."

Sweet. Not an adjective used to describe him possibly ever. It was enough to make Cole laugh as he took his change from Lou and put his wallet back into his pocket.

He took the bowl from her while she grabbed some packs of crackers and her hot chocolate.

Rather than go to one of the few tables set up to try to squeeze in around folks already eating there, Sophie went to the garland-and-white-lights-draped gazebo with its big red bows at the top of each section. A fully decorated Christmas tree was in the center of the gazebo. Several people sat around on the seats along the perimeter, so Sophie sat down on the steps.

Cole handed over her chili. If he was going to walk away, now was his chance.

Only, he wouldn't leave her to sit alone on the gazebo steps.

What kind of person would he be if he did that? After

all, she'd always been nothing but kind to him, despite knowing what she knew.

He sat down next to her, the cold from the steps cutting through even the thickness of his utility pants. In her thinner clothes, Sophie had to feel as if she was sitting on an ice block. But rather than complain, she awarded him another happy look.

Meeting her gaze, the smile he'd been fighting broke free. He didn't even know why he was smiling, just that he felt the lifting of his facial muscles as his mouth curved.

"Finally," she breathed. "I thought you'd forgotten how."

Still feeling a bit like a puppet with her holding his strings, as if she controlled his body more than him, Cole grunted, "That makes two of us."

Looking a little caught off guard at his response, her smile wavered—but that only lasted for a moment. He could almost have missed it because she recovered that fast. "Well, I'm glad you remembered, because I like your smile."

"Why?" Wasn't that the million-dollar question? Why was Sophie so nice to him? Why did she light up brighter than the square's Christmas tree when she looked at him? Was it all a ruse? All founded in benevolence?

Blowing on a steaming spoonful of chili, she eyed him. "What do you mean, why? Doesn't everyone prefer smiling people to unsmiling people?"

She had a point.

Cupping his gloved hands, Cole blew into them, as if he thought that was going to warm them. Had he been hoping her answer would warm his soul right down to his fingertips? He wasn't physically that cold, so he must have been hoping for something.

"I guess so."

Sophie ate her spoonful of chili. "Mmmm, this is good enough to make the whole world smile. Yum. Want a bite?"

She planned to spoon-feed him? Neck muscles tensing, Cole shook his head. "I already ate."

"Don't say I didn't offer to share."

"No worries. Those stars in your crown are safe."

"What does that mean?" She gave him a blank look as she wrapped her lips around the spoon again.

"Nothing," he murmured, feeling guilty that his own shortcomings were seeping through.

"Did you see the tree lighting earlier? Wasn't it gorgeous? I was at the booth, so I only saw it from a distance, but it's always so impressive."

Cole had gone to the tree lighting by default as he and Andrew had been canvasing the square at the time.

"What's your favorite Christmas memory?"

"Huh?" Cole turned back to Sophie, wondering how it was even possible for her brain to jump from one subject to the next so quickly.

She waved her spoon as she spoke. "Your favorite Christmas memory, what is it?"

"Same as any kid. Christmas morning and unwrapping presents."

"Presents are good," she agreed, taking another bite, then asking, "Did you get lots of presents or was it mostly lumps of coal? Coal for Cole. Ha, ha."

Cole's lips twitched. Yeah, he'd been hearing all types of coal jokes from his buddies, now that they were in the Christmas season. Usually in conjunction with something about Sophie.

"I deserved lumps of coal," he admitted, "but never found any in my stocking."

"Tell me about Christmas morning at your house."

Cole frowned. "Why?"

"Because I want to know. And don't ask me why I want to know!" she said, pointing her empty spoon at him. "Just tell me."

"It was me and my parents."

"You're an only child?"

"I was for a while. My parents divorced when I was ten, but up until then, it was the three of us. They both remarried and had more kids. Now I have four half-sisters. Two from each parent."

"Four? Wow. That's lucky." Sophie sounded as if she truly believed that. "I just have Isabelle but would love to have a dozen more of her."

Cole wasn't sure he'd ever viewed himself lucky for having sisters. More indifferent, really. He'd been a teenaged boy when his parents had remarried, and he had joined the military as they were starting their new families. They'd written to him on occasion, the letters and postcards eventually catching up to wherever he was stationed, but he'd never been close to his siblings. Both parents had new families, and he'd never quite belonged as part of either one.

"Do you ever see them?" she asked between bites of her dinner.

"Occasionally." He'd gone home a few times on leave but had felt awkward and out of place with his parents' new families, as if he was the outsider, a reminder of a failed first try. "They all live in Georgia."

"Georgia isn't that far from Kentucky."

"Far enough."

"Was there a favorite Christmas morning?"

"Not that I recall. They were all about the same. Wake up, wake the parents, open presents, then spend the rest of the day playing with whatever they'd gotten me while they did their thing."

Sophie placed her empty bowl beside her on the step. "Being an only child sounds boring."

"I was never bored."

"I can't imagine not having Isabelle to spend the day with. We had so much fun on Christmas, with Mom, too."

He noted she didn't mention her father but decided not to ask. He wasn't much on people asking about his private matters, so he sure wasn't going to push into someone else's.

"How about you? Do you have a favorite Christmas morning memory?"

Her eyes took on a sparkly faraway look. "I was six. It's the last Christmas we spent as a family before my dad left."

Left as in actually left, by choice? Or left as in passed away? Cole kept his questions to himself. If Sophie wanted him to know, she'd elaborate.

"Isabelle and I wanted this dollhouse with all this furniture in it. Dad worked at a local factory and Mom at the salon. They didn't have any extra money, and this dollhouse was the Cadillac of doll houses with all the bells and whistles." Her eyes took on a faraway look. "Thinking back, I don't know how they did it, but that dollhouse, and furniture for every room in it, were waiting for us under the tree. We played and played with that gift. It's probably still in the attic somewhere."

"Sounds like it was a good investment on their part if you both played with it that much."

"It was." She stood, brushing off her backside. "Lots of happy memories associated with that dollhouse and Christmas mornings."

They tossed her trash in the appropriate bins, then rambled through the crowds.

She hadn't linked her arm with his again, but instead had her gloved hands shoved into her coat pockets except when she occasionally paused to point someone or something out to him.

Touching or not, he imagined they still looked cozier and closer, more intimate, than what they were as Sophie smiled frequently and chatted a mile a minute about whatever she'd last called his attention to.

Cole hadn't meant to walk her back to her booth. But when he'd spotted Andrew, his friend had been talking with Bodie and Sarah rather than the sheriff, so Cole had steered clear. Sophie had looked longingly that way but must have sensed that Cole hadn't wanted to go over to the church booth, and for once, she hadn't forced the issue.

Hopefully, the trio hadn't spotted him and Sophie walking together.

Otherwise, Cole was in for some teasing when they got back to the firehall that night.

What was he thinking? Whether Andrew had seen him or not, it wasn't as if his friend wouldn't be able to make an educated guess as to where Cole had disappeared to—and who he had disappeared with. If nothing else, the Butterflies probably had a whole slew of informants watching their every move. He wouldn't put it past them. And yet, he couldn't make himself pull away from Sophie, no matter who was watching.

When she and Cole arrived back at the booth, Sophie stared at the empty table where stacks of brochures had been when they'd left.

Going around the table, she bent to pull out the box where extras were, and her mouth fell open as she lifted the empty box.

"Wow. They're all gone!"

"Well, of course they are all gone." Rosie waved off Sophie's surprise as if it were no big deal.

How had Rosie given away five hundred brochures that quickly?

"I wasn't expecting you two back so soon," Rosie admitted, her gaze going back and forth between Cole and Sophie. "I figured you'd be at least another thirty minutes or so."

"We looked around a little, but I'm fed and ready to take back over. Thank you for giving me a break, Rosie." She turned to Cole. "And thank you for feeding me."

Rosie's eyes lit up at Sophie's comment, and the woman's gloved hands clasped together.

"No problem." He paused a moment, looking uncertain, then tipped his head slightly. "Night, ladies."

"Night, Cole," she said, watching him walk away.

"That there is a fine man you've gotten yourself."

"Agreed that Cole is a fine man, but he's not mine."

"Then, child, you need to up your game and make him yours."

Spoken like a true Butterfly. Sophie laughed. "You're assuming I want him to be my man—and that I even want a man to begin with."

Rosie gasped. "Are you saying you don't?"

Sophie lowered her gaze. It landed on the empty display table. Rather than answer Rosie's question, she glanced up at the older woman and said, "I'm blown away that we ran out of pamphlets."

"I recruited a little help, but each one found a home," Rosie said proudly. "And there you go, clever girl, changing the subject again."

Recruited a little help?

Sophie eyed her friend suspiciously. "What kind of help?"

"Well, Sue Ellen Harvey came by and said she'd like some to put out at the farm, so I gave her a whole stack of them. She said she'd make sure they ended up in the right hands to get us more volunteers."

"Ahhhh," Sophie said, beginning to understand. "Well, I guess I can stick around to talk to anyone who drops by and has questions."

Rosie shook her head. "Child, you've done your good deed for the night. Go, find that young man whom you may or may not want to be yours, walk around and have some fun." Her eyes lit with excitement. "Maybe you could go for a ride in the Harveys' carriage. I'm sure I can arrange something special, especially after all the free publicity they've gotten out of Lou's proposal during our carriage ride last year."

Sophie shook her head. She seriously doubted she'd get Cole to agree to a romantic carriage ride. She'd seen how he reacted when they got near the church booth.

He hadn't wanted his friend to spot them.

She knew Ben and Andrew teased him—she'd heard them when they'd rescued her from the tree—but she hadn't thought he cared. Maybe it bothered him more than she'd realized.

"No, I'll stay here in case more come by. I wouldn't want to miss anyone who wants to know more. Plus, Cole's on duty, so I doubt he'd be able to go on a carriage ride even if I could convince him." She was pretty sure she'd have to set herself on fire while in the carriage to get Cole anywhere near it and her at the same time. "Thanks anyway."

"Speaking of Lou, was that Alberta Jennings still slurping down the chili when you were getting your snack?" Rosie attempted to look nonchalant, but her tone dripped with icicles.

"I didn't actually see her, but Lou did mention her a time or two while I was there," Sophie answered honestly.

Rosie's lower lip dropped. "Why that...what did he have to say about that woman?"

Sophie pretended like she didn't want to say.

"Tell me," Rosie insisted. "If that woman is starting to get to my man, I need to know."

"Well, he said he gave her dessert—a pie, I think?" Sophie pretended to wince, as if it pained her to have to tell Rosie. "Because she's so sweet."

"What?" Rosie huffed, then did a little indignant shimmy and lifted her chin. "We'll just see about him giving dessert to that woman when we both know she's hanging around just hoping..."

"Just hoping what, Rosie?" Sophie prompted, hoping to force Rosie's acknowledgement.

"That Lou will get tired of waiting on me." Rosie's

expression shifted from indignation to concern. "Sorry to run, but I've got to go talk to my fiancé about what qualifies as 'sweet.' He should certainly know that it isn't Alberta Jennings!"

Sophie bit back a giggle as she watched Rosie stomp off.

Sophie hung out for another hour at the booth, talking to a few more folks who wandered by, sharing her enthusiasm, the photos of past recipients, and giving out business cards. As the crowd thinned, Sophie decided to pack up her precious quilts.

One by one, she took the cherished material down, starting with the ones she'd attached to the sides of the tent. She folded them and placed them on the table in a neat stack.

When she'd folded the last one, she realized she had a problem.

She couldn't carry them all to the shop by herself. Isabelle had helped her set up the tent, but she wasn't around now. Sophie would need help to get the quilts safely back to the shop in one trip, since there were too many for her to carry.

She picked up her phone to see if Sarah and Bodie had anyone extra they could send over to give her a hand.

"Need help?"

At Cole's question, she spun toward him. "Cole?"

"Andrew and I were headed back to the truck when I spotted you packing up. You were staring at the stack of quilts as if you weren't quite sure what to do with them."

Sophie blinked. "You specifically came to help me?"

"Do you need help, Sophie?" he repeated.

Feeling bubbly inside that he was there, Sophie nodded. "Looks like you're making a habit of rescuing me, Cole Aaron."

"That's why they call us Fire and Rescue."

"Good point." She laughed. "And, yes, I absolutely could use some help with these. Thank you."

Cole picked up a stack of quilts. The softness of the material surprised him. He wasn't sure what he'd expected of the red, white, and blue material, but for some reason he'd thought it would be coarser, stiffer.

Sophie gathered up a stack of photos and a banner that had previously been taped to the display table and put them inside a storage bin. "I'm so glad you spotted me. I was just about to call for backup because I didn't want to leave any of the quilts behind."

"It's not a big deal. Andrew needed to make a detour before we headed back to the station. I was just killing time while I waited."

"Well, your timing was perfect."

Once Cole was laden with quilts and Sophie was pulling a wagon loaded down with her wares, they crossed the blockaded street, pausing outside the shop. Her key chain jingling, she unlocked the deadbolt, sighing with pleasure as she opened the door and was met by the smell of pine needles and cinnamon.

Mmmm, she loved the smells of Christmas.

"Give me just a minute to turn off the alarm," she said as she took off toward the back of the store.

She shut down the alarm and dumped her bag she held onto the cash register counter.

When she turned back, Cole was close—so close she almost bumped into him.

"Sorry!"

"I thought you'd want the quilts back here."

"Um, yeah." She gulped as she realized they were alone. She wasn't frightened by him in the slightest, but she still felt a little on edge to be alone with Cole. It had her heart pounding overtime. "Do you mind helping while I put them back on display?"

He followed her to where she had patriotic material for sale.

Sophie partially unfolded one of the quilts and draped it over a rack, rearranging it until the stars were perfectly aligned.

He studied the detailed pattern on the quilt as she tweaked the positioning.

"Did you make these?"

Pride filling her at his question, she nodded. "Yes, I did."

She took another quilt from him, then quickly had it back in its place, too. She changed the quilts out as she made new ones, but always tried to have several samples made up prior to their being awarded. She liked to keep at least a couple around the shop as examples she could show their customers.

"You're very talented."

Her heart warmed at his compliment. "Thank you. Do you sew?"

His taken-aback expression had her laughing. "Men do sew, you know," she pointed out.

He looked skeptical. "None I've ever known."

"We have male volunteers when we do sew-ins."

"Sew-ins?"

"Days where volunteers get together to sew. We make as many quilts as we can in an allotted time frame. Sometimes we go for twelve hours, sometimes twenty-four hours, sometimes a weekend. We try to schedule a couple every year." She took a third quilt from him and refolded it to where it showed a particular bit of the pattern. "It's a lot of fun, and we always end up with several completed quilts."

"And men attend?"

"We had a few in attendance this past summer." She put the next folded quilt on a shelf, making sure a full block could be seen. "Mostly husbands of some of our volunteers, but we'd like to get more men involved. Hint, hint."

Cole shook his head. "Not interested."

"Give me time." She waggled her brows at him. "I'll change your mind."

"Not on this."

"But on something else?"

His lips twitched. "I just meant that I won't ever be sewing or attending a sew-in."

"Never say never." Sophie got each quilt situated as she wanted, then turned to him. "Give me a minute, please."

She took off for the small bathroom in the back, checked her hair in the mirror, pleased to see the pink that being outdoors for so long had added to her cheeks. Or was it being with Cole that had given her face color? She looked happy, excited to be alive.

She was. Because of the man waiting on her.

She hurried back out of the bathroom, planning to set the alarm, but she caught sight of Cole via the lit security camera monitor screen as she passed Isabelle's open office door.

He stood next to the patriotic materials and had the corner of one of the quilts in his hand, examining the stitching.

Not casually, but really looking, a plethora of emotions on his handsome face.

Sophie's heart squeezed as he ran his fingertip over the pattern, tracing out the intricate details. A faraway look settled into his eyes as he let the material fall through his fingers.

Then, as if unable to resist, he picked the corner back up and held it tightly in his hand, as if he didn't want to let go of the red, white, and blue material.

Oh, Cole, she thought. *If ever someone needed to be wrapped in one of my quilts, it's you.*

If only he'd let her give him one. She thought of the quilt she'd been working on at home, of the time and effort she put into every stitch, of how much she'd love to wrap it around him and welcome him home.

Because he did need a quilt, even if he didn't think so.

Just as she suspected he needed her. Even if he didn't think so on that, either.

As his friend, she added, before she let any other connotation attach itself to her thought.

Cole needed her as his friend.

CHAPTER FOURTEEN

EAR THE SHOP'S CLOSING TIME, Sophie and Isabelle set up tables for the Make Your Own Stocking class. Each attendee had the option of using one of their display sewing machines or bringing their machine from home. They'd had to turn away a few interested participants due to lack of space and Sophie wanting to make sure they weren't too crowded for her to be able to give individualized attention as needed.

Once everyone had arrived and was situated, Sophie went to the front of the open area.

"Welcome, everyone," she told the friendly faces sitting at the tables. Rosie, Maybelle, Aunt Claudia, Ruby, and Mrs. Harvey were among them. Yeah, those ladies did not need her help sewing, but she still wanted to make sure her class was a lot of fun for them.

She gestured over to their table. "Part of me feels I should go sit down and let one of you teach, as each and every one of you have more sewing experience than I do," she admitted as she prepared to start the class.

"That doesn't mean we're too old to learn a new trick," Ruby said, smiling at Sophie.

"She's talking about you," Rosie stage-whispered to Maybelle.

Maybelle pursed her lips. "That's odd. I could have sworn she meant *you* when she said 'too old'."

"Who are you calling old?" Rosie complained as she fluffed her blue locks. "Just because I'm an experienced seamstress doesn't mean I'm a day past forty."

"Forty? Well, at least you got the experienced part, right," Maybelle said drily, then checked her perfectly manicured fingernails.

"Good grief, she's so old, she's suffering memory loss," Ruby said at the same time, elbowing Sophie's aunt.

"Lost a good fifty years," Aunt Claudia agreed, shaking her head in a sad gesture.

"Fifty years?" Rosie shrieked, completely ignoring Maybelle. "You take that back, Claudia."

"Think of it this way," Maybelle continued, giving a prim smile. "You look great for ninety, which is more than you can say if you were claiming to be a single day younger."

"At least you admit I look great," Rosie huffed resituating herself in her chair. "We all know you three are just jealous of my youth and beauty."

The three Butterflies snorted.

"Ladies," Sophie said, trying to get their focus back on her and not each other. "There are eighteen of us here tonight. I'm going to review the steps we'll take making the stocking, then we'll divide up into pairs."

"Just so long as I'm not paired with *certain individu-*

als, that's fine," Rosie stage-whispered to Mrs. Harvey, gesturing toward Maybelle.

Maybelle didn't look concerned, just smiled in that stately way she had that said she knew more than everyone else in the room. She usually did, too. Maybelle made things happen. Sometimes in plain sight, but oftentimes behind the scenes, so carefully and strategically that a person didn't even realize what she was up to until she'd already maneuvered them toward the direction she'd decided they should have been going to begin with. Her uncle and Aunt Claudia traveling was just one exmaple.

"To make everything go quicker, I've precut fabric into the pattern. There are plenty of extras, so hopefully everyone will find one they like, but for those who don't, see me and I'll demonstrate how to use the cutting machine to cut your stocking shapes in any fabric you choose. I also made a handout for each of you to take home with you that has a pattern you can use for future stockings."

Sophie smiled at the group, glad they were mostly familiar faces that seemed engaged.

"Once we've all selected our material, we'll get started at our machines. If anyone wants names embroidered, or the like, on your stocking, see me after you've selected your material so we can get that done prior to sewing your stocking together."

Sophie took two precut pieces of fabric of varying colors and sewed them together inside out, flipped them right side out via the small area she'd left unstitched near the toe of the stocking. She then did the same for a second piece. When done, she ironed both pieces, pinned them together inside out, then sat down at a machine and stitched them together, while explaining what she was doing to the women. When done, she turned it right side out and folded the top down, revealing a wide swath of the second colored fabric.

"Voila. You have your stocking." She continued to push against the seams to remove any puckers as she showed the women what she was doing. "But let's be real. As beautiful as this is, it's not overly exciting. So, as I mentioned earlier, we could have embroidered a name or a saying across the top prior to attaching the two pieces." She picked up an example that she'd made earlier. "Or we can add rick-rack or a fuzzy trim." She picked up further premade samples. "Or you can get creative and come up with your own way of making your stocking fun and unique."

The next hour passed quickly as the women picked their material, embroidered, sewed, and decorated their stockings.

Maybelle's forehead scrunched as she stared at Rosie's stocking. "Did you seriously make a stocking that says, 'Fourth of July'?"

"What about it?" Rosie flung back.

"Other than that you put a summer holiday on your Christmas stocking?" Maybelle snorted, then cut her eyes to the woman on the other side of her who was happily sewing and had been ignoring her friends' bickering with the ease of long experience. "Ruby, call Doc Evans tomorrow. We need to get our girl in for a checkup. She's off her meds again."

Rosie smiled, pretty as you please. "You're the one who's off her meds. I know exactly what I embroidered, and it was intentional."

"You purposely put America's Independence Day on your Christmas stocking?" Maybelle arched a brow.

"It may be America's Independence Day, but it's my anti-Independence Day. Lou's, too." She gave a little laugh and flip of her blue hair. "Not that the lucky devil knows yet, but he will after I give him this."

"Rosie!" Sophie exclaimed, realizing what her friend was implying.

Understanding dawned in Maybelle's eyes. "It's about time you put that man out of his misery."

"That's great," Ruby said. "Being married to the right man is such a blessing, and Lou's a good one. Not as good as my Charles, mind you, but Lou's a keeper."

"I'll send you my travel agent's name and number," Aunt Claudia offered. "You'll want to start looking at honeymoon spots immediately. I can make a list of travel do's and dont's that George and I have picked up over the past year."

The women continued back and forth. Sophie half-listened, fighting a smile every so often as she helped one of the other ladies attach gold trim to her stocking.

"By the way, Sophie," Maybelle said, snagging her attention, "Triple B Ranch For Kids called. We've added thirty more kids to our list."

Sophie's gaze cut to Maybelle's. "Thirty more kids? At this late date?"

They were already worried about having enough toys and contributions to buy the usual necessities they gave. Adding thirty more kids...*Oh, wow.*

"Why not?" the older woman asked, clearly not seeing it as a problem. "The ranch asked for help providing their kids with a good Christmas experience. We've never turned away anyone asking for help. Why would we start with thirty foster children?"

Rosie, obviously thinking the same thing Sophie was, opened her mouth, then clamped it closed. She and Sophie locked gazes, then both gave little shrugs at the same time.

Maybelle knew about the decreased donations last year. But maybe she knew something they didn't know and had a reason for not sharing their concerns on having enough gifts for the kids.

Regardless, thirty more kids needed a Christmas morning.

They'd make it work. Somehow.

"Hi," Sophie said a bit breathily as she climbed into Cole's Jeep. "Sorry I'm running late. We had several customers, and one needed multiple pieces of material cut. I took care of her order as I didn't want to leave Isabelle and Thelma in a bind."

"Not a problem."

She snuck a look at where he sat in the driver's seat. He wore a white pullover that loosely hugged his broad shoulders, arms, and chest. She wanted to touch the material, find out for herself if it was as soft as it appeared. The urge was so strong that she slid her hands beneath her legs. Maybe being tucked between her outer thighs and the leather truck seat would help her remember to keep her hands to herself.

He had to sense her watching him, but he didn't say anything.

"Thanks for doing this with me today," she told him

while buckling her seatbelt then sticking her hands back beneath her legs for safekeeping.

He started the engine. "Just because I've dropped my Santa suit off at the cleaners, you thought I'd say no to helping out when there's a possibility we won't have enough toys?"

"No, that's not what I meant." She stole another glance at him, realized he was half-grinning. "You're teasing me."

His brow lifted. "You think?"

The stress from her busy morning melted away into a giddy fluffiness. Cole was teasing her. She liked his teasing. It made her happy and the smile on her face let him know.

What didn't make her happy was how worried she was about making sure they had enough donations for the toy drive.

Which was why she'd called her toy drive partner and asked for his help.

"Okay, Mr. Santa Smarty Pants," she was smiling, "we'll go around to the businesses that have collection boxes and pick up what's been donated thus far. We still have almost two weeks before collection ends, but at least we'll have an idea of what's come in so far."

Keeping his eyes on the road, he nodded. "Have you ever not had enough toys in the past?"

"No, but Maybelle just agreed to add thirty more kids to the list. The total number now is higher than it's ever been before."

Of course, Sophie agreed with Maybelle's decision, and would've done the same thing. No way could they have said no to helping with those kids' Christmas.

"Donations were down last year. We had enough,

but barely," Sophie admitted. "Plus, several of the On-the-Square Christmas Festival vendors reported that their sales this year were down from past years. That's the first time I recall that ever happening, so yes, I'm a little worried."

"Not sure what the ones in the past were like, but it looked busy."

"The parade and the tree lighting were hits, as was the whole evening, really," Sophie agreed. "I don't think the number of attendees was down, just that people weren't spending as much money as in past years."

Cole shrugged. "Maybe they already had all the Christmas stuff they needed."

"Bite your tongue. A person can never have enough Christmas stuff."

Cole half grinned. "If you say so, Santa Sophie."

Sophie practically floated off the SUV's passenger seat. What was it about the man that a simple smile from him lightened her insides so completely?

And what could she do to return the favor? She wanted Cole to be happy. She wanted...

"Ha. I'm not the one who wore that red suit during the parade," she reminded. "Do you have a tree, Cole?"

Not glancing her way, he shook his head. "Do you?"

"Of course." Sophie studied his profile. He looked relaxed and ready to take on whatever she threw at him. "Will you put up a tree?"

"Nope." He focused on the road as they made their way through town.

"Why not?"

"Why would I?"

"You deserve a Christmas tree, too, Cole."

He laughed. "Why's that?"

"Because everyone deserves to enjoy the miracle of Christmas."

"Not that I buy the idea that a tree is any guarantee that I'll be able to enjoy the miracle of Christmas, but it's just another day in my world."

Sophie gasped, covering her mouth with her hand and shaking her head. "Say it ain't so."

Cole laughed at her exaggerated reaction. "When I'm home, I'd rather focus my energy on things other than putting up and decorating a tree just for me. It would be a waste of my time."

Sophie couldn't hide her disappointment. His "just for me" echoed through her heart. Didn't he think he deserved to experience the magic of the holidays?

"Giving yourself the gift of Christmas is never a waste of time. Life is about celebrating every moment, but especially times of goodwill toward mankind."

"That's what Christmas is?"

"It's what it should be."

He glanced her way. "You seriously think I should have a tree for no one other than myself to see, knowing it'll just be a bunch of work putting it up and then having to take it down again when I care nothing about having it up in the first place?"

He obviously didn't think he should, but Sophie nodded anyway.

"I'm positive you should."

Christmas filled a part of one's soul in a way that no other time of year did. He just had to embrace the magic to feel its powers spreading joy throughout his being. Cole needed Christmas.

Which made Sophie wonder where his past Christmases as an adult had been spent. Had he been alone?

Stationed somewhere on a military base? Or on one of his assignments off base?

"If it makes you feel any better, I'll be working on Christmas Day."

"Actually, it does make me feel better." Because she wouldn't be worried about him sitting at home treeless. Everyone should have a Christmas tree. At least they had one up at the firehall. "Wait, you had to work on Thanksgiving Day and on Christmas day, too? I thought the firehall rotated who was on shift for the holidays?"

She knew this from Ben's involvement in church activities over the years. If he worked one holiday, he was always off the other.

"They usually do, but several of us single guys volunteered to swap so those with families can be home with their wives and kids on both Thanksgiving and Christmas day. It's not a big deal."

Sophie's heart swelled at his admission.

"It's a big deal to the firemen who get to be home with their families, and for the kids whose parents are there when they wake up."

Her dad had always managed to hold it together on the Christmases he was home, which was likely one of the reasons Sophie liked the holiday so much. Or maybe it was just that it was such a great time of year when everyone seemed to go out of their way to be kinder.

And the decorations. She liked the decorations, too. Especially the lights. The more lights, the better.

"That's a nice thing to do," she pointed out. A lot of the things Cole did were nice. Although she suspected "nice" wasn't an adjective he'd use to describe himself. Having read his journal, she knew the thoughts he associated with himself. They weren't pretty.

The more time she spent with him the more she believed the things he'd written weren't really a true reflection of him. Obviously, they had been once upon a time, but the anger and anguish she'd read on those tragic pages weren't what she saw when she looked at Cole. Weren't what she imagined him feeling.

Obviously, he had. *But not ever again*, her heart whispered. Not ever did she want Cole to return to that grim place he'd once dwelled within.

Nor would she let him. She'd surround him with goodness and light so bright, his thoughts would never step in the shadows again.

Which gave her an idea.

"You should come to church with me on Sunday."

Cole pulled into Lou's Diner's paved lot and put the engine into park. "What?"

"On Sunday. Come to church with me." It was a brilliant idea, one she should have thought of sooner. She clasped her hands together in excitement as she flashed her biggest smile. "Afterwards, several of us are going to the assisted living home to decorate trees for the residents. If you don't want to decorate a tree for just you, then help decorate a tree for someone who isn't able to decorate their own tree but wants one all the same."

"I..."

"Are you working at the station?" She already knew he wasn't. Not unless he'd swapped schedules with someone again.

"I'm not, but—"

"But you're not into helping the elderly who aren't physically able and need help making one of their last Christmases special?"

229

His gaze narrowed as he regarded her. "You don't pull your punches, do you?"

"Not if it means I get to spend the afternoon decorating Christmas trees with you while helping others." Sophie fought smiling. "I mean, come on, that's a win-win."

Perhaps she shouldn't have admitted the part about wanting to spend time with him.

Only, she *did* want to spend time with him. And what better way than while decorating for the elderly? Plus, she suspected the white knight in him wouldn't be able to say no. Cole liked to help others. That came through in everything he did, despite anything he might say or think otherwise.

"I'm not much on church."

"Have you actually been to church?" Sophie wasn't backing down, not when she believed he needed what she was offering him. Friendship, peace, a sense of community and belonging.

"Not in years."

"That's your problem. But even if you had, you've never been to church with me," she reminded as if that was something great and wonderful. Maybe if she acted as if it was, he'd buy it. Probably not, but she pressed on. "Sitting next to me in church brings the experience up to another whole level. You shouldn't miss it."

"You have me curious," he admitted, eyeing her. "But I'm not sure. Church really isn't my thing."

"You'll at least think about it?"

He took a deep breath, then nodded. "I'll think about it," he promised. "But don't hold your breath."

Sophie wouldn't. She knew it was a long shot, but that he was considering it made her smile.

Cole carried another box into the church community room and put it with the other donations that had been collected. "That's the last of them."

Sophie eyed the various toys and games. When her gaze met Cole's, she looked concerned. "At first glance, it looks like a lot, but we're going to need way more with taking on the Triple B Ranch for Kids."

Cole's chest tightened at the worry in her voice. "There will be more toys donated between now and the end of the drive. We'll get the word out about the increased need—maybe it'll make people want to give a little more. We've still got time."

"I hope Maybelle doesn't come by here before then, because there are a lot of kids on our list needing presents." Her gaze skimmed the toys. "There's definitely not enough to do as much as we usually do."

Seeing the anxiety etched on her face knotted his stomach. Sophie was twinkling Christmas lights and happiness, not frowns and worrying. He didn't like it. Nor did he like the realization of the lengths he'd go to put the sparkle back into her eyes.

"What about the cash donations?" They'd collected a few checks on the first day they'd gone around to businesses and had gotten a few more today. "Will those be used to buy more toys to help fill the gaps?"

Sophie shook her head. "At least, we never have bought toys with the money donations in the past. We use the cash to purchase clothes for each kid. A shirt, pair of jeans, socks, underwear, and a pair of shoes. Plus, it's used to buy the wrapping paper, ribbons, etc.

that we wrap each kids' gifts in. The toys have always been donated directly and the other things purchased specifically for each child on our list."

"It'll all work out."

With one last glance at the stack of donated items, Sophie nodded. "You're right. No Pine Hill kid is going to go without a magical Christmas morning."

Cole suspected that Sophie would personally ensure each kid had plenty of gifts even if it meant emptying her savings account.

Cole suspected he'd give up quite a bit to ensure Sophie didn't have to.

Although worry still shined in her eyes, she smiled at him. "Thanks for going with me today. We'll keep our fingers crossed that everyone ups their donations this year and that on our last collection, the bins are so overflowing with goodies that we can't carry them all. I'd say *our* bins, but hopefully, all the bins will be full. I don't even care if it means losing your challenge with Andrew and Ben."

Cole hoped that, too. And not just for the kids to get a merry Christmas. But because he knew full bins meant a merry Sophie.

He'd figure something out. Maybe he could talk to the guys at the firehall and see if they could come up with a little extra. Sure, they'd rag him, but seeing the joy that would light in Sophie's eyes and knowing every kid had a special gift would make it worth their teasing.

The realization of how much fulfilling this goal of Sophie's mattered to him, and how much he'd be willing to do to see it happen, made him feel a little as if he were walking into a burning building without his gear.

Would her belly please quit doing acrobatics? Sophie placed her hand over her stomach for the dozenth time that Sunday morning in hopes it would calm the nervous gurgling.

Although she rotated out on teaching a children's Sunday school class, she was currently on an off cycle, so she sat with her mother and Isabelle in a ladies' class after arriving early at church.

When class finished, they headed to the auditorium for the main service. Sophie spoke to most everyone she passed as she, Isabelle, and their mother made their way to a pew near the front where they typically sat. Her mother and Isabelle would be fine regardless of where they sat, but Sophie found that if she sat near the back, she got distracted too easily with people watching, baby watching, and mind wandering. People were so interesting, and their church had the cutest kids ever.

Her family knew that as long as she was up front, Pastor Smith would hold her attention. Usually.

Today, that might be difficult for the pastor to do.

Would Cole show?

Of course, by the time Pastor Smith started his lesson, Sophie would know whether or not he'd come, so maybe she could focus. Until then, though, she was a bundle of nerves.

She told herself not to get her hopes up. Cole had never said he would attend.

He never said he wouldn't, either, she countered, determined she was going to think positively. Wasn't that why she'd taken extra time in choosing what she was going to wear today? She'd ended up in a comfy red dress decorated with a cute penguin with a Christmas scarf around its neck, paired with black tights and boots, and a pair of dangly Christmas wreath earrings that would be great for decorating later.

"What's up with looking behind you?" Isabelle turned to try to see what Sophie was looking at. "Expecting someone?"

Sophie's face heated. She needed to stop checking. If he arrived, he'd find her. Any of the ushers could direct him toward where she and her family always sat.

"Isn't that just the sweetest?" she asked, ignoring her sister's question as she gestured toward the front of the church.

"Holy, holy, holy," one of the church's little cuties sang from where he stood near the front podium, singing and waving his hand along with his song.

Despite being on edge with wondering if Cole would show, Sophie smiled. She adored watching the toddler's love of singing.

"Precious," Isabelle agreed, smiling, too.

Once her sister was occupied with watching the child, Sophie's mind went back to Cole. Maybe he would visit. She hoped so. If not, she'd invite him again. She'd text him another invite that afternoon, let him know she'd missed seeing him.

"Sophie?"

Knowing she was antsy and had almost turned to look over her shoulder again, Sophie nodded at her sister and told herself to settle down. "Sorry. Just thinking about what I'm planning to do this afternoon."

Isabelle seemed to accept her answer, then turned to

listen to something their mother was saying. *Thank you, Mom.*

Sophie's thoughts went right back to Cole.

As she often did, she'd thought about him a lot the night before while she'd been working on her quilt and talking to the cat watching her from her window ledge. Stitches hadn't offered up any ideas on how she could make Cole's Christmas better when he truly didn't seem to see the holiday as anything more than another work-day. Still, she'd appreciated what a good listener he'd been. Lately, the cat had been keeping her company nightly, even if from the other side of a glass barrier. She only wished that Cole was as constant of a presence in her life.

The more she got to know Cole, the more she wanted to make every day better in his world—and to include him in her world.

When it was time for services to start, Sophie let out the breath she'd been holding.

Cole wasn't coming.

Had she really thought he would? That he'd walk into church and sit beside her and listen to Sarah's dad talk about the most amazing and loving God who was the reason why Sophie believed in ultimate goodness?

Part of her had believed he would.

Because she felt this crazy connection to Cole, and whether he wanted to admit it or not, she was certain that he felt it too. The way he'd looked at her when she'd invited him...

It was likely the journal that made her feel so close to him: the fact that she'd read it and gotten that inner look at such raw emotions combined with her knowledge that her father had suffered a similar torment.

Whatever, she just knew the connection between them existed and that it seemed as fragile as a butterfly's wing and yet as powerful as a raging river.

It was both.

The only positive to his not showing up was that she didn't have to explain her invitation to Isabelle, who'd been suspicious all morning, commenting on Sophie taking much longer in the bathroom than she typically did while getting ready.

It was no wonder her sister thought something was up since Sophie had spent ages doing her hair and make-up.

Too bad her efforts to dress up had been wasted. Because she'd wanted to dress up for Cole and see that spark of male appreciation flare in his pale blue eyes.

Sophie bit into her lower lip and reminded herself that she only wanted to be friends with Cole.

Except she was in church so she really shouldn't lie to herself that way.

What was Cole doing at church?

He certainly didn't belong inside these hallowed walls. Not because he didn't believe in a higher being, but just because the things he'd done had permanently tainted him inside. Some things were unforgiveable.

He was unworthy to have stepped foot inside the doors.

And yet, here he was. Cole wasn't a man who felt fear often and gave in to it even less, but Sophie sure had a way of pushing him outside his comfort zone. Not that he was necessarily afraid of being at church;

it was more the woman who had motivated his donning his only pair of dress slacks and a white button-down that made him nervous. He'd topped his best attempt at "church clothes" with a black dress coat that had belonged to his uncle and somehow made him feel less vulnerable in his unaccustomed attire.

Or at least, it *had* until he'd actually walked inside the building.

He shouldn't be here.

"Welcome," a thin, mostly bald man who had to be knocking ninety said, holding out his frail hand to Cole. Smiling, he introduced himself, then leaned in close so he could hear Cole's name. "We're glad you're here, son. Go find yourself a seat. It's just about time for services to start."

Cole entered the auditorium, hesitated in the back as he scanned the room. A young boy, probably close to two, swayed in rhythm to his song at the podium in front. He held a song book and enthusiastically sang until his mother scooped him up, kissed his forehead, and carried him to a seat a few rows back.

Cole's gaze lingered as he watched her hand over her still-singing boy, still clutching his song book, to a man whom Cole assumed was the boy's father.

Something inside Cole shifted as he watched the young family.

Something that felt a lot like longing.

That couldn't be right, though. He'd never wanted that. Not really.

Only, he couldn't lie to himself, not inside a church, and say that he didn't feel envy at the wholesome goodness and love he sensed surrounding the three.

Then again, those emotions overwhelming him might

have less to do with the young family—and a whole lot to do with the woman sitting in the pew in front of them.

Sophie. Sweet, full-of-Christmas-sparkle Sophie.

Of course, she would sit in the front of the church. In order to join her, he'd have to walk all the way down the aisle. Everyone would see him sit beside her. Ben would see. There would be no slinking into the back row and hoping no one noticed he was there, that no one realized he didn't belong.

Not that he thought anyone would ask him to leave. But wasn't he scuffing up something clean and perfect just by being here?

Eyeing the aisle that would take him to where Sophie sat, Cole swallowed. Logically, he knew the distance wasn't more than forty or so feet, yet it felt miles away. Miles and miles that were laden with obstacles all along the way.

Obstacles? Or emotional traps? Cole gulped back the bile rising in his throat.

He should leave.

He turned, planning to do just that, but when his eyes collided with the older greeter's, he froze.

"There's several open seats to choose from, son. You're welcome to sit anywhere you like."

Cole's temples throbbed as he nodded awkwardly, berating himself for being a coward. Because why else would he have tucked tail and planned to run?

He was there to attend church, then help decorate Christmas trees for the elderly at a nursing home of some sort. No big deal. He volunteered all the time via the firehall. This was similar.

Just in the house of God.

Maybe lightning wouldn't strike him for daring to step inside the sanctuary.

Then again, if it did, that would save him from having to go forward, from being embarrassed that he was there at Sophie's bidding. Not to mention, the shame that he felt so unworthy.

To be in church. To sit beside someone as good as Sophie.

Sucking in a deep breath, Cole reminded himself that she had invited him, that she wanted him there, that when she looked at him, she saw someone worth inviting, someone she deemed worthy of spending time with, someone she frequently smiled at with so much warmth shining in her pretty hazel eyes.

Her light called to him, warmed him, calmed his need to turn and leave. Just the thought of her smile gave him enough strength to forge forward.

Like a ship lost at sea, he kept his gaze trained on the back of her head. Using her inner light as a beacon to guide him, he made his way to her pew without looking around to any of the other parishioners. He didn't want to know who was there or wasn't there.

It didn't matter. Sophie was right in front of him. Sophie was who mattered.

Admitting that was scarier than being inside a church.

When he stood beside her pew, she looked up. Upon seeing him, her entire face transformed with delight.

"Cole," she whispered, scooting closer to her sister to make room for him to sit down beside her.

Relief filled him.

It hadn't been any altruistic motivations of helping others that had brought him to the church. Sure, he wanted to help others. Always had. But he was there because Sophie had asked him, because she wanted him there.

Because whether he should or shouldn't, he liked how her face had just lit up brighter than any Christmas tree they'd decorate later that day when she'd seen him.

She'd said he needed a Christmas tree. Did she have any idea she was his Christmas tree? That it was her that had already made this holiday season brighter and sweeter than any he could recall since early childhood?

He liked that seeing him was what triggered the pleasure shining on her pretty face and made her look as if she was going to bubble over with happiness.

He liked it much more than he should, as a man who'd sworn to never be in a serious relationship due to what lurked inside him.

Only, where Sophie was concerned, "should" didn't seem to be enough to keep him away.

CHAPTER FIFTEEN

"**Y**OU'RE HERE," SOPHIE WHISPERED AS Cole sat down next to her on the church pew. Pure joy filled her. "I wasn't sure you'd make it."

"You asked me to be here," he reminded, his gaze locked with hers. She could see the mix of uncertainty, embarrassment, and something more in his eyes.

"I can't leave those assisted living residents Christmas treeless," he continued. "You'd never let me live that down."

"There is that, Santa Cole." She grinned, automatically reaching to take his hand and giving it a squeeze. "I'm so glad you're here."

Warmth filled her at the strength in his callused fingers and rather than let go, her gaze dropped to where she held his hand.

It was one of the few times she'd intentionally touched him. She liked touching his hand.

She also didn't want to let go. Because holding Cole's hand left her a bit in awe, as if she were holding a precious gift and should cling to it for as long as he'd let her.

Her gaze lifted to his, perhaps asking silent permission, perhaps wondering if he felt that warmth coursing between them, too. Sophie wasn't sure, so she waited for his response, for something letting her know that he was okay with holding her hand.

He gave a little squeeze back, even half-smiled, and Sophie's heart leapt. *Yes.* She'd invited Cole to church, and he'd come. He hadn't wanted to, but he still had. Because of her. He was next to her, holding her hand, and they were about to begin worship services.

Giddiness threatened to have her floating off the pew.

Today was an excellent day the Lord had made.

Then, Cole's gaze went beyond her to Isabelle and her mother, and his partial smile faded. He pulled his hand away to reach for a hymnal.

"I'm not much of a singer. Hope it's okay if I just listen."

"That's fine," she assured, looking him in the eyes as she said it because she wanted him to know she truly meant it. It was more than fine.

She glanced in the direction of her mother and sister, wondering what it was about them that had Cole pulling away. As expected, they were watching them. Her mother had a smile on her face. Isabelle's expression, however, was fretful.

Oh, Isabelle. Not all military men are Dad. With Cole, Sophie was going to trust her instinct rather than give in to her big sister's worries.

Cole needed her friendship. She needed his.

Based on those wonderful brief seconds that their

hands had been laced, she'd guess that her emotions were tangled up with the firefighter in ways that went way beyond just friendship.

Guessed? Ha. She was so entrenched in her emotions for Cole Aaron that not even the child's sweet little voice singing from behind her was enough to distract her from the man sitting next to her, holding his song book, and staring down at the words in such a way that Sophie wanted to wrap her arms around him and hug away every bad thing that had ever happened to him.

Sophie and Cole finished putting together a large artificial blue spruce in the assisted living center's dining hall. Sophie stepped back to inspect their work.

"Hmm, that branch needs to be fluffed up a little."

Eyeing the tree to figure out which branch she referred to, Cole then reshaped the branch while Sophie pulled decorations from a box. She plugged in a string of colorful lights to make sure they all lit up. Each light twinkled with a burst of color that filled Cole with a bit of nostalgia.

"Yay. They all work."

His lips twitched at her happy little dance moves.

"Laugh if you want to, but the lights are my favorite part," she asserted as she handed one end of the strand to him.

"Why's that?" he asked, surprised by the feelings swamping him.

He acted as if Christmas had never been a big deal, but memories of Christmases with his parents pre-divorce, decorating their tree, flashed through his head for the first time in years. Maybe the young family he'd seen that morning in the church had triggered thoughts of himself as the child he'd once been, a part of a loving family.

"Because it's the first layer of magic," Sophie informed as if he should have known the answer all along.

"First layer, huh?" He couldn't resist smiling at how she swayed her arms out, stretching the lights out across her pretty red dress and down the long sleeve covering her arm. "How many layers of magic does a Christmas tree usually have?"

Not nearly as many magical layers as Sophie Grace Davis. She overflowed with goodness.

"Let's see," She pretended to be considering her answer very seriously as she twirled, slowly winding a bit of the light string around her waist and making him think yet again that she was his own personal Christmas tree. "There's the lights, then the ornaments, and then the most magical layer of all—the star."

"I see."

Eyes twinkling brighter than any star in the sky, she laughed and stretched out her arms, lights and all. "What do you see? That I look like a beautiful Christmas tree?"

Had Sophie read his mind? Sometimes, it felt as if she could. Perhaps because she'd read his journal and knew the inner ticking of his thoughts. Or perhaps it was something more he felt zinging between them.

Cole studied the vision she made with the lights wound loosely around her a few times. She was beautiful.

His heart sped up as he wondered whether the lights truly were magical. He couldn't deny that something was happening inside him at being near her, at looking at her, at getting wrapped up in Sophie's joy.

Magic. That was as good a word as any for what happened when he looked at her. She made him feel things he'd have thought impossible. That had to be magic.

"You think I'm being silly," she laughed as she twirled herself free of the strands twisted around her. "I know I'm a kid at heart when it comes to Christmas—and a lot of other times of the year, too, actually. But you have to admit, this is fun."

"You have a strange idea of what embodies fun," he countered, just for argument's sake. In truth, he knew she was right. He was enjoying her company and was glad that they were doing something good in the process of their "fun."

The assisted living crew had been excited when they'd arrived to decorate, and the looks of appreciation on the faces of the elderly residents they'd come in contact with thus far had made him feel ashamed he'd ever even considered not coming to help.

He glanced at the boxes he'd carried to the room. The contents were now spread out on a table. He and Sophie were the only ones here in the dining room, but there had been a large group that had come out to the facility. While this tree was going up here, others had been paired off to go to various resident rooms to decorate mini trees.

Which was fine by Cole, as he felt more comfortable being away from the group.

Although being alone with Sophie held an edge as well.

Truth was, he'd been on edge from the moment she'd held his hand at the beginning of the church service.

Those few seconds had rattled him, though not necessarily in a bad way. It was more that he was excited to be in this moment with her—excited enough that it had him feeling edgy.

Sophie had wanted to hold his hand. He'd wanted to hold her hand.

Which was possibly how he ended up brushing his hand against hers as he took the lights from her.

Her gaze jerked to his as if she'd felt the same zing as he had when their skin grazed. Her eyes sparkled more beautifully than any of the lights, giving off more magic than any tree that had existed in the history of Christmas trees.

Good grief. She was turning him sappy and he could barely even bring himself to mind.

Sophie's throat worked as she swallowed, then she looked away from him and back at the tree. "If we work together, this will go much faster."

"Are we in a hurry?"

She shook her head. "No, I...no...no rush, we just want to make this tree amazing for the residents, so that when they come to the dining hall tonight, they'll oooh and aaah and feel Christmas spirit fill their hearts."

"I'm sure it will be, and that they will."

She nodded then, turning toward the tree. She sounded a little breathy when she next spoke. "When decorating, it works best if we start at the top and work our way down with the lights. That okay?"

"Fine." He didn't have tree-decorating preferences. He didn't recall having ever decorated a tree at all before, though perhaps he had helped his mother at some point in the period between his parents' divorce and his mother's remarriage.

"I'll go up the step ladder to where I can reach the top and get the lights started. Will you move them around the tree for me, so I don't have to go up and down over and over again?"

She climbed several rungs up the step ladder, reached out and wove the lights in and out of the fake evergreen branches. When she indicated, Cole moved around the tree, trying not to feel nervous as she leaned in to reach far branches. But he was unable to squelch the uneasiness in his stomach.

"Be careful."

"Afraid you'll have to catch me if I fall?" she teased, shooting him a look that could only be labeled flirty.

Lord help him.

"More like I know how you are with trees," he countered, holding onto the ladder to help keep it steady. "I don't want to have to come up there to rescue you."

Sophie giggled. "No worries. You're safe. I doubt I'll go climbing on these little branches in search of Stitches."

Cole arched his brow. "You've officially made friends with your tree cat and given him a name?"

"He comes to visit me every night, but I don't fool myself that it's for reasons other than that I feed him," she admitted, sighing a bit dramatically. "He's never let me get more than a few feet away but now sits outside my bedroom window every night. Sometimes, he's still there when I wake in the mornings."

"That's better than his waiting on a tree branch for you to come save him," he teased.

Pausing in draping the lights to look his way, Sophie's eyes danced. "Ha, ha, you're so funny."

"Not that I ever saw him in the tree that night," he mused, "but I suppose I'll give you the benefit of doubt."

She laughed. "You think I was walking home that night and just thought to myself, 'Hmm, it's been a few years since I climbed a tree, I should try my luck with that one'?"

Had she said that was what had happened, it wouldn't have surprised him. Sophie had an impulsivity that had probably gotten her into a bind on more than one occasion.

"I'm a firefighter. That doesn't sound too farfetched to me. Have you heard about some of the rescues we've assisted with in this town?"

As they wound the lights around the tree, then began placing ornaments, Cole told Sophie a few stories of the more unusual rescues he and the guys had made. He'd never been much of a talker but recounting the tales to Sophie was easy.

"I know I shouldn't laugh," she admitted as he told her about a person they'd had to rescue who'd gotten stuck on Halloween when he'd tried to slip through a narrow row of metal fences so he could surprise his pregnant wife. "But the image of you and Andrew having to rescue a grown man wearing a diaper, bonnet, and booties strikes me as hilarious."

"Once we knew he was okay, we found it funny, too. Apparently, his wife had found out she was pregnant a few days before, and he hadn't taken the news so well, initially. He was trying to make it up to her with the costume and gifts he'd stashed in his goodie bag."

"Strange man."

"We thought so, too, but hey, by the time we got him out, his wife wasn't mad at him anymore, so I guess it worked out for him in the long run. What about you? Any funny tales at the quilt shop?"

"We have some interesting customers, but none who get stuck in iron fences."

"Just trees?"

"That would be our workers," Sophie corrected with a smile flashed his way.

While talking, they finished the lights and made a good dent in the ornaments on the table.

Sophie stepped back and surveyed their work. "Hmmm, we need more near the top."

"Plus, the star."

"The star is last, the icing on the cake, so to speak." She climbed back up the step ladder and rearranged an ornament that Cole had thought looked fine the way it was. "Hand me that box of ornaments, please."

She pointed to a plastic tray that held half a dozen big red balls adorned with gold flecks.

"This would work better if I was on the ladder and you just handed me what you wanted hung higher," he suggested, not liking that she was balanced precariously on the ladder again, leaning toward the tree.

She stretched to straighten an ornament. "How would that be better?"

"You know which ornaments you want put where and I don't. If I was up there, you could supervise me from down here."

"That's not a problem. You will know which ones to hand me because I'll be telling you. I have no problem ordering you around. Now, get me that box, Marine," she purposely made her voice deep and harsh. "Snap to it or I'll make you drop and give me twenty."

Snorting, Cole glanced at the array of ornaments still

on the table, then picked up the box she'd indicated. "Auditioning to be a drill sergeant?"

Eyes sparkling, she asked, "You think I'd cut it?"

He gave her a get real look. "Nope. Too soft. You'd go down as the nicest drill sergeant in history."

"Apparently, my tough voice wasn't nearly tough enough." Sounding a little self-conscious, she laughed. "But I'd be okay with being known as the nicest drill sergeant in history.".

Studying where she'd placed the ornament and rearranged it on the artificial tree, she decided she didn't like where it was hanging and removed it.

"I'd cover the whole world in niceness if I could," she continued when she finally got the ornament positioned just as she wanted it.

At least, Cole thought she had. Instead, she leaned back to get a better look.

"Be careful, Sophie."

Turning, probably to assure him she was fine, she lost her hold on the top of the stepladder, then lost her footing.

Grateful he'd always had quick reflexes, Cole caught hold of her waist and put her firmly on the ground in front of him. Just as her hand had lingered against his earlier, his did now at her waist.

She'd grasped his shoulders to stabilize herself. How could catching her steady him and make his knees wobble at the same time?

Her gaze locking with his, Sophie swallowed.

She had that look again. The one that conveyed things she shouldn't think, shouldn't feel. The one that clouded his good intentions.

"Sophie," he began, his hands leaving her waist to

cup her face as he stared down into her eyes. "My beautiful Sophie. What are we doing?"

The emotions swirling in her gaze branded his soul.

"I'm no good for you," he insisted.

She shook her head. "You're wrong."

"Sophie." They couldn't do this. Only, as Sophie stretched on her tiptoes, intending to touch her lips to his, he didn't move away or make any attempt to stop her.

Just held his breath in anticipation of her lips against his—

"How's it coming in here?"

At Isabelle's voice, Cole jumped back from Sophie.

Or had it been Sophie who'd leapt away?

Cole inwardly grimaced. What was he thinking? Of course she was embarrassed. He wasn't a "bring home to meet the family" kind of guy. He was a guy who was so messed up in the head that he still occasionally had nightmares that left the sheets sweat-drenched. No wonder her sister was giving him an evil eye.

He didn't say anything, just met Isabelle's unhappy gaze and braced himself for whatever condemnation she hurled at him. What could he say in his defense? Nothing. He didn't blame her for not being happy about what she'd walked in on.

Sophie had almost kissed him.

Would have kissed him had her sister not interrupted.

And him? He would have let Sophie kiss him.

Thank goodness Isabelle had chosen that moment to walk in.

Or maybe not. Because Cole couldn't help but wonder if Sophie's lips would have been as soft against his as he suspected. If her kiss would have been full of sugar and everything nice.

Spice? He suspected there would have been that, too. Sophie certainly spiced up his life.

But he hadn't even decided he and Sophie could be friends beyond the toy drive. He definitely shouldn't be kissing her.

It didn't matter that she'd been the one going to kiss him. He should have been strong enough to resist. Instead, he'd been powerless to step away.

Powerless to do more than stand there, knowing what she intended, and feeling the greatest, sweetest anticipation of his life.

When what he should have been doing was taking charge of the situation and putting a halt to what was happening for his sake and Sophie's.

Only...

"We're actually finishing up. We just have the star left," she continued, her voice a higher pitch than her normal tone. If Cole recognized that telltale sign, no doubt her sister did, too. "It'll be the perfect topper for this one."

When Isabelle didn't say anything, Sophie turned to look at her, but didn't back down beneath her sister's unhappy glare.

For that, Cole was grateful. He'd have hated to witness Sophie's regret. His own was more than enough.

She would regret what had happened, but not as much as she would have had her sister not interrupted. He needed to put some distance back between him and Sophie. For both their sakes.

"Everyone else is finished with their mini trees for the residents' rooms," Isabelle informed, her gaze going back and forth between them. She might not be say-ing anything condemning aloud, but her expression conveyed she knew exactly what had happened, and that she didn't approve. "We're all in the foyer, about to decorate the big tree there. We thought we'd do it as a group and take photos for the church website. I didn't want you to miss being in the pictures."

"We'll be there in a few," Sophie told her sister, then looked toward him. "Cole, if you'll get me the star, I'll put it on the tree."

Cole got the star, but rather than hand it to Sophie, he climbed the few steps up the ladder himself.

"Hey, I said I'd do it," she reminded.

"Humor me," he asked of her, needing to be doing something—and also knowing there was no way he was letting her back on that ladder. "I've always wanted to put a star on a Christmas tree."

Despite the tension of their almost-kiss and her sister's near tangible unhappiness from the other side of the room, Sophie laughed. "Yeah, right. Don't think I don't know exactly what you're doing."

"What's he doing?" Isabelle asked, coming to stand next to Sophie as they both watched Cole put the star on the tree.

"Keeping me off the ladder. He's afraid I'll almost fall again, and he'll have to catch me. Again. Over just a little to the left, Cole," Sophie informed, her attention tuned to what he was doing. "Oh, that's perfect! You're an expert tree topper, Cole Aaron. Don't you think so, Isabelle?"

Isabelle sighed, "I'm headed back to the foyer. If you want to be in the group photos, gather up your leftover decorations and come join us."

"She doesn't like me much."

Fighting frustration at her sister's untimely inter-ruption, Sophie shrugged at Cole's comment, wondering where to start in explaining Isabelle's attitude toward him.

Wondering also if she should comment on the almost-kiss, ask him what he'd been thinking, feeling.

She knew what she'd seen shining in those pale eyes.

Eyes she'd once thought of as an icy blue.

They weren't.

There had been nothing cold about the eyes she'd stared into as he'd caressed her face. They'd been blue fire scorching her insides and flaming her confidence to kiss him. Now, that confidence was gone and looking at him, she wasn't sure of anything except that his expres-sion was full of regrets.

Oh, Isabelle. Why did you have to interrupt at that precise moment?

"It's not you," she began, searching for words to make him understand what she'd never fully under-stood herself.

Cole snorted. "Maybe you missed it a few minutes ago, but it's definitely me she doesn't like."

"I should have said that it's about much more than you, personally." Sophie started over, glancing around the empty dining area. She felt torn, as if she was be-traying a secret, but she also felt obligated to attempt to make Cole understand. She didn't want him judging Isabelle unfairly or making assumptions about her behavior. "Isabelle respects military personnel, past and present. She's appreciative of all of you, but she doesn't trust letting any of you get close—to her and most especially to me."

The confusion on Cole's face said he didn't understand. No wonder. She was completely botching her explanation. Taking a deep breath, she went for broke, trying to explain in the most direct way she knew how.

Even if that way hurt.

"My father was in the Army. When we were little, he was gone more than he was home. When I was six, he left and never came back." She sucked in a deep breath to make up for the lack of breathing while rushing through her explanation.

"I'm sorry for your loss."

Sophie winced. "I...Cole, this isn't easy to talk about. He wasn't lost in action—at least, not on a battlefield that anyone could see. He was fighting a battle inside his own head that we couldn't help him with. He left, filed for divorce, and disappeared from our lives. Because of him, Isabelle isn't keen on having personal relationships with past or present military. And because she's my big sister and thinks she's in charge of me, she doesn't want them for me, either."

If anyone could understand, Cole would probably be the closest, thanks to what he'd gone through.

His confused expression deepened. "But you're both involved in your quilts for soldiers organization, aren't you?"

"Quilts of Valor Foundation," Sophie corrected. "Isabelle supports me and my work with them because she knows how important it is to me, but she's never made or donated a quilt to the foundation," she admitted, sadness hitting her anew at her sister's resistance to the idea. Sophie firmly believed her sister would find healing in the making of a quilt and wrapping a soldier in it. Believing that was easy, but convincing Isabelle to ever do so seemed an impossible task. "She doesn't do the sew-ins or that type of thing, but she's okay with the shop supporting the foundation. We always have at least one sample quilt on display, along with pre-made kits, and information available. Well, you know that," she laughed a little nervously, "you helped bring the quilts back from the festival booth."

"I remember. I could see the patriotic fabric display in my head while you were talking."

"Really?" Part of her wanted to ask what he thought of the display—wanted to talk to him about anything other than her father, and the impact his leaving had had on her and Isabelle. But this conversation needed to be had. Because she wanted him to understand why Isabelle was so distrusting. Mostly, she didn't want him to not like her sister. That he liked Isabelle was impor- tant. "My sister doesn't mean any harm. She just..."

"Doesn't trust any military person to stick around because your father left."

Sophie hated talking about Isabelle's hang-ups or her father's choices. Some things just felt as if they were supposed to be kept private. The Davis women always kept quiet about their lives even prior to Cliff Davis's abandonment.

Talking about him now felt like opening doors that had been kept shut a long time because scary things lurked on the other side.

Finally, she said, "He never wanted to hurt us. That's

why he left, so he wouldn't. Isabelle has never forgiven him."

"Have you?"

"Isabelle took his leaving harder than me. Probably because I was younger and had her and Mom showering me with love, making sure I never felt abandoned. Whereas I want to offer every soldier comfort and healing, she sees them all as extensions of Dad." Sophie sighed. "Any lingering anger I may have had toward him disappeared when I read your journal."

Sophie glanced around the dining hall, feeling that the space was much too open to be having this conversation.

Sophie took a deep breath, shook off her melancholy, and pasted on a smile. "Help me carry these boxes, please, so we can go join the others. We wouldn't want to miss being in the group pics."

"Yep, wouldn't want to miss that." His tone implied otherwise.

His phone rang just as they entered the main lobby where the others were gathered. Pulling it out, he glanced down at the number, then excused himself to go outside to take the call.

Sophie watched as he paced the sidewalk, talking to whomever was on the other end of the line.

During all the times they'd been together, he'd never gotten a call or taken a message, she realized, wondering who the caller was.

"He's cute, Sophie," one of the other volunteers praised as they packed up the Christmas decoration boxes into a plastic bin they'd tuck out of the way until it was time to repack everything after New Year's.

Cute. Bleah. Dragging her gaze away from the window, Sophie shrugged and wished her friends would come up with a better way of describing Cole. She wasn't going to call him cute when to do so felt as if it would be an insult rather than compliment. Cute was for bunny rabbits and puppies. Cole was...Cole.

"A bit quiet, perhaps, but definitely cute," the volunteer continued. "How long have you been seeing him?"

"We're just friends," she said, not sure if that was true. Were they friends? More than friends? She'd almost kissed him.

"Seriously? Y'all were so fun sledding, and then when I saw him show up at church and come sit right next to you, I thought the two of you must be an item. I was like 'Go you, Sophie Davis.'"

Sophie smiled at her friend's encouragement but wasn't sure what to tell Laura, wasn't sure what Cole would want her to say. Something wonderful was happening between them, but she didn't fool herself into thinking that she knew how to label it. If he believed he wasn't good for her, would he ever really embrace a relationship between them?

The answer wasn't one she wanted to acknowledge.

"He's new in town," she commented, knowing her friend was waiting on her to say something. Cole had been in Pine Hill less than a year. That counted as new, right? "He doesn't know a lot of people. I thought it would be nice for him to come to church and meet all of you today. You know, get involved in the community and make friends." She tried to look casual, as if their conversation wasn't a big deal. She didn't want to trigger a lot of gossip. Any discussion about their relationship should first occur between her and Cole. Only, she'd seen Cole's face after Isabelle interrupted. His regret at what had almost happened had been obvious.

"That's great." Laura sounded genuinely pleased by Sophie's answer, then asked, "You're sure there's nothing more to it? You looked so happy to see him when he sat down beside you this morning."

How many people had zeroed in on her reaction to Cole joining her at church?

"I was happy he came to church. He told me hasn't been in a while." Ecstatic. "Shouldn't we all have been glad he was there?" She gave her friend a pointed look. "Seriously, he's a bit of a loner, so I was pleased that he came this morning."

Isabelle had been listening with interest. Sophie had been all too aware of that fact, so she wasn't surprised when her sister joined the conversation.

"Sophie's interest in Cole stems from the fact that she feels sorry for him because of what he went through during his military career." Isabelle's tone brooked no argument. "You know how she is about wanting to wrap every soldier in one of her quilts."

Sophie frowned at her sister. She didn't feel sorry for Cole. Hearing her sister say that she did just didn't ring true.

"I do feel badly for what he's been through," she began, meaning to continue explaining from there—that she was saddened by all the hardships he'd faced, yet that she admired his strength and resilience—but Laura interrupted when she paused to collect her thoughts.

"You gave him a quilt?" Laura sounded impressed. "That's great. I love all the charity projects you do. I just don't know where you find the time, though."

"Um, no, I haven't given a quilt to Cole." Sophie

didn't point out that people made time for the things in life that were most important to them. For Sophie that was family, church, work, and Quilts of Valor. "Not yet. I hope to award him a quilt someday. He needs one so badly but doesn't think he does because he doesn't really understand what it is we do, how our quilts heal. He doesn't believe he deserves to be wrapped."

Because Cole didn't believe he deserved anything good. He might not have said the words out loud, but she was sure they were true.

He thought he was no good for her. He was wrong about that, too.

"I just have to convince him to let me award him one." She sighed, then resolved herself. "I'm working on convincing him, slowly but surely. Someday, I will give him one and he will feel better."

A quilt with prayers set into every stitch she'd sewn. The quilt she'd designed and was making currently. A quilt she was making specifically for him, even if she was just now truly admitting it to herself.

As she sewed, her head, and her heart were filled with thoughts of Cole and how the material would soon wrap him in a forever hug.

"That's wonderful," Laura said, placing the last of the ornament boxes into the bin. "I'm sure he appreciates all you're doing to help him get acclimated to Pine Hill. If you truly aren't interested in more than friendship, send him my way."

Still distracted by her thoughts, it took a minute before Laura's comment sank in. When it did, Sophie fought to keep from frowning at her friend.

Um, no. That wouldn't be happening. Laura was a great person, but Sophie wouldn't be sending Cole in any direction that involved another woman.

Because the thought made her a little crazy.

A lot crazy. Crazy jealous.

Because she thought Cole belonged to her? He didn't. Not even close.

And yet, she had almost kissed him. And he had almost let her.

Their almost-kiss had been more special than the few real kisses she'd experienced, although, to be fair, those few instances hadn't been anything spectacular.

Would Cole's kiss have been spectacular?

Sophie thought so. *Knew* so. Cole was spectacular. She didn't want to share him with Laura. Or anyone.

Realizing she was staring off into space, daydreaming, Sophie reined in her thoughts and her gaze. Unfortunately, the latter landed on her sister.

Isabelle eyed her suspiciously, as if she'd read every thought that had popped into Sophie's mind.

Heat flooded her cheeks, because they both knew that no matter how much Isabelle protested, no matter how much either of them said otherwise, Sophie was hooked on Cole Aaron.

Isabelle opened her mouth, but whatever she'd been going to say was forever lost as her gaze flickered behind Sophie. Without looking, Sophie knew Cole had come back into the room.

Wondering who his call had been from, happy he was back, Sophie turned, smiling and planning to make sure he knew she was glad he was there.

The chill from his time outside had his cheeks and nose a bit pink, but those indications of the cold didn't compare to the frosty edge to his pale blue gaze.

Sophie's smile faded. "Everything okay?"

Chapter Sixteen

Cole had overheard everything—all about how he was Sophie's latest charity project.

He'd known.

From the beginning, when she'd shown compassion and pity rather than disgust after reading his journal, he'd known.

He'd also known better than to let his emotions get all tangled up with an impulsive, do-gooder, church-going, got-to-fix-the-world, bright-eyed, big-hearted small town girl. Yet that's exactly what he'd done.

"Cole?" She stared at him with those hazel eyes that threatened to pull him in.

Good thing he'd gotten splashed with a bucket of frigid reality.

"That was the fire hall. I've got to go."

Sophie's disappointment was palpable as she searched his face. "Oh. Okay. Can you stay for the group photo?"

Was she kidding? He hadn't wanted to do the group

photo even before he'd gotten the call asking if he'd cover for someone needing to go home.

Before he'd overheard a conversation confirming what he'd known but had let himself ignore, wanting to enjoy the moment because he'd gotten sucked into Sophie's the-world-is-a-happy-snow-globe bubble.

No more.

"No, of course not," she corrected herself before he could answer. "You've got to go."

Everyone in the room seemed to be watching them as if his leaving were some drama playing out. Perhaps it was. Because whatever insanity had possessed him to go to church with Sophie, to think maybe they could be friends, was gone.

She wanted to wrap him in a quilt because she thought it would fix him. But there was nothing that could fix him—and if that was all she was after, then they might as well end things between them now. Without another word, because none were necessary, Cole tipped his head a little in acknowledgement, then turned to go.

Once outside the assisted living facility, he sucked in a deep breath of air, the cold hitting his lungs hard. He blew out slowly as he made his way to his Jeep.

What a fool he'd been.

"Cole!"

As he was opening the door, she rushed up to his SUV.

Why didn't it surprise him Sophie had followed him outside? It was just the kind of impulsive thing she'd do despite the fact everyone, including her sister, was probably watching them through the windows.

Hand on the handle, he paused.

"Please be careful."

Careful? Did she think he was headed out on a call?

"Always."

She stared at him, her eyes begging him to say something, to acknowledge things he never would.

"I'm glad. I—"

"I've got to go," he interrupted, knowing it was true for so many reasons.

Sophie swallowed, nodded, then stepped back from his vehicle.

A thousand things he could say hit him, but he held his tongue.

Some things were better left unsaid.

"You have to talk to me at some point," Sophie insisted the following day, from the passenger seat of Cole's truck.

Cole had been doing his best to keep his eyes on the road and not on where she fidgeted with her seatbelt. She'd chatted non-stop from the moment he picked her up at her shop, smiling and acting as if nothing had happened at the nursing home. Nothing had. "It's making for a long trip with you not talking."

Should he point out that they were almost finished collecting the boxes and their Christmas charity 'partnership' was coming to an end? Just one more business, then he'd drop her back off, and he'd take the toys they'd collected to the church. Alone.

The toys, along with the funds donated by the fire department crew. Cole wasn't sure how much was needed, but the crew had come through generously.

Hopefully, it would be enough to cover gifts for the kids at the Triple B Ranch.

Maybe it wouldn't be as much as what Sophie had mentioned they usually did for the kids, but each kid could get a gift, surely.

He'd thought about canceling this last toy collection pickup with her, but each time he'd told himself he'd see this through. Initially, he'd approached the toy drive as a mission. One where he did his job, and then he walked away. He was back to seeing it that way again— and now, it was a mission that was nearly complete. After today, the toy drive would be over, other than wrapping and distribution. He shouldn't have reason to be alone with Sophie again.

"Cole, talk to me."

"You seem to be doing just fine by yourself," he pointed out. She had talked enough for the both of them, chatting about anything and everything as if nothing was wrong until she'd apparently had enough of his silence.

"Ah-ha. You said something. Finally." Her face took on a proud look as if she'd accomplished some grand feat in pulling the words from him.

"Had something to say."

"And you hadn't up to that point?" She glanced at her watch. "We've been picking up collection boxes for over an hour, and you've barely said two words."

He shrugged.

"See. There you go again. Nonverbal."

Not talking was easier and way less painful than getting pulled back into the fantasy that something had been happening between them. That something even *could* happen.

How could he have forgotten all the reasons why that was impossible? If nothing else, her talk about her father leaving should have been reminder enough. Instead, it had taken hearing her admit she was throwing a pity party for him to jar him out of his Sophie sunshine euphoria.

"Don't be this way." Her voice held such a pleading quality to it that Cole's insides twisted.

"What way would you have me be?"

"The way you were when we were sledding, or playing the game at Sarah and Bodie's. Or while we were at the On-the-Square Christmas festival, or while we were decorating the tree. Or—"

"Let me stop you," he intervened. "I told you in the beginning that I wasn't interested in being your friend."

"I—Yes, you did say that," she admitted, her expression a mixture of uncertainty and stubbornness. "But I thought...Why would you say that? I mean, who doesn't want more friends?"

"Me—I don't. The way things are now is how they need to stay."

"Says who? Because that's not what I think you need."

No, she thought he needed her to make a big deal of his past and wrap him in one of her blankets.

"I don't need your emotional charity, Sophie. I'm just fine."

She looked shocked. "I never said you weren't fine."

"But you think it."

"Obviously, you have no clue what I think."

"I heard you say you wanted to give me one of your quilts."

Her jaw dropped open a little. "That's what this is about?"

"You read my journal and rather than be disgusted as you should have been, you felt sorry for me instead, probably because of your father. You've made me into a pet project who you want to fix. Thanks but no thanks, Sophie. I don't need or want anything you have to offer."

Sophie grew quiet, then said in the most even tone he'd heard her use, "I can't undo that I read your journal, Cole."

"I'm not asking you to." Although if he had it to do over, he'd have destroyed the book so no one could have ever found and read it.

"Then what are you asking of me? Because I don't understand."

Cole drummed his thumbs against the steering wheel, wishing he could magically transport himself anywhere other than sitting next to Sophie and having this conversation. "Nothing."

"But...I..." Her breath caught. "'Nothing' doesn't work for me."

"This isn't just about you."

"Exactly," she agreed, her expression stubborn. "It's about us."

"There is no us."

"There should be."

He shook his head. He didn't even want to hear her say such foolishness. She still thought he could be fixed, but he knew better. His darkness would overpower her goodness and dim her light forever. He wouldn't allow that.

Sophie deserved better.

She said, "If you'd only—"

He shook his head again. "Let's just get through collecting these toys and see what we still need, okay?"

"I...you're not really giving me a choice, are you? Even though this isn't what I want, you're going to push me away?"

"No, and yes." For her own good.

"Then fine, let's get through collecting these toys. But just so you know, I don't agree with you and think you're making a big mistake, because I like you, Cole. I really like you. And not because you're a 'pet project' or because I feel sorry for you, because I don't." Her gaze narrowed. "Or, at least, I didn't. Now, I guess I do because you're pushing me away and, say what you will, I'm good for you."

That had never been in question. The issue was that he wasn't good for her.

"Sure of yourself, aren't you?" he couldn't resist asking.

She lifted her chin. "Tell me I'm wrong."

"You're wrong, Sophie," he said without hesitation. He put the SUV into park in front of her shop, realizing only after he'd done so that he hadn't gone to the last business on their list. He'd go by himself later. "Forget whatever it is you think you feel for me, because I'm not interested."

"You were."

Now that the car was parked, he held her gaze.

"I got distracted. I never should have let that happen. Not in my line of work."

Making sure to keep the inner turmoil, the doubts he struggled with hidden, Cole ended what shouldn't have began

"We aren't friends. We never have been, and we never will be. The sooner you accept that, the better things will be for all involved, especially me."

"He didn't mean it," Sophie assured Stitches through her open bedroom window.

The cat's meow in return seemed to sound a little doubtful. Or maybe she was just projecting because, despite her brave claim, she worried that Cole had meant every word.

She'd seen how quickly those walls had gone up, had seen how thick they were, had seen his refusal to let her back in.

"He's going to miss me," she said out loud, although her brain's version went more along the lines of how *she* was going to miss *him*.

She glanced over at the quilt she'd yet to finish, neatly folded on her dresser. The quilt she'd put so much appreciation and love into stitching long before she'd admitted she was making it for Cole.

The quilt he didn't want.

"Meow."

Sophie glanced up just in time to see the cat make the jump from the windowsill onto the foot of the bed.

"Oh wow," she breathed softly, almost afraid to say anything, worried she'd scare her guest away. "This is an unexpected surprise."

The cat meowed again, then, seeming content at the foot of her bed, lay down and watched her.

"Um, yeah, so am I supposed to not move now for the rest of the night for fear of scaring you off?"

Just as she'd scared Cole off.

"Seriously, he's an ex-Marine. Nothing I do should scare the man," she mumbled to herself, to the cat, to the wall.

This was pathetic. She was pathetic.

"I guess if it means you staying in here with me, listening to me pour my heart out, then I can do my best to lie here and work on these puzzles the way he never did. Why buy crossword puzzle books, then never do them? Tell me that."

None of the ones she'd seen in his SUV had contained a single filled-in space.

The cat just blinked.

"Obviously, he can't even commit to penciling in his answers."

Sophie piddled with the crossword puzzle book for another ten minutes or so before sitting it on her dresser.

Cole might not be able to commit to even answering a crossword puzzle in print, but Sophie didn't have that same fear.

Her fears went just as deeply as his, though. Her fear was caring about a man who could never let himself care back because of all the protective walls shielding his heart.

It wasn't a new fear. When she was a child, it had been her father. Now, it was Cole.

Closing her eyes, she lay back on the bed and prayed Cole someday found peace and met someone he deemed worthy of tearing those walls down for.

Even if that person wasn't meant to be her.

She'd be just fine. The past month with Cole had opened her eyes to a lot of things about herself. She was strong enough to care for him. And strong enough to let him walk away if that was what he needed to do.

She'd be fine. It hurt, but she would be fine.

If only she could convince herself that he was doing the right thing when her heart insisted that he wasn't.

"What's up with you and Sophie?"

Not looking up from his crossword puzzle, Cole shrugged at Ben's question. "Nothing, as far as I know."

"You weren't at church Sunday."

Cole snorted. "I haven't been at church a lot of Sundays."

"You've been a pain lately," Ben added.

"Who wouldn't be, having to put up with all these questions?"

Ben shot him a serious look. "You don't plan to see her again?"

"It's a small town. I'm sure our paths will cross."

"We've still got the 'wrapping and delivering the presents' party. Maybe you'll get lucky and she'll forgive whatever your sorry self did."

Cole shrugged. Sophie forgiving him wasn't the issue. Never had been. From the beginning, she hadn't judged him harshly. He'd prefer her anger and disgust over pity. Pity was the one thing he couldn't deal with.

"You must have done something if you and Sophie are no longer a couple," Ben pushed.

"We were never a couple."

"Sorry, man." Ben slapped him on the back. "I really thought she was the one for you."

Andrew came back into the room, carrying an envelope that he handed to Cole. "This is for you."

"What is it?"

Andrew shrugged. "How would I know? Open it and see."

Cole took the business-sized envelope, noted his name written in bold print across the front. No address, no return address, no postage. Just his name.

"Someone hand-delivered it?"

Andrew shrugged. "I guess. It was in the office, and I was asked to give it to you."

Cole frowned. He'd seen Sophie's flowy, curvy handwriting, and this wasn't it.

Not that he had any reason to automatically assume it might be from Sophie...except that who else would send him mail at the firehall?

Aggravated with himself for the direction of his thoughts, he opened the envelope and pulled out two slips of paper.

One was a cashier's check for more money than he made in a month. The other was a note that simply said, "Have fun shopping for the toy drive. Make the donations from the fire department."

Stunned, Cole turned the check to where Ben and Andrew could see.

"I know you want to beat us, but come on man, a cashier's check made out to you?"

"I didn't do this," Cole assured, racking his brain to decipher who had.

Andrew narrowed his eyes. "Who do you know that we don't know?"

"Do you recognize the handwriting?" Ben asked.

Cole shook his head. "Why would anyone send this to me rather than directly to the committee?"

"Maybe they heard how you rallied our crew to pitch in money to buy the items still needed, so when they decided to donate to the cause, they thought you'd be the best one to handle it," Ben suggested.

Andrew crossed his arms, pretending to be annoyed. "Whoever it is wanted you and Sophie to win our competition. Don't think I'm not grateful for the donation, but I'm not amused it was sent to you."

Cole snorted. "I don't know anyone with this kind of money."

Andrew shrugged. "It seems that they know you."

"Apparently."

"You may need help spending all that and getting the gifts to the church tomorrow evening." Ben's smile was wide. "You want some shopping buddies?"

"Why not?" His brain was racing. The check was a lot of money. He wanted to spend it wisely but wasn't sure what was needed. Who would know?

Sophie.

No. He...he just couldn't.

Maybelle Kirby. She was head of the committee. She'd know what was needed.

He glanced down at the check in his hand, wondering...no, it wouldn't make sense for Maybelle to have been the person who sent the check.

But she'd be able to let him know what was needed, might even have a list of the Triple B kids' genders and ages and wish lists—or at least be able to get one to him in a hurry.

"Looks like we're shopping." He glanced at the figure

on the check and shook his head in disbelief. "Lots of shopping."

Ben rubbed his hands together. "This is going to be fun."

Ben was right. But what Cole looked forward to most was seeing Sophie's look of surprise when he and the guys walked in tomorrow laden down with toys.

Or maybe, right or wrong, he most looked forward to seeing Sophie, period.

"Can you hand me a piece of tape?"

Without looking up at Maybelle, Sophie tore off a piece of tape and handed it to the older woman. "Here you go."

Volunteers were lined up, wrapping and sorting presents that would be delivered on Christmas Eve. They'd ended up with enough donations for the original requests.

But not enough to meet the needs of the Triple B Ranch for Kids.

After Rosie and Sophie had a long heart-to-heart, Rosie had contacted Triple B earlier in the week to let them know that they would be delivering presents, but not as many as they'd hoped. Still, they'd make sure each child had something to open.

"So many children who are going to be so excited on Christmas morning," Ruby said, finishing with the package she held. "It's going to be so wonderful.

"Agreed," Aunt Claudia added. "Almost as wonderful as the trip I'll be taking come January. We're headed to Greece, you know."

"We all know because you won't be quiet about it," Rosie said, rolling her eyes. "How about you find something different to talk about? Like Sarah and Bodie's honeymoon."

"Ha. If you had any sense about you, we'd be discussing where you and Lou are going on your honeymoon," Maybelle said drily.

Ruby looked up from where she was wrapping a gift. "Any luck on getting a location out of either of the happy couple?"

"I have Sheriff Roscoe on it," Maybelle assured. "But so far, he says Bodie isn't talking."

"I can hear you," Sarah called from a nearby table where she placed wrapped gifts into large plastic bags labeled with each child's name and address.

"We know, child," Rosie assured. "We're hoping if you hear us bring it up enough, you'll feel bad and tell us."

Sarah gave her friends an amused look. "I don't know where we're going, so you won't be getting any information from me."

Sophie smothered a smile.

"And good luck on getting a clue from Bodie," Sarah told them. "His lips are sealed, and not even the Butterflies can get him to crack, because as much as he loves you all, he doesn't want you accompanying us on our honeymoon."

Maybelle harrumphed. Rosie snorted. Ruby just smiled. Aunt Claudia was still talking about her upcoming trip to Greece even though no one was really listening.

"Is this everything?" Maybelle asked when she picked up the last toy. "We've still got the foster kids from Triple B Ranch. We've not crossed any of them off our list."

Sophie's stomach plummeted. Rather than divvy up the gifts they had, leading to them being more thinly spread, Sophie had decided to proceed as normal, then see what was still needed. She'd hoped more toys would come in, that her estimates would prove to be much lower than the reality and there would be plenty for all.

With a sinking heart and her eyes threatening to spill tears, Sophie stepped forward, then paused. No, she wasn't giving up. She wouldn't let those kids not have a Christmas. No way.

"Not yet, but we're working on more last-minute donations." She would get them, too. Even if it meant going to every business in town and begging for additional contributions. Plus, she'd raffle off one of her quilts. She'd find a way. "No worries, Maybelle. Every child will have a gift and—"

The church community door opened and Cole, Andrew, Ben, and several other firemen came in carrying boxes and bags.

Huge, overflowing boxes and bags.

"What's all this?" Sophie asked, her eyes still blurry with unshed tears, but her gaze not able to leave Cole.

She hadn't seen him since they'd collected the last boxes and he'd told her he didn't want to be her friend. Again.

Her stomach twisted at the memory.

Oh, how she'd missed this man who had come to mean so much to her so quickly.

And oh, how amazing he looked in his uniform as he said, "The rest of the donations."

"These were at the firehall?" Sophie asked, stunned. Where had Cole and the crew gotten all the gifts?

"They're from the fire department," Andrew clarified. "There was a flurry of new items right at the end, thanks to a friendly rivalry on getting donations."

Sophie fought choking up with emotion. The guys had bought these? Thank goodness Cole had tossed out that challenge, then. She wanted to hug them all.

"Perfect," Maybelle praised, never having looked overly worried.

"This is wonderful," Rosie clasped her hands together. "There's more than enough for all the Triple B Ranch kids."

"With extras in case we have last minute requests." Ruby beamed at her grandson.

Sophie's gaze stayed on Cole. He hadn't looked her way, but she knew he was aware of her, was aware that she was watching him, that she couldn't pull her eyes from him.

Seeing him was almost as wonderful as seeing the gifts they'd brought in.

Eventually, he met her gaze. Sophie smiled, holding her breath in hopes he'd smile back.

He gave a slight nod of acknowledgement, then looked away.

No. He couldn't do this. He couldn't push her away.

She stopped what she was doing, marched over to where he stood with the other firemen and wrapped her arms around him.

"Thank you so much, Cole."

He was so stiff in her embrace that Sophie thought he might freeze into place.

When he didn't respond in any other way, she inwardly sighed, ignored the giant crack forming in her heart at his continued rejection, then stepped over to hug Andrew and thank him. He was almost as uncomfortably stiff as Cole. Ben hugged her right back, though.

"No problem, Sophie," Ben said, his expression proud. "We were glad to help." Sophie smiled back, thankful for the friendly face. "But for the record, next year, Andrew and I will win our competition."

Sophie's gaze cut to Cole, but he was studying something across the room and didn't say anything. She'd assumed Ben and Andrew had collected most of the remaining donations. Apparently not.

"Where did all this come from?"

"Cole got a big donation."

"Can't Cole talk for himself?" she asked, then wanted to slap her hand over her mouth.

"Children," Maybelle scolded, clearing her throat to get everyone's attention. "Snap to it. We've more toys to wrap. Lots more toys, thanks to the fire department."

As they usually did when Maybelle spoke, everyone got to work, including Sophie, although her gaze strayed over to the firemen who'd help carry the items in. One in particular.

Whereas the others were talking to various people, and several had jumped in to help wrap gifts, Cole quietly helped carry toys over to the table to be sorted and wrapped.

Cole kept his eyes and his hands on the toy he wrapped, taking care to make each fold precise and each piece of tape perfectly sealed.

"For the record, we're already plotting our new strategy," Andrew told Sophie from where he wrapped presents next to Cole. "We won't be outdone again by you and this holdout who came through at the last minute."

"Who was the donation from?" Sophie asked.

"Nobody knows," Ben supplied. "An anonymous cashier's check came made out to Cole with a note to buy things for the toy drive on behalf of the fire department."

"Wow. That's awesome."

Sophie's gaze cut to Rosie. Did she think Rosie had donated the check?

"Good of them," Maybelle said, then gave Cole a nod of approval. "And of you for doing the right thing, since the check was made out to you."

Cole felt a little embarrassed under her eagle-sharp gaze. Something in her stare clicked, and although she didn't say another word, just turned from him and started talking to one of the other Butterflies, Cole knew.

Maybelle had sent the check. It made no sense, but he was sure she had.

Which meant the woman had wanted Cole to come to the rescue. Which only made sense if...

Blasted matchmaking Butterflies.

But in this case, he'd take it without arguing since it had meant more than enough toys for the kids.

The firemen volunteered to help deliver the presents, so they stuck around until every gift was wrapped, labeled, and tucked in a bag tagged with where it would go.

"Cole?"

He'd used every ounce of strength in him not to respond to her sweet hug. Had dug deep for even more strength to keep from looking at her, especially when he'd sensed her gaze on him.

He reached inside and hoped he had enough strength for whatever it was she wanted as he turned to face her.

Her bright eyes searched his. "Thank you."

"I didn't do anything. Had I not been here, the check would have been sent to someone else." Or deposited directly, if he was right about his Maybelle suspicion.

"Maybe, but you *were* here, it came to you, and you saved the day yet again."

"Don't make me out to be a hero, Sophie. I'm not."

She gave him a small smile, but for the first time since he'd known her, that smile held a sadness to it. The realization that he'd done that gutted him.

"Real heroes never think they are." She reached up, touched his cheek, then seemed to realize what she was doing and let her hand fall away. "I hope you have a merry Christmas, Cole. For whatever it's worth, through my eyes, you've always been my hero."

Chapter Seventeen

"Q uit that," Isabelle ordered from beside Sophie as they finished cleaning the shop before closing it for the holidays.

"What?" Sophie asked, wiping down a countertop and tossing some stray threads into the trash bin.

"Thinking about him."

If only it was that easy.

"I miss him," she admitted, not bothering to deny her sister's claim. Isabelle knew her too well not to suspect the truth.

Isabelle sighed. "I know. You're almost as sad a sight as that cat hanging around the house."

Sophie's mouth dropped open. "You know about Stitches?"

Isabelle rolled her eyes. "Did you seriously think I wouldn't notice? He's on our front porch every night, along with a box, blanket, water, and food bowl. What was I supposed to do? Just ignore him?"

Sophie's eyes widened. "You've been feeding him, too?"

"No," Isabelle quickly denied. "I've told him over and over I'm not going to feed him because he doesn't live at our house, and to not give me those pitiful meows. But somehow, I still end up petting him—"

Giving up all pretense of cleaning, Sophie's mouth fell open. "Stitches lets you pet him?"

Isabelle gave her a *duh* look.

"I can't sit on the porch without the thing rubbing all up against my legs until I let him in my lap." Her gaze narrowed. "Why? Am I not supposed to pet him? Please don't tell me something is wrong with him. I don't like him, but I...well, I don't want anything to happen to him, either."

"Nothing is wrong with him, as far as I know," Sophie hastened to say, still staring at her sister. "I'm just surprised Stitches lets you pet him, that's all."

"What's that mean? You think he only likes you?"

Sophie watched the play of emotions passing over her sister's face as she went back to cleaning with a suspicious vengeance, and realization dawned.

"Oh my goodness, you say you don't like Stitches, but you do!"

"I didn't say that," Isabelle defended, her cheeks going pink as she averted her gaze from Sophie and focused on straightening a bin of discounted thread spools.

"You didn't have to. Stitches has you wrapped around his furry paw."

"Don't be ridiculous. The fact that I've been petting that pesky cat for the past couple of weeks doesn't mean anything."

"The past couple of weeks?"

Leaning against the countertop, Isabelle shrugged.

"Quit making a big deal of it. I am not wrapped around that cat's paw."

"Yeah, well, for the record, Stitches has yet to let me pet him and I'm the one feeding him."

Straightening, Isabelle's eyes widened, then a grin spread across her face. "Seriously?"

Sophie nodded.

"Then why would he let me pet him?"

Okay, so she was a little peeved that Stitches had been holding out on her while loving on Isabelle, but the pleasure on her sister's face was enough to have Sophie smiling.

"Maybe it's all that catnip-scented lotion you've been wearing."

"I have not—" Isabelle countered before realizing Sophie had only been teasing her. "You're just jealous because he likes me better than he does you."

"That's true," Sophie admitted. "So much for loyalty. I mean, I'm the one feeding him, not to mention the one who got stuck in a tree trying to save him, and he chooses you to love on. Great."

"At least we know he has good taste," her sister teased.

Sophie snorted. "Yeah, right."

"Unlike you."

"Let up on Cole."

"Because he's the man of your dreams?"

He *was* the man of her dreams. Or at least, the man she dreamed of.

Because he might be done with her, but her dreams weren't registering that, and he continued to star in all of them. Dreams where they laughed together, played together. Dreams where Cole looked in the mirror and saw the man Sophie saw.

A good man. A hero. *Her* hero.

Dreams where he looked at her and didn't fight what was between them.

Because she wasn't crazy. She'd seen how he looked at her, how he'd stepped outside his comfort zone—going sledding, going to church—for her. He hadn't done that because he hadn't cared. He *did* care, whether he'd admit it or not.

"My relationship with Cole is complicated," she admitted. She and Isabelle had always talked about everything, but regarding Cole, Sophie had bit her tongue, knowing her sister's bias.

"Because he's former military?"

Sophie shook her head. "Cole being former military isn't a problem for me."

"I know that," Isabelle assured. "I'm saying it's a problem for him, which in turn makes it a problem for you."

Not really surprised at her sister's insight, Sophie glanced at her and nodded.

"I know he cares about you," Isabelle continued, "but—"

"What?" Sophie asked, having been caught off guard by her sister's comment. "How do you know he cares for me?"

Isabelle rolled her eyes. "Anyone can see that he's crazy about you, but that's—"

"You think he's crazy about me?"

"Sophie," Isabelle said in a completely exasperated tone. "You're missing the point."

"Which is?"

"That you shouldn't be crazy about him."

Sophie bit into her lower lip. "But what if I am anyway?"

Isabelle was silent for long moments, then said, "Then I pray God guides you in whatever decisions you make, and that you find true happiness in life. It's all I've ever wanted for you."

Cole made her happy.

"Thank you, Isabelle. For loving me, and loving on my cat, too."

Her sister gave her a pointed look. "I'm pretty sure Bobbin is actually my cat and not yours."

Christmas morning arrived bright and early. Although Sophie and Isabelle didn't rush from their rooms to wake their mother as they'd done as children, they both still made their way to the living room when the smell of Christmas breakfast began drifting through the house.

Since they'd gotten big enough to contain their exuberance, Darlene had started the tradition of cooking a mini feast for the three of them. They ate first, then opened presents while sipping on Christmas coffee.

"Mmmm, that smells wonderful," Sophie praised as she walked into the kitchen. "What can I do to help?"

"Grab plates and set the table. Isabelle is making coffee."

Breakfast was a hit, and soon they were in the living room, sitting around their tree.

Their mother got them items from her salon, a new sweater apiece, and some books they'd mentioned wanting to read. Isabelle went next and handed out her gifts—beautiful crafting aprons she'd made for them.

"Oh, wow, Isabelle, this is amazing."

"Yes, I love it," their mother agreed. Both Sophie and her mother put theirs on and posed for photos.

"I'm next," Sophie squealed, excited to give them their gifts.

She'd made her mother a heating pad filled with rice that she could wrap around her neck to ease her often-achy muscles after being at the salon for long hours. She had also bought her a new set of scissors and had topped her present with a Butterfly-made snowflake.

Fighting her smile, she handed Isabelle a box.

"Quit smiling so big. You're scaring me."

Sophie laughed. Her sister would laugh, too, when she saw what Sophie had chosen for her.

Gently removing her own Butterfly-made snowflake, Isabelle just as carefully removed the wrapping paper from her present, folding the paper once it was off the gift.

"Just rip into it," Sophie encouraged. "You're taking too long. We'll miss Sarah's wedding if you don't hurry."

"Only if you take as long getting ready for it as you did for church the Sunday morning Cole came to visit."

Ouch.

"For that, I should take your gift back and give you coals."

Isabelle lifted the box's lid, looked at the contents, then shook her head, laughing. "You shouldn't have."

"I thought you might say that."

Isabelle pulled out a "To-Do List" scratch pad with a dragonfly emblem in each of the corners, along with a dragonfly pen and several other stationary items, all emblazed with dragonflies. At the very bottom of the box was a cat bandana with a tiny dragonfly embroidered on it and a cat collar Carrie had helped Sophie find last minute.

"Those are lovely," Darlene said, leaning over for a closer look. "Cute collar. About time y'all got one for Bobbin."

Bobbin? Which meant their mom knew all about Stitches...a.k.a. Bobbin, apparently. Sophie shouldn't be surprised. Moms usually knew everything.

Laughing, Isabelle cut her gaze toward Sophie, then hugged her. "Thank you, I think."

Sophie, Isabelle, and their mother were early to Sarah and Bodie's wedding, but the church was already packed. Not that Sophie had expected anything less. It might be Christmas Day, but sharing this special moment with the couple was a gift all their friends and family would cherish.

After just a few minutes, Bodie, his best man, and Bodie's dog Harry appeared at the front of the church. Harry wore a bowtie and stood beside the men as if he knew exactly why they were there and what he was supposed to be doing. Both men were dressed in military blues, their chests decorated with various pins and medals in acknowledgement of their service to their country. The trio looked sharp, like they could take care of anything that came their way. Today, their mission was to have a good time, and based on the smile on Bodie's face, they were succeeding. Even Harry seemed to sense the excitement in the air and be anxiously awaiting Sarah's appearance as he eyed the back of the church.

Sophie closed her eyes and imagined Cole in full formal military uniform. She'd never seen in him his uniform and imagined it might never happen now that he was no longer in the service. Too bad, because he'd look handsome, like he could take care of business, too. Then again, he looked that way in everything she'd seen him wear—even when she'd gone to the firehouse to return the journal and had seen him in a Santa suit that hadn't fit him at all.

She liked that about him, that he made her feel safe, as if he could take care of her no matter what.

She glanced around the church, wondering if he was there, then berated herself. She knew where he was—he'd told her. Cole was at the fire department, filling in so someone else could be home with their family. A hero to yet another family, although he wouldn't see it that way.

But even though she knew where he was, she wished he was beside her, just as she'd wished the same thing every time she'd entered the church's sanctuary since Cole's visit.

She wished he was there, holding her hand and sharing her day.

She sighed, garnering a questioning look from her sister. The look turned knowing as Isabelle reached over, took Sophie's hand and gave it a squeeze.

Sophie smiled back. No matter what, she was going to be fine. She had such an amazing family and friends. Life was good.

Even if Cole chose not to be a part of that good life.

Within minutes, Butterflies began walking down the

aisle, one at a time, dropping flower petals as they did. Aunt Claudia, Ruby, and then Rosie—who made dropping her petals more into a dance as she sashayed and waved at wedding guests—and then Maybelle, looking beautifully elegant.

When all four Butterflies stood at the front of the church on the opposite side of Bodie, Harry, and his best man, the music changed. Everyone stood, turning to look at the bride, including the dog.

"Wow," Sophie breathed when Sarah and her father appeared in the entranceway.

"She's a beautiful bride," Isabelle whispered.

Sophie nodded, her gaze going back and forth between a giddily smiling Sarah whose arms were linked with her father's as they made their way down the aisle and her groom who looked completely besotted at the vision his bride made.

It was clear that Sarah wasn't seeing any of her guests. She only had eyes for the man waiting on her.

As Bodie only had eyes for Sarah.

What must it feel like to be loved like that? To know that you'd found a person to love you through thick and thin? Through the good and the bad? That the one who you loved, loved you back with all their heart?

"We're gathered here today for the blessed union of my daughter and this fine young man. Her mother isn't here, but she'd be so proud of the woman Sarah has become, as would my sister, her Aunt Jean. It is with great joy as her father that I give her in marriage to Bodie to be his wife."

Sarah's father spoke to the crowd, then handed her over to Bodie and changed role from father of the bride to the preacher performing their ceremony.

Sophie sniffled more than once as Sarah and Bodie exchanged their vows, especially when they knelt and Harry placed his paw upon their entwined hands.

Truly, Harry was the smartest, most perceptive dog Sophie had ever encountered. Unlike Stitches, who apparently preferred Isabelle over the person feeding him.

"I now pronounce you man and wife," Pastor Smith told the couple, then looked at Bodie, all smiles. "You may now kiss your bride."

Bodie kissed Sarah and a collective sigh sounded around the church, to be followed by a round of laughter when he lifted his head for a moment only to be pulled back into the embrace by Sarah.

"Ladies and gentlemen, I present to you my new son and my beautiful daughter, Mr. and Mrs. Bodie Lewis."

Sophie swiped away a happy tear rolling down her face as cheers and clapping resounded throughout the church building.

Hands clasped, smiles wide, Bodie and Sarah made their way down the aisle, followed by Lukas escorting Maybelle, then Harry leading the other three Butterflies from the church.

Sophie's mom sighed. "What a beautiful wedding. I can't wait until I get to throw one of you girls a wedding and see you that happy."

Isabelle put her finger to her nose. "Not it."

Rather than address what her mother had said, or even think about how it made her feel, Sophie rolled her eyes at her sister, then looked at her mother. "Sorry, but I'm afraid you may have a long wait ahead of you since neither of us are even dating."

Her mother looked confused. "What about that nice

fireman who sat with us a few Sundays ago? He was a cute thing."

Cute? Even her own mother? Sophie sighed. "Sitting with us in church one time doesn't qualify Cole as my boyfriend."

"I was under the impression you spent quite a bit more time with him than just that Sunday." Ah, mothers really did know everything. "Just so you know, I approve."

That got Isabelle's attention. "You do? But he's former military. I thought you would—"

"What does his being former military have to do with anything?" Their mother seemed genuinely surprised that Isabelle considered that to be an issue.

"Dad—"

"Goodness, Isabelle, Sophie's friend has nothing to do with your father."

"But—"

"Some of the best people I know were in the military," Darlene continued. "There's that sweet Mr. Johnson who lives over on Baker. I do his hair once a month. He served in the Vietnam War and the things that man has seen." She paused, then took a deep breath. "Then there's Ella Stewart. Did you know she was a nurse in the Army back in the day? I bet she turned all the boys' heads, because even in her eighties, she's a looker."

Sophie and Isabelle exchanged looks. The wedding must have done something to loosen their mother's tongue, because she didn't usually talk about their father or the military unless Sophie was discussing her quilts.

"Sophie, you should make them both quilts. I can't believe I haven't thought to mention them to you before." Darlene smiled at them. "Now, let's head toward the reception. You know how much I love wedding cake."

Their mother linked her arms with them, much as she might have done when they were younger, and led them out of the church sanctuary.

Christmas morning with her mom and Isabelle had been perfect. Sarah's wedding had been perfect. But after arriving back home that afternoon, a nervous energy buzzed inside Sophie that she couldn't ease.

She knew why.

Cole's quilt. She stared at where it sat on the dresser, only lacking a small area of binding to be finished—yet she hadn't done the final few stitches.

It wouldn't take her five minutes to finish. Why hadn't she?

Because when she finished the quilt, she'd have to make a decision on what to do with it.

She'd made the quilt for Cole. It had been his from the start, even if she hadn't realized that right away. He didn't want to be awarded a quilt, but that didn't make it any less his. Every stitch had been placed with him in mind. She couldn't, wouldn't, give it to anyone else, not when it belonged to Cole.

Walking over to the dresser, she picked up the quilt, eyed the ten-inch section needing bound, set down on her bed, and went to work.

Tap. Tap. Tap.

"Meow."

"Hello there, traitor," she teased the cat who'd started tapping on her window when he wanted inside. Sophie sat the quilt down long enough to open her window so the cat could take its place at the foot of her bed.

As expected, the cat came in and settled in his usual spot.

Sophie closed the window, then sat back on the bed, picked the quilt back up, and worked on the binding.

The cat meowed, stood, moved to where Sophie sat, giving her an expectant look.

"What?"

He meowed again.

When Sophie held out her hand, he rubbed up against it, moving back and forth so Sophie stroked him from head to tip of the tail.

Wow. Excitement filled her.

"About time, don't you think?" she asked, as she grew bolder in petting the cat. He continued to allow Sophie to pet him until he decided to nestle in next to her to go to sleep.

"Merry Christmas to me," she murmured, reaching for her phone so she could take a photo to commemorate the moment.

Once she'd gotten a couple of shots, smiling, Sophie went back to sewing, finished the binding, then hugged the quilt to her.

Cole's quilt. She wanted him to have it. Needed him to have it. Today. On Christmas.

He didn't want the quilt presented to him officially? Fine. That didn't mean she couldn't give it to him as a Christmas present. What he did with it after that was up to him.

"Sorry I'm about to disturb your nap," she told the cat as she stood from the bed. To her surprise, the cat stood also, leisurely stretched, then jumped off the bed to the floor and rubbed against her legs as if it were the most natural thing in the world for him to do so.

She paused long enough to give him some loving, then went to get a box and wrapping supplies.

The cat helped—sort of—as Sophie folded the quilt, placed it in the box.

Just as she was preparing to tape the box, she paused.

There was one more gift she needed to give to Cole.

Chapter Eighteen

"**D**UDE, I'M GOING TO START charging you delivery fees," Andrew warned as he came out into the break room of the fire hall. Confused, Cole glanced up from his crossword puzzle. "Or at least expect a tip."

"I've got a tip for you," Cole said wryly. "Quit accepting gifts from strangers."

"Hey, that last gift saved the day for the toy drive," Andrew reminded him. "Unfortunately, this feels too heavy to be a cashier's check, but maybe you'll get lucky and there's one tucked inside."

"You just want another excuse to go buy toys," Ben teased his friend.

"Who needs an excuse?" Andrew grinned, gently shaking the package and listening to see if he could figure out the contents.

Cole watched him come to a conclusion, then grin as if he knew something they didn't.

"Where did that come from?"

"No 'from' name," Andrew said, holding out the beautifully wrapped package.

"A present showed up at the door, and you just happened to be the one to find it?" Cole eyed the box with the same trepidation he'd eye a booby trap. He suspected this might be one.

An emotional booby trap.

"Something like that."

Cole rolled his eyes. "Yeah, right."

His buddy knew more than he was admitting to.

"Here."

Cole reluctantly took the present, glanced down at the flowy, curvy way his name was written in handwriting he recognized instantly. Fighting to keep his breathing even, he sat the present on the table beside him.

"Open it," Andrew said. Cole shook his head. "Dude, that's not funny."

"Yeah, we want to know what Santa brought you," Ben chimed in.

"If he thought it was from Santa, he'd open it," Andrew pointed out with a chuckle.

"True." Ben poked Cole. "We want to know what Sophie got you. Open it. Come on, before our holiday shift ends."

Cole glanced at his watch. Rather than work a full twenty-four hours, they'd be swapping out with another crew at four. Which was only about twenty minutes away.

His gaze shifted to the present. From the size of the box and its weight, Cole didn't have to open the package to know what was inside. He knew.

Despite his friends' complaints, Cole didn't unwrap the present at the station. When his shift ended, he placed it in his SUV passenger seat and still didn't want to open it. He sat there for a while, considering whether to drop it off on Sophie's front porch before driving back to the farmhouse. The package remained unopened as he placed it on his coffee table and sat staring at the shiny gold ribbon that made him think of the streaks in her hair, the sunshine of her soul.

Sappy. He should open the present and be done with it.

Why had she even gotten him a present? He'd pushed her away. Because he didn't want her pity. Because he wanted to protect her from himself.

The hurt in her hazel eyes had haunted him every moment since, but pushing Sophie from his life was the best thing he could do for her. She deserved better, would find better so long as he stayed out of the way.

Maybe now that Ben and Susan had broken things off, Sophie would turn to his pal. They definitely had more in common than she and Cole ever had, and Ben was a great guy.

But the idea of Sophie with Ben, with anyone, made Cole want to run in the opposite direction as fast as he could, for as long as he could, until he collapsed in exhaustion.

Sweat popped out on the back of his neck as if he really had gone for that run.

"Just open the present," he ordered himself out loud. "You know what's inside."

Cursing his cowardice, Cole opened the package. Then, sitting back down on his sofa, he lifted the lid off the box, not surprised to see the quilted red, white, and blue fabric.

He *was* somewhat surprised to see the journal and envelope on top of it, though.

And was completely surprised at a twelve-inch-tall windup music box shaped like a Christmas tree with a plastic drum as the base, garland branches and tiny packages as the decorations. On top was a twinkly gold star.

Knowing he was about to hear a rendition of "O Christmas Tree," Cole wound the handle one time and wasn't disappointed as the music filled the silence of the room.

Ignoring the journal, he picked up the card and slid it out of its envelope.

A Christmas card. On the cover was a sled covered in glittery snow with a red ribbon tied around it. Inside was a note from Sophie.

Every stitch in this quilt was put there for you, one at a time, and each was meant to mend broken pieces. You may never choose to use it, but I made it to wrap around you, to be a forever hug and reminder that you are loved no matter how dark the moment. Merry Christmas, Cole.

P.S. Everyone deserves a Christmas tree.

Cole closed his eyes. *Sophie. Sophie. Sophie.*

Setting the journal on his coffee table, he lifted the quilt from the box, shook it out, and then stared at it in awe.

Stars. Stripes. Arrow points that probably had some quilter's name he didn't know.

He'd never seen anything like it.

Had certainly never been given anything like it.

"Oh, Sophie." He shook his head, trying to clear himself of the emotions threatening to overwhelm him. "I don't deserve this or what you think you feel for me."

She'd said he was loved. Did she mean friendship love? Christian love? Or did she fancy that she felt something more for him?

He feared it was the latter, even though she deserved so much more than he was or would ever be.

Put the quilt away, he ordered himself.

Instead, he wrapped it around himself and pulled the material tight.

It was as close as he could get to another real hug from Sophie.

Pulling a corner of the quilt to his face, he breathed in, relishing the scent of the laundered material because it smelled of her.

He rubbed his thumb over the stitching and recalled what she'd written. Every stitch was made to mend. To mend him.

Cole sank back onto the sofa, quilt still wrapped around him, and stared at the journal.

The journal he'd written in a haze, set aside, and never opened again.

That book told of the things inside him that left him unable to ever be with Sophie. Or anyone. It contained memories of life and death, pain and sorrow, blood and gore.

Of his biggest failure when he'd waited too long to pull his guys out. That decision had cost him and his men dearly and had triggered his decision not to reenlist.

The guilt pressed on him heavily, dragging him back

into grim place where he'd nearly lost himself. He'd managed to claw his way back from it, but the fight never stopped. He always feared he'd find himself slipping back to it again. That misery filled the pages of the book.

Sophie had read it all.

She was too good inside to see the bad in him, so it was no wonder she'd felt sorry for him.

Pity or not, he pulled the quilt tighter around him, letting the material hug him as Sophie had promised.

The music box clicked off. Cole picked it up. This time he wound it as far as it would go, set it down on the table, and watched as the tree slowly spun to keep his eyes from going to the book.

And yet, it seemed to glow with urgency in front of him, calling to him in a way he wasn't strong enough to resist. He picked it up and cracked the spine for the first time in almost two years.

Two years that seemed like a lifetime ago.

The deeply embedded words on the first page could have easily been carved onto his heart, they pained him so. The second page hurt just as intently.

Taking a deep breath, Sophie's scent filling his nostrils, the music from her tree playing in the background, he read on. Page after page. Word after word.

Moisture stung his eyes, ran down his face, as surely as if he was back at basic and had just been gassed.

He read on, rewound the tree as needed to keep the music going, then read some more.

When he came to the last page, hands shaking, he closed the journal and leaned forward, resting his head in his hands as memories and emotions swamped him.

Not just of his time in the military but the days following his return to civilian life when he'd drifted from one job to another, not fitting in anywhere, not having a sense of purpose. Not until he'd seen an advertisement to train as a firefighter.

Fighting fires had put out more than external flames. It had helped restore balance and a sense of purpose. It had helped him become who he was supposed to be.

Not a hero, as Sophie labeled him. But not a complete failure, either.

Cole picked up Sophie's Christmas card, reread the words she'd written.

He was loved. By Sophie. Whether that love was friendship, Christian fellowship...or more, he'd take it. Welcome it. Cherish it.

He knew what he had to do. Right then. Because some things couldn't wait. Gathering up the journal, card, and his tree—keeping the quilt around him—he practically ran to his SUV.

He had to see Sophie, to thank her for his gift, and to wish her a Merry Christmas before it was too late.

As he was getting into the vehicle, something hanging from the coat rack caught his eye.

Yeah, he needed to give her that, too.

Sophie fed the material beneath the sewing machine foot, making scant quarter-inch seams all the way around her latest Petdana.

She hadn't been able to sleep, and not because of the cat sharing her bed, so she'd decided to go for a walk. Which had turned into deciding to sew at the shop for a while. If she couldn't sleep, she could at least get some work accomplished.

She'd texted Isabelle so her sister wouldn't worry when she didn't show back up at the house for a while, and then she'd started sewing.

And sewing.

Because sewing was her therapy. It had been her entire life. Her grandmother had started her sewing with the idea that it would help with her inability to focus, and it had worked.

When she felt badly, she sewed and felt better. When she felt mad, she sewed and felt glad. When she felt drained, she sewed and was rejuvenated at the creation of something new. When her mind raced, she sewed, and usually, it helped calm her.

Tonight, she sewed in sorrow at losing something she supposed she'd never really had. Because if Cole had cared for her as she'd thought, he'd have at least texted her a funny Christmas meme or a thank you.

An *Oh wow, Sophie, this quilt is amazing and so are you.*

Ha. Her imagination really was on overdrive.

Because the reality was, he'd gotten her gift—she knew he had because she'd texted Andrew to ask him, and the firefighter said Cole hadn't even opened the present.

For all she knew, he'd gone home and started a Christmas bonfire with it. Because he didn't want her gift, or her.

Sophie finished the pet bandana she was working on, reached for the next set of embroidered material she had already pinned together, and had just started to sew it when something tapped against the front door.

Panic hit her. She was at the shop. Alone. On Christmas night. Was someone trying to break in? Did bad guys knock?

Just as she was preparing to sneak behind the counter so she could go to Isabelle's office and check the security camera, her phone rang.

"Oh!" She jumped, wondering if whoever was at the door could hear her phone, and scrambling to answer it, especially when she saw who the caller was.

"Cole?" she whispered as she answered, relief filling her that she'd at least be able to tell someone what was happening. "You may have to rescue me again. I— Someone is knocking at the shop's door and I'm here alone and—"

"It's me, Sophie. I'm the one knocking at the shop's door."

Cole was at the door?

"What are you doing here? You scared me."

"Sorry. I figured Isabelle called you to let you know I was on my way from the moment I left your house."

"Isabelle—you were at my house?"

"Sophie, open the door and I'll tell you everything."

"I...okay."

Still holding the phone to her ear, Sophie walked to the front of the shop, amazed to see that Cole truly was standing at the door.

Even more amazing was what he was wearing.

She quickly undid the deadbolt and opened the door.

"What are you doing here? Dressed as Santa?" Then what he was holding registered. His quilt. His journal with her Christmas card stuck inside, and his Christmas tree. "Cole?"

"Can I come in?"

She stepped aside, letting him enter, then out of habit, made sure the door completely shut and turned the deadbolt.

"Locking me in?"

"I...sorry, habit." She reached for the lock, meaning to turn it back, but he stopped her.

"I'm teasing, Sophie. Leave it locked in case your sister decides to interrupt."

"Interrupt?"

"She has a habit of interrupting us. Leave the door locked. We need to talk."

"About?" Sophie didn't point out that Isabelle had a key, just stared at Cole and the sight he made dressed in his Santa suit minus his eyebrows, wig, mustache, and beard, holding his presents and his quilt. The fire department must have had a Christmas party where he'd had to play Santa.

"My gift."

Her gaze dropped to the stuff he held and understanding of why he was there hit. Her heart sank.

"I'm not taking those back, Cole." Hands going to her hips, she huffed out a breath. "If that's why you're here, just leave. Leave now."

Cole watched the play of emotions flicker across Sophie's face, watched as she lifted her chin, put her hands on her hips, and put on the most stubborn expression he'd ever seen her wear.

"I'm not here to return my gifts," he assured her. Far from it.

Driving to her house, he'd thought he'd known what

he wanted to say, had mumbled words to himself the entire drive.

Now that he stood in front of her, dressed in his Santa suit, the words seemed muddled in his head. No wonder with the way his formerly solid bones seemed to have turned to water. Especially his knees. How was he even standing?

"I'm waiting."

"Isabelle didn't call?"

"No. My sister is how you knew I was at the shop?"

"She answered the door when I went to your house a few minutes ago. I didn't believe her at first when she told me you weren't home. What are you doing here?"

"Sewing."

"On Christmas night?"

"You're seriously asking me that? You, the man who believes Christmas is just another day...despite the fact that he's currently dressed as Santa?"

"Christmas isn't just another day for me. Not ever again. That's why I'm wearing my Santa suit. Why I'll wear it next year and the year after and for however long the fire department, or anyone, needs me to be Santa."

Sophie's stance shifted. "What happened?"

"*You* happened."

Her lips parted, but she didn't seem to know what to say, so she just stared at him.

"You swept into my mostly-content world with your Christmas magic and joy and turned everything upside down."

She blinked as if she didn't quite believe what he was saying. "I did that?"

He nodded.

Forehead wrinkled with confusion, she studied him. "Is that a bad thing?"

"I thought it was," he admitted.

"Thought, as in past tense?"

Shifting the items in his hands, he held up her card. "Did you mean what you wrote?"

"I asked my question first," she reminded him, frowning.

Despite the anxiety filling him at what was happening, Cole half-laughed. "You're right. You did. Yes. As in past tense." He took a deep breath. "Thank you for my quilt, Sophie. It's amazing."

Her smile lit up her eyes. "You're welcome."

"And my card," he continued.

"You're welcome for that, too."

"And my tree. "O Christmas Tree" is now my all-time favorite song."

"Well, it is a great song," she conceded, looking more and more happily stunned by what he was saying.

"And for my journal."

Realization dawned in her eyes. "You read it?"

"I wrote it," he reminded her.

Her hands fell away from her hips and she stared at him in awe. "But you'd never read it, had you?"

He shook his head. "I didn't like the man who wrote that book. More than that," he continued, "I was ashamed of him, ashamed you'd read his words. Ashamed that my darkness had ever sullied the goodness of your mind, showing you the mistake I'd made and the terrible price that was paid for it."

He had been so embarrassed that she'd read those tormented thoughts, had wished he'd destroyed the journal before it could pass into her hands. Now, he recognized Sophie finding that journal may have been the best thing that had ever happened to him.

She was the best thing to have ever happened to him.

"The man who wrote that journal...he is a part of you, I know that, but you shouldn't be ashamed of him or the decisions he made. You did what you were sent to do, and even in the worst moments, you were willing to lay your life down to save others. There was no way for you to know that ambush was going to happen, nor was it your fault."

Cole's throat tightened at her words.

"You need to forgive that man, Cole. He's the part that made you grow stronger and become who you are today. He's the clay that was molded into a man who still would think nothing of laying his life down to save another, but whose life is so very precious and such a blessing to everyone who is fortunate enough to know him. That's the man I see."

"Tell me more about who you see when you look at me, Sophie."

"I certainly don't see someone I feel sorry for, except for when he pushes away anyone who gets too close."

He didn't deny her claim.

"I see a man who is good to his very core."

Despite all the emotions that had led him to Sophie that night, he automatically recoiled at her words, having believed for so long that he was dead inside.

Sophie studied Cole's face as she continued to tell him all the things she'd been longing to tell him, hating that he'd flinched at her assessment of his character, of who he was.

"You are a good man. You're kind and generous, loyal and honest, and have the greatest sense of honor of any man I've ever known."

"There you go with those blinders on again," he deflected, attempting to make light of her words.

Sophie was having none of it. He was here. He had opened his gift, had read his journal, and had come to her. Wearing a Santa suit while carrying her quilt and his Christmas tree, card, and journal.

That had to mean something.

"Possibly," she admitted. She opened her mouth to tell him, and he stopped her.

"I shouldn't have asked you to tell me what you see."

What? She'd loved that he had asked. Loved that he'd given her the opportunity to tell him all the things in her heart.

"Instead, I should have told you how I feel." He swallowed, then took her hands into his. His shaking hands. "What I see when I look at you."

Sophie bit into her lower lip, swallowed in effort to keep her throat from closing entirely.

Was this really happening?

"Sophie, you are the greatest gift I've ever received. Meeting you, knowing you, having your joy in my life has changed me in ways I can't begin to describe. It's no wonder that no matter how hard I tried to keep my distance, I fell for you anyway."

"You fell for me?"

"Like a ton of green candy canes."

"I...I thought..." Tears formed in Sophie's eyes.

Happy tears. "I was afraid you weren't ever going to let me in."

"Let you?" He smirked, then shook his head. "There was no letting. From the moment I first laid eyes on you at that Fourth of July picnic, I never got you out of my head. And then you showed up at the firehall wearing that red reindeer sweater and Christmas-shined your way into my life." He squeezed her hand. "Into my heart."

He recalled what she'd been wearing when she'd come to the firehall?

Happiness blossomed in Sophie's chest, spreading throughout her entire being.

"I can't believe you're really here, saying these things," she mused, truly wondering if she'd fallen asleep at the sewing machine and was dreaming all of this. "Santa must have left me on his nice list this year."

Cole's smile was so endearing that it couldn't possibly be real.

"You're the only girl on this Santa's list."

She smiled up at him and sought words to tell him what was in her heart. "Reading your journal, feeling the emotions you felt, the struggle you went through," she continued, trying not to choke up, "and traveling with you as you moved from deep despair to that last hopeful entry where you'd been accepted into the fire academy, pulled me in. I fell for you, Cole. When we met, I felt such a powerful connection that I was a bit devastated when you didn't give any indication that you instantly felt it, too."

"I felt it," he assured. "I didn't want to feel anything, but I knew you were different from any person I'd ever met."

"But, for all that I felt from reading your journal, getting to know you, seeing your smile, hearing your laugh, witnessing your generous heart, looking into your warm eyes—all of that has made me love you more than I ever dreamed possible."

"You love me?"

Heart pounding to the point she worried that her heart might burst, she nodded. "I'm so in love with you, I can barely think straight."

"Christmas really is the most magical day of the year, because none of this feels real," he admitted, his beautiful pale eyes sparkling like rare blue gems.

She glanced at her watch. It was still Christmas. Barely.

"Because you love me, too?"

"You know I do." He lifted her hand to his lips and pressed a kiss to her fingertips. "I love you more than life itself."

"That's almost enough," she teased softly, smiling up at him.

"Almost?" He laughed. "I'll keep working on it, then," he teased, then his face grew somber. "I admit, I worry that the darkness in me will surface from time to time. I hate the thought of you ever witnessing one of my nightmares."

The raw concern in his voice hurt her heart for him.

"It'll be okay, Cole. We'll face whatever happens together."

He cupped her face. "I never want to hurt you, Sophie."

"Then don't ever leave me."

"That might be the easiest thing you've ever asked of me."

Smiling, Sophie leaned over to where he'd set down the quilt she'd made him, a quilt of comfort and healing and love, and she wrapped it around his shoulders and pulled her very own Santa to her.

As their lips met, Sophie whispered, "Welcome home, Cole."

Moments later, Cole's forehead resting against hers, he smiled. "If home is where the heart is, then I am home. Merry Christmas, Sophie."

THE END

DILLY DUCHESS POTATOES

A Hallmark Original Recipe

In *Wrapped Up in Christmas Joy,* Cole experiences his first Thanksgiving in Pine Hill. While Sophie regrets not inviting Cole to dinner, Cole spends Thanksgiving with his fellow firefighters at the station...who ask him if he's sweet on Sophie. It's a little uncomfortable, to say the least, but the taste of Grandma Ruby's renowned cooking makes up for it. You can make Grandma Ruby's Dilly Duchess Potatoes for yourself—it's the perfect dish to share with your friends, family, and loved ones, and it's sure to have them coming back for seconds.

Prep Time: 30 minutes
Cook Time: 60 minutes
Serves: 10

Ingredients

- 4 large Russet potatoes, peeled, quartered
- 2 eggs, large, beaten
- 7 tablespoons butter, melted
- 1 1/2 tablespoons dill, fresh, chopped
- 1 tablespoon flat leaf parsley, chopped
- 1 teaspoon garlic powder
- Salt and Pepper to taste
- 3 tablespoons Parmesan cheese, grated
- 1/2 cup or more of heavy cram (to get desired consistency)
- 1/3 cup butter melted

Preparation

1. Preheat oven to 400°F.
2. In a large saucepan, cook the potatoes in boiling water until fork tender, about 25 minutes.
3. Drain and place in a large mixing bowl to cool, about 20 minutes
4. Add in eggs, butter, dill, parsley, garlic powder, salt, pepper and Parmesan cheese.
5. Blend well and add cream a little at a time until it is smooth. Taste for seasoning and adjust if needed.

6. Spoon the potato mixture into a pastry bag with a large star tip.

7. Pipe onto a baking sheet or sheets.

8. Melt remaining butter and drizzle on top.

9. Bake 20-25 minutes or until golden brown.

Thanks so much for reading
Wrapped Up in Christmas Joy.
We hope you enjoyed it!

You might like these other books
from Hallmark Publishing:

Wrapped Up in Christmas
Christmas in Evergreen
A Timeless Christmas
An Unforgettable Christmas
A Royal Christmas Wish
A Gingerbread Romance
Journey Back to Christmas

For information about our new releases and
exclusive offers, sign up for our free newsletter at
hallmarkchannel.com/hallmark-publishing-newsletter

You can also connect with us here:

Facebook.com/HallmarkPublishing

Twitter.com/HallmarkPublish

About the Author

USA *Today* bestselling author Janice Lynn loves to spin a tale that puts a smile on her reader's lips and a tear in their eye as they travel along her characters' journey to happy ever after. Her favorite read is one with a strong heroine who is able to laugh at herself and a hero who appreciates the heroine's strengths and imperfections.

Janice's books have won numerous awards including the National Readers' Choice Award and the American Title, but she is most proud of her seven children. From actor, engineer, nurse, student, to Army National Guard, they are her greatest accomplishments.

Janice lives in Tennessee with her family, her vivid imagination, lots of crafting and quilting supplies, and numerous unnamed dust bunnies.

Turn the page for a sneak peek of

Christmas
CHARMS

A small-town Christmas romance
from Hallmark Publishing

TERI WILSON

Chapter One

*E*VERYONE TALKS ABOUT CHRISTMAS MAGIC as if it's an actual, literal thing. As real as silver tinsel draped lovingly from the stiff pine needles of a blue spruce tree. As real as snow on Christmas morning. As real as the live toy soldiers who flank the entrance to FAO Schwartz, the famous toy store now situated in Rockefeller Plaza, right at the center of the bustling, beating heart of Manhattan.

But here's the truth—as authentic as those costumed soldiers seem, they're really just actors killing time until they land a role in an off-Broadway play. I know this because a pair of them stood in line behind me last week at Salads Salads Salads during the lunch rush. Dressed in their tall black hats and red uniforms with glossy gold buttons, they piled their bowls high with lettuce, cucumber slices and shredded carrots while discussing their audition monologues for the upcoming revival of *West Side Story*. It was all very surreal and not the least bit magical.

Genuinely magical or not, though, New York is undeniably lovely during the holidays. After four Christmases in Manhattan, I still go a little breathless every year when I catch my first glimpse of the grand Rockefeller Center Christmas tree. Every time I stand on the frosty sidewalk in front of Saks Fifth Avenue for the unveiling of their big holiday light show, I feel my heart grow three sizes, just like a certain green you-know-who.

I love this time of year. I always have, but this particular December is special. This Christmas will be my best yet. I just have to make it through my last day at work before taking off on my first real vacation in eight years—to Paris! My boyfriend, Jeremy, has family there, and this year, he's invited me to spend the holidays with them. Christmas magic, indeed.

Oui, s'il vous plaît.

I pull my coat tighter and more snugly around my frame as I jostle for space on the busy midtown streets. The very second the floats in the Macy's Thanksgiving Day parade pack up and go home, Christmas shoppers and holiday tourists descend on Manhattan in droves. The switch is kind of jarring. One minute, a sixty-two-foot inflated turkey is looming over Central Park West, and the next, his giant, colorful plumage is nowhere to be seen. Swinging shopping bags are the only thing in sight, all the way from one end of 5th Avenue to the other.

The Christmas crowds are predictably terrible, so I always leave extra time during the holiday season for my walk to the upscale jewelry store where I work, just a few blocks from FAO Schwartz and its not-so-magical toy soldiers. A snowstorm blew in last night—the first of the Christmas season. And even though I'm in serious danger of being swallowed up by the crush of people headed toward the ice-skating rink at Rockefeller Center, I can't help but marvel at the beauty of the season's first snowfall.

Manhattan looks almost old-fashioned covered in a gentle layer of white. Frost clings to the cast iron streetlamps, and icicles drip from the stained-glass windows of St. Patrick's Cathedral. Huge Christmas wreaths have been placed around the necks of Patience and Fortitude, the massive stone lions that flank the main branch of the public library like bookends, and when a winter storm is sprinkled on top, the tips of their front paws and noses are the only visible glimpses of pale gray marble beneath a blanket of sparkling snow. I can almost picture them rising up to shake the snowflakes from their manes and prowling through Midtown, leaving a trail of paw prints in the fresh powder.

I smile to myself as I near the toy store. One of the actor soldiers out front pauses from saluting at passersby to pose for a selfie with a little girl bundled up in a bright red snowsuit. It's an adorable scene, and I let my gaze linger longer than I should. Before I register what's happening, I plow straight into a man exiting the store.

Oof.

We collide right at the edge of the red carpet stretched out beneath FAO Schwartz's fancy marquee. Technically, I'm only partly to blame. The man's arms are piled so high with gift-wrapped packages that I can't even see his face, so I doubt he can tell where he's going or who might be in his way. My gaze snags on the sight of his hands in the seconds just before impact. They're nice hands—strong, capable. The sort of hands that can probably steer a car using only two fingers. Cradle a sleepy puppy in a single palm. Loosen a necktie with one swift tug.

I blink, and then impact occurs and the packages scatter. The rattle of what sounds like airborne Lego bricks and who knows what else snaps me back to attention.

"I'm so sorry. I wasn't watching where I was going," I say. I drop to my knees on the sidewalk to try and collect as many of his gift-wrapped packages as I can before they get stepped on. "Here, let me help you."

We reach for the same box and when our fingertips collide, I realize there's something almost familiar about those nice hands of his. Something that makes my stomach do a little flip, even before I look up to meet his gaze. And when I finally stand and get a glimpse of his face, I'm more confused than ever.

Aidan? My arms go slack, and all the presents I've just scrambled to pick up tumble to the ground again. *Aidan Flynn?*

No. It can't be. Absolutely not.

One of his packages must have conked me on the head or something and made my vision go wonky, because there's no way my high school sweetheart just walked out of FAO Schwartz. The Aidan Flynn I used to know wouldn't be caught dead in New York City. He was a hometown boy, through and through—as much a part of Owl Lake as the snow-swept landscape. Hence, our awkward breakup.

"Ashley," Aidan says, and it's more a statement than a question. After all, he shouldn't be as surprised to see me. I'm the one who belongs here. This is my city, my home—the very same city I left him for all those years ago.

Still, he seems to be almost as stunned as I am, because he makes no immediate move to pick up the remaining gifts scattered at our feet.

"Aidan, what are you..." I clear my throat. Why is it so difficult to form words all of a sudden? "What are you doing here?"

This can't be real. It's definitely some sort of Christmas hallucination. Not magic, definitely not that. Even though I can't exactly deny that there's a pleasant zing coursing through me as we stare at each other through a swirl of snowflakes.

I shake my head. *Get ahold of yourself.* I've moved on since Aidan and I dated, obviously. Eight years have passed, and now I'm practically engaged...sort of.

In any case, I shouldn't be wondering why Aidan looks as if he's just bought out an entire toy store. Is he a father now? Is he *married*? Is he a married to a *New Yorker*? All of these possibilities leave me feeling a little squeamish. I wish I could blame my sudden discomfort on something gone off at Salads Salads Salads, but alas, I can't.

"I'm working," he says, which tells me absolutely nothing. He could be one of Santa's elves for all I know. Or a professional gift wrapper. Or a personal shopper for a wealthy Upper West Sider who has a dozen small children.

Somehow none of those seem like realistic possibilities. Against my better judgment, I sneak a glance at his ring finger.

No wedding ring. My gaze flits back to his face—his handsome, handsome face. Goodness, has his jaw always been that square?

"Oh," I say. Ordinarily, I'm a much better conversationalist. Truly. But I'm so befuddled at the moment that I can't think of anything else to say.

Plus, I'm pretty sure Aidan noticed my subtle perusal of his most important finger, because the corner of his mouth quirks into a tiny half smile.

My face goes instantly warm. If a snow flurry lands on my cheek, it will probably sizzle. When Aidan bends down to scoop up the packages I dropped, I take advantage of the moment to fan my face with my mittens. Out of the corner of my eye, I notice one of the toy soldiers smirk in my direction. As if I need this surprise encounter with my Christmas past to get any more awkward than it already is.

Aidan straightens, and I jam my mittens back into my coat pocket. I really should get going. My shift starts in less than ten minutes, and Windsor Fine Jewelry is still a good eight-minute walk this time of year.

But something keeps me rooted to the spot, and as much as I want to blame it on simple nostalgia, I'm not sure I can. Aidan is more than my high school sweetheart. He's the personification of another place and time. And every now and then, the memories sneak up on me when I least expect them—now, for instance. Whenever it happens, I feel strangely empty, like one of those chocolate Santas you don't realize are hollow until you bite into them and they break into a million pieces.

That's silly, though. I'm fine, and my life here in Manhattan is great. I'm certainly not on the verge of breaking.

I square my shoulders as if to prove it, but when I meet Aidan's soft blue gaze, my throat grows so thick that I can't speak. Not even to say goodbye.

"It was good to see you, Ashley," he says.

And then he's gone just as quickly as he appeared, and I'm once again standing alone in a crowd.

Read the rest!
Christmas Charms is available now!